51GN5 OF L1F3

A comedy fantasy novel by

Nigel Peace

Local Legend Publishing UK

A Record of this Publication is available
from the British Library

ISBN 978-1-907203-20-6

Local Legend Publishing 2010
Park Issa
St Martin's Road
Gobowen, Shropshire
SY11 3NP, UK
www.local-legend.co.uk

Cover Design by Titanium Design
www.titaniumdesign.co.uk

What's it all about, then?
Life.
Why does stuff happen and is there any point anyway?

Does anybody have a Plan?

Well, actually, they do.
But it may not be quite as well thought out as you might hope…

From The Author

I've been thinking about death ever since I found myself born. I mean, being alive is so *wonderful* that you just want it to go on forever, don't you?

Unfortunately, the more life I got the more I began to get the horrible feeling that Heaven might just be like Earth, with a lot of the same idiotic people. I've been an engineer, tour guide, social worker and teacher, so I've met some of them. Still, maybe there's a few Good Guys too, the odd hero and a nice dog, like the one in Willesden. What do you think?

This book has taken sixty years to write, so I hope you like it. And please visit me at

www.spiritrevelations.com

With heartfelt gratitude to Beth for all her support with this work.

To everyone who ever wished there was a plan.
Good luck. You're going to need it.

Chapter Plan

Chapter One ~ The Call-Up

Why was he here? Benedict slowed the car almost to a stop at the sight of his old school's redbrick buildings, somehow much smaller than he remembered them. There was the angry blast of a horn from behind. Turning in through the open gate, he edged along the gravel drive and checked off the memories. On the left was the crazy paved path to the headmaster's house, bordered by neatly trimmed hydrangeas. He was out of bounds. Through the twilight to the west he saw the first floor windows of the Sixth Form common room where he'd learned to play bridge. "Six no trumps." Beddows had had to clean his football boots for a month after that. And yes, there was the pitch where he'd been invincible that drizzly January afternoon, diving fearlessly, flying across the goal to palm the ball away, taking school into the regional final. Just beyond… oh, the Music School had gone, and out of a grey mist rose a huge and ugly modern building, all concrete and glass…

Another turn revealed the quad. Something was wrong. It was littered with paper rubbish and plastic cartons, and the Refectory stood cold and derelict, every window broken, glass lying in a jagged carpet outside. Then another blast shattered his thoughts as a black saloon with lights flashing sped right at him from nowhere. He crunched into reverse and swerved away just in time, knuckles white on the wheel, watching the driver's grinning face as she flashed by. The car's controls didn't seem to be where they should be now. He couldn't find a gear.

Benedict threw open the door and almost fell over the old red bicycle left lying there, the front wheel buckled, the chain hanging uselessly from rusty cogs. He found himself near a set of weathered stone steps leading up to a polished oak door. To one side, a glass-covered notice-board held a single piece of paper headed 'AL' in heavy gothic print and followed by a list of names. Yes, the Advanced Level exam results of course. Leaning forward to take a look, Benedict found his own name at the bottom and, unmistakably, the word 'Disqualified' next to it. Despite the evening, he was sweating now, heart pumping. The door swung open easily at his touch to reveal an art studio, in the centre of which stood an easel displaying a naïve charcoal portrait of himself.

"Come on. We can't wait any longer." The soft voice came from the left. She sat in a swivel chair on a raised dais, and now turned towards him, slim and pretty, wearing a mortarboard perched on long fair hair and nothing else. He opened his mouth but nothing came out except a shrill bell announcing the end of lessons.

Benedict woke up instantly and threw a hand out onto the alarm clock, knocking the glass of water at his bedside onto the floor. He lay back, his breath coming in short, deep gasps, his body stuck to the moist sheets as he replayed the dream in his mind, unable to move. Mary came into the bedroom, already dressed and well into her day, and glared impatiently at the pool soaking into the carpet.

"I've been calling you. Breakfast is going cold. Come on, I can't wait any longer."

He shook himself free of his inner world and eased himself out of bed, legs unsteady and... too late, there was blood on the carpet too now. He tried to tell her about it all, later at the kitchen table, but she was listening with only half an ear, busying herself with papers and tidying.

"I can hardly describe how powerful it felt. It must mean something, don't you...?"

"For heaven's sake, it's just a dream," she retorted over her shoulder. "You've had them before. We all do. You're in the grown-ups' world now and you're going to be late for work."

He drove very carefully today, admitting to himself that Mary was indeed less than interested lately. She always had things to do and somewhere to go, and yes, they'd hardly touched for months. He supposed that most couples must experience this after twenty years, the marriage boat drifting in a quiet backwater. But Benedict really should have realised that storm clouds were gathered over this water and a flood tide was approaching. He had, after all, been warned.

Φ

Archangel Gabriel blew into the room like a tornado looking for something to pick up, toss about a bit and then smash just for fun. He really had better things to do than check up on Second Level Witnesses. That was supposed to be the Celestial Operational Planning Service's job, but can you ever find them when you need them? Manpower shortages! Honestly, who needs compassionate leave when you're already dead? So this Benedict chap was having a crisis but that's hardly the end of the world. Happens all the time. Everything was under control and... He glared at the only occupant of the room, a thin balding man apparently in middle-age, dressed in the standard issue pale green habit with yellow belt. He was intently watching a small screen with slow, misty images like a football match being played in heavy snow.

"Anthony? What's the news?"

"Oh, England are two-nil down. It's awful, you should see the state of the pitch and -"

"I didn't mean that. Aren't you supposed to be watching something a little less trivial at the moment, like some rather major life trauma for your guidee?" He winced as he uttered the dreadful word. What was Heaven coming to nowadays, all committees and Mission Statements and Celestial Correctness and nobody spoke proper English any more. His protests were ignored of course. Archangels were regarded as dinosaurs in this modern electro-cyber-Interthingy era. There was no respect. What was the use of experience when you have electronics? So here he was, reduced to chasing up feeble pension-chasers like Anthony who wouldn't know a God Moment if it ran up his leg and blew raspberries in his chakra. He took, as it were, a deep breath and tried again.

"I believe Benedict is almost at his Point of Spiritual Initiation?"

Anthony sat up and took notice, suddenly realising who his visitor was and that the room had gone very cold.

"Yeah, the shit of enlightenment is about to hit the fan of destiny, sir. Pretty soon. Probably."

"I should have thought that with all this," Gabriel made a sweeping gesture towards the banks of high technology that occupied an entire wall, "you could be a touch more precise? Time may not mean very much to us but I seem to remember that it sure as hell does to them. Didn't you have those bleak days when you didn't know how you were going to get through the next few hours and there was nothing to believe in?" Anthony considered this thoughtfully.

"Oh yes, but it was the nineteen-fifties. Skiffle, the Home Service, holidays in Bognor. Every day was like that. 'Course, things have accelerated now. 'Frinstance, did you know there's this chap, Roddick, who served an ace at -"

"Be that as it may, perhaps your chap could do with some input from you, given The Plan that's been put in place?"

"Yeah, well, 's not easy is it?" Anthony wheedled. "Due respect to Moses, but life is not set in stone. There's all sorts of other people involved down there who make all sorts of silly choices and, well, just interfere with things. Witnesses can only do so much, eh?" Gabriel's heart sank further. A fraction more determination would not go amiss. Nobody, but nobody, knew better than he how tricky things can be to organise. After all, he'd done the logistics for some of the biggest projects ever. Life may well be messy, but that's the nature of it and you just got on with it.

"What have you done so far?" he sighed.

"Well obviously, the dreams to start with, the usual stuff. The first few never got through but last night's biggie got him shaking in his socks all right. He even wrote it down."

"Did you get all the archetypes in?"

"Most of `em, uhu. School, car, alarm, bike, nudity… Even managed the initials this time. Though I say it myself -"

"And did he understand it?" The self-satisfaction froze.

"Well, that's another matter. Y'see, advertising executives with posh houses in Hertfordshire and three-hour lunch breaks aren't really used to PSIs. He's still got a few things to work out for himself… There's a limit to what I can do, y'know."

"Ah yes, that reminds me." Gabriel consulted his notes. "You're right, this is too big for one man, so he's been assigned another Witness. We hope you won't feel put out?" The CC was very nice but Anthony wasn't in the least put out. Perhaps he could put his feet up a bit now, shift some of this responsibility. There's a lot of stress in Witnessing.

"Fine by me, if you say so," he replied, trying to make it sound humble. "This *is* a Big Deal, needs a sensitive touch. Experience. Wisdom. Who's it to be, then – Tibetan monk perhaps, Chinese magus?"

"Er, not exactly -" began Gabriel. But then with one of those extraordinary synchronicities that happen all the time in spiritual circles, at that very moment the door burst open again.

"Yo, rude boys, is I late for de raga? Bruv, ent this just *bangin*?" Ranjit did a twirl so that the oversized habit that enveloped him like a tent billowed up and filled half the room. The white belt was knotted round his head to hold back the long, black, fine hair strung with multi-coloured beads. The other two gaped, trying to take in the dozen or so silver rings, the painted toenails, the nose stud and the sheer irreverence.

"Jus' call I RJ, bruv. I is your new man, innit."

Gabriel tottered quietly from the room and left them to it.

Φ

Harold Arthur St John Markham DSO was glad when he died. It was possibly one of the best things he'd ever done.

It was at first assumed in the village of Buckley Rise that the colonel was an idle old soak whose liver had outgrown its usefulness, but this was far from the truth (except that he did die in the bath). He'd kept himself in trim and up to form with twenty press-ups and twenty bicycle kicks every day while stripped to his vest in front of the bedroom mirror. He kept his mind active by rereading Plato's Republic and by writing occasional fierce letters about sexual permissiveness to the editor of the Gazette. He had bearing. He was alert, and he never wore tweeds.

It was his own fault if the neighbours got it wrong. The truth is that he'd pretty much cut himself off since everything worthwhile in life had disappeared. The disbanding of the regiment had been closely followed by that of his marriage, when an exasperated Barbara had left him for a pork butcher in Maidstone. For a while, he'd pottered in the vegetable patch and vegetated in the potting shed, brooding on the socioporosis of the country's backbone and watching the steady decline of morality with a deep sense of personal loss. Self-discipline faded, and so did Harry.

Society filled up with wishy-washy sociologists moaning on about disadvantages and free school milk. No fibre. Then there were the personal liberty apologists wittering about wealth-is-good and realities-of-life. No heart. It almost made him vote Labour, just the once. Nobody was doing anything about discipline.[1]

Lathered and pink, he'd stretched out in the bath and turned on the radio for the evening news. The headlines were, in order: an American actress had got married for the fourth time, school teachers were on strike for a thirty hour week, the Chief Executive of a water company had been awarded a half million pound bonus, and two million people were feared dead in an African famine. Harry decided that he no longer wished to be part of this world and, without either considering the matter further or turning off the radio, slid gently beneath the bath water and stayed there.

He hadn't left a note, of course, assuming that no-one would care or even notice that he'd gone. As it happened, Mrs Gardner, who tidied and shopped and cooked a bit, was considerably put out to discover her pale, late and very cold employer next morning. Indeed, she felt it necessary to help herself to a large Amontillado before covering his privates with a flannel.

Harry waited patiently in the queue for the Level One Natal Reception Centre. Having been a colonel in the British Army, he'd had plenty of experience of waiting about. There seemed to be some sort of disturbance up ahead.

It had been a long session already for the Control Clerks and Boris would have been fed up to the back teeth if he'd had any. Of course, one did not become an NRC[3] without thorough training in cool dispassionate

---

[1] That's what the Army was for, of course, nothing more. Whatever else it did was a mere ripple on the surface of history. The Army simply bred men. Granted, it also killed men but that was just unfortunate and might as easily have happened under a bus.

staring, the total suppression of subjective emotion, and the mastery of the Standard List. One loved one's work however humble, every task essential to the great machinery of the afterlife, to The Plan. One received one's reward in Heaven. The facts that he hadn't the faintest idea what The Plan was, and that he'd been in Heaven for ages and to his knowledge had received nothing, only occasionally troubled him. The odd break at a Joy Of Being Centre did help to reinvigorate him with a new sense of purpose, but he'd only just got back from his last stay and things were already getting him down. First there was that woman from Arizona who absolutely refused to believe that she was dead – the RC not doing their job properly again – and then there was the chap from Nepal who insisted he should go straight to Level Two at least, and eventually had to be carried over the barrier shouting that he was going to get his guru onto them.

You'd think people would be a little grateful that they'd survived. But no, one problem after another and the queue just wasn't getting any shorter. There was something, as it were, in the air today. An astral ripple. An etheric undercurrent. And there was also John Clarke.

Now, aside from moments of frustration, Boris was genuinely proud of his work. An NRC[3] has a certain status and responsibility; after all, one was the first trained spirit that most deceased encountered normally. He took pride in his skill at fending off pathetic questions and getting everyone processed before they could think twice. He'd won a Productivity Award in the Western European Sector three times. He might look forward to promotion one day soon if there were no cock-ups in the meantime. That's why Boris now had this very strange sensation, uncommonly like sweat tingling all over his scalp. For without doubt John Clarke was a living, walking cock-up.

No records, no files, no identity. Nothing. He shouldn't be there. But there he was, standing meekly on the other side of the counter, cap in hand, fawn gabardine raincoat over one arm, mild and apologetic and holding up the queue. Nothing in Boris's training had prepared him for this. Obviously, the only way the system could work was if everyone had records and everyone was expected. Even the woman from Arizona had been expected, however rare a raven attack on American tourists at the Tower of London might be. And it wasn't even as if John Clarke was reluctant or argumentative or anything. Quite the opposite – he seemed perfectly willing to accept whatever fate might befall him. But without records, nothing could befall him. Eventually, Boris did what any self-respecting official, spiritual or otherwise, has to do. He passed the buck.

NRC[4] Jones was just tidying his desk and sipping the last of his tea from a floral paper cup. Old habits die hard. He leaned back reflectively in his padded mock leather chair and looked at the fishing prints on the wall, the medal cabinet and the ten square metres of magenta pile carpet, while the personal Thought Module chattered quietly to itself on the desk beside him. All the satisfying trappings of his position. Yes, there was, as it were, something in the air. But he hadn't got where he was today without being able to deal with things in the air.

He patted the day's pile of record cards contentedly. Another three and a half thousand souls despatched. Well, it wasn't the big time but that was the price you paid for dealing with England. They were so stable and unexciting. Still, he ran a tidy ship.

He strolled over to the two-way mirror. Watching the feeble expressions of bemusement on newly-deceased faces never failed to entertain him. But what was this nagging instinct? He hadn't got where he was today without careful attention to nagging instincts. Perhaps someone famous or important was coming up the line? He always liked a quiet word and a handshake with them. The personal touch. No, he couldn't see anyone worth mentioning, though there did seem to be a bit of a commotion, some jostling and complaining...

Boris entered.

"We have a bit of a problem, NRC[4] Jones, sir," he announced. Jones clasped his hands behind his back, spread his legs slightly and rocked on his heels. It was a rather good posture he'd copied from a member of the royal family.

"You mean, *you* have a problem, Boris." He was a decent man, NRC[3], but he had no imagination. He'd never have any chance of promotion. "If it's about that chap from Nepal, I've already been onto the Spiritual Guidance Bureau and they're -"

"No sir, it's John Clarke."

"Who?"

"Exactly, sir. That's just it. I don't know. No records."

"Nothing?"

"Not a scrap."

"Then he's not here."

"Yes, sir. I mean, no, sir. Er, he's behind me, sir."

It didn't take too long for Jones to concede that there was a problem. He scratched himself, fidgeted, and glared at the slight figure across the desk.

"Let's get this straight. Who are you?"

"John Clarke, sir. B.A. (Sussex). 14 Acacia Stree -"

"Yes, yes, but what are doing here? You're not supposed to be dead. You're not on our list. In fact, you don't seem to be on *any* list."

"Sorry, sir, I just found myself here. It was a bit sudden, granted. About tea-time. Should I have brought my passport?"

Jones didn't answer, but buzzed his secretary to check if he'd double-checked the lists.

"`Course I `ave, an' gone through Past Records an' Forward Estimates an' bin onto the RC. `E don't exist, guv."

"`E do. I mean, he certainly does. He's sitting in front of me. And don't call me that in front of other people, please."

"But if `e don't exist then -"

"Look Ziggie, you'll never get anywhere with that logic. Get onto the FEW, will you, and get them to check the Destiny Control registers."

"Come on, guv, that'll take aeons. You know they never answer. They're not even *supposed* to answer. An' I was `oping to slope off a bit early to meet this nice -"

"Do it, Ziggie. We can't have souls wandering about willy-nilly."

"They won't like it, guv. They'll only tell the SGB…"

Jones hissed something not very spiritual back down the Module before replacing the receiver on its hook, and his highly trained smile back on his face. But something quite unprecedented was going on. Not credible. He studied Clarke again – the man was totally unremarkable. So why did he seem so dangerous?

"We'll have to wait," said Jones, reaching into his drawer for a couple of paper cups. "Tea?"

Φ

If the NRC was in trouble, so was Benedict.

"I'm in trouble," he said to himself. He stared at the computer screen in disbelief and punched a few keys. Nothing happened. And when he pushed his chair back from the desk in frustration, there was a small cry of pain from behind. "Oh… I… I'm so sorry. I didn't realise…" He helped the young woman to her feet and retrieved the papers scattered on the office carpet. It was magenta. "Are you all right?" She winced slightly as she put her left foot to the ground but smiled anyway.

"Yes, fine, sir. I did knock, but you were miles away."

Benedict sheepishly helped her to a chair and handed her the file, which she immediately gave back to him.

"They told me in Reception to bring these up for you. Something about a new campaign?" He dimly recognised her now, one of those cheerful, anonymous faces you pass every morning when you go in and every evening when you go out. Someone who isn't very important. Late twenties, he supposed, pretty enough in a quiet way, very clear eyes of some indefinable greenish colour. And somewhere at the end of a long, dusty corridor of Benedict's mind, on the other side of a polished oak doorway, a bell rang.

He glanced at the file she'd given him with incomprehension. It was labelled Very Urgent in red and bore a title that meant absolutely nothing to him.

"Yep, I really am in trouble," he muttered, leafing through the pages. "There's no way I can get this done today. There hasn't even been a Planning... well, you don't want to know about my problems. Look, you'd better get back." He offered a hand to help her up but she gave another small cry and sat down again. Benedict fetched tea from the machine in the corridor.

"Everything seems to be top priority lately," he said ruefully. "I've no idea what's going on. Even the computer's acting up. I was on the Internet when you came in. There's this bridal wear campaign, so I typed in some keywords for a search of famous weddings – you know, 'celebrity' and 'marriage', that sort of thing. All I got was some historical archive page about the Mary Celeste. I ask you. Then the damn thing froze on me. And my laptop at home has been acting up as well. It's like a conspiracy."

"Bugs."

"Or a virus."

"Or you."

"Eh?"

"Maybe it's just you. These things are only happening around you, right? So perhaps it's your energy doing it. You do seem pretty stressed -"

"Come on, that's nonsense. How could... do you really think that's possible then?" She shrugged and sipped her tea.

"I know nothing about how computers work. They're alien creatures. I mean, I can do basic things... But I do think that anything's possible." They sat in silence for a minute while Benedict turned over in his mind his rudimentary knowledge of electromagnetic fields. The thought took him back to school, and to last night.

"I had this really weird dream, too. Very powerful. It's still swimming around my in head, like someone's trying to tell me something."

"Then that's what it is. Except it's you, I mean, your own mind. There's something inside trying to get out." Benedict struggled with the idea. He may be an advertising executive, but he was the pragmatic sort, organised and rational, the one who got things done. Creativity wasn't his department and the paranormal definitely didn't happen. But something was happening.

"So how come the Internet's got it in for me too?"

"Quite the opposite. It's trying to help you. What do you know about the Mary Celeste?"

"Only what everyone does – found drifting in the Atlantic, abandoned, big mystery…"

"And her captain's name was Ben." Something very cold and with a lot of small legs started crawling up Benedict's spine.

"And my wife's name is Mary." It was almost a whisper. "We met when we were at school and… grief, the dream was about school and come to think of it she was in it, driving a car…"

"I read some of the page over your shoulder when I came in. The ship was found in 1872… is that relevant?"

"Aah," he groaned. "Only that Mary's birthday was 1972…"

"So all I'm saying is that if there's a signpost maybe you should read it?" Benedict shook his head as if to clear it, and sat back down at his desk.

"Look, none of this is making any sense," he said abruptly, "and we're wasting time. I've got Very Urgent stuff to do and you'd better get back."

Alison wandered back downstairs but she was in no hurry. The HR woman had it in for her so she'd probably already lost her job for spending too long away from Reception. It didn't matter. Anyway, she'd been having a recurring dream lately, about Bees.

Φ

"PSI countdown starting… now." Anthony pressed a purple button and watched the numbers flicker across the screen in an apparently random sequence. Seven, seven, two, eleven… Since they made no sense whatever to him, he switched back to the football.

"Hey bruv, I is watching that, you fassy," complained Ranjit. Anthony gave him a withering glare. The atmosphere had been decidedly frosty since Gabriel's departure in a cloud of undisguised despair.

"Mean a lot to you, do they, interpolatory chaos derivative field patterns?" he suggested with more than a touch of sarcasm. Actually they meant nothing to him either but he'd been around long enough to pick up the jargon.

"Sure, bruv. I is eddicated y'know. Maffs is my ting, yeah, like I done my time at uni. Man, chaos is cool."

"Ah yes," Anthony countered, establishing his authority by opening the beige file Gabriel had tossed onto the table as he left. "Uni. Now that would be the academically prestigious University of Burnley, wouldn't it? Where you attended precisely one lecture and spent your entire student loan in two weeks, before – and do correct me if any little details are wrong – dissolving three Es in a pint of rum, climbing to the top of the Manchester Airport observation tower, taking all your clothes off and shouting 'Capitalism sucks' as you toppled not very gracefully onto the tarmac. Not exactly a distinguished higher education, was it?"

"Don't mean I don't know nuffin," muttered RJ. "Ok, I was a prat den."

"The airport was closed for eighteen hours," Anthony read on. "They thought you were a terrorist. Thousands of people missed their holiday flights. Angry parents, crying children. The restaurants ran out of chips. Well, maybe you do know something about chaos, then."

"Yeah, well that's it 'bout Heaven, right? I got nuvver chance, like, to mek up. C'mon Tone, our brer's in seeerus shit down there. We gotta do summat!"

The whistle blew for half-time and Anthony switched off the monitor, standing up for a good stretch. The boy hadn't been here five minutes, didn't know how it was. He thought back to his own arrival, trampled underfoot outside a Rolling Stones concert when he's only popped out for the Daily Mail, and his first flush of enthusiasm for the job. Well, true, he'd never actually been the enthusiastic sort, but it all did seem like a decent responsibility, overseeing a soul's progress. Until you realised that there's practically nothing you can do about any of it. On the one hand you had your destiny, so things were planned out anyway, and on the other hand you had your free will which always screwed up the plan. And obviously it's not CC to interfere.

In any case, communication was hardly straightforward. If it were, spiritualist mediums wouldn't be blathering on about Auntie Joan says the cat is happy but thinks you should get some new socks. No, the best you could hope for was to slip in the odd dream and leave the rest to them and chaos. What's the fuss? You can always have another go later anyway.

That reminded him. His own Witness had mentioned at their last review some possibility of a turn as a politician in New Zealand. It sounded good, nice and quiet, plenty of sport. Anthony decided to go and make a few enquiries.

"Don't touch anything," he ordered coldly as he ambled out.

A deflated Ranjit sat glumly for a while, twisting his rings and twirling his belt. Heaven was not going to be a breeze, then. Perhaps getting shacked up with Anthony was a punishment. Perhaps he wasn't in Heaven after all, and this was all a very, very bad trip.

But then his eyes took in the banks of flashing, twitching, beeping technology around him and, despite himself, the excitement rose again. This was seeerus cool stuff. This was his generation. Surely it wouldn't hurt if… He sat himself down in front of what looked like a multi-DVD drive and saw a piece of paper sellotaped to the side of it. Anthony's password. A few keys later and he was in.

Ranjit might know fairly little about quite a lot, but he did know about computer systems. Specifically, how to hack into them. Within moments he was watching Benedict being sacked, apparently for not dealing with some urgent job, damaging company equipment and having an affair with a Receptionist on company time. As Benedict cleared his desk, RJ saw his boss, Michael, make a telephone call to Mary arranging to meet her in the usual place that evening.

"Dick'eds!" hissed RJ to himself. "The brer got jacked!" These were not holy observations but they were accurate. The young man's natural outrage at the injustice – he was after all of ethnic minority with piercings and long hair so he knew about injustice – flared up and burned out all the cautions he'd been given earlier. Something had to be done about this. Benny-baby was not going to be dealing with this on his own. Fingers flashed across keyboards as Ranjit gave himself a crash course in second level astral software.

Φ

The barrier gave way under the weight of the crowd's indignation at being kept waiting to enter the afterlife. More than fifty souls had got through unprocessed by the time Boris and the NRC[1] security team restored control. The colonel looked back sadly at the sight and shook his head, before strolling forward to who knew where. No discipline.

Φ

From flavour of the month to persona non grata in ten minutes flat. Life can be like that. Colleagues you've worked with for years turn away and busy themselves in the middle distance as you pass. Tight-lipped ex-friends shoot accusing stares. Silence and fear, as if misfortune were contagious. The doorman you exchanged friendly banter with this morning now walks beside you with a self-important smile and a puffed out chest and a grip on your arm like he's NYPD. You balance your pathetic cardboard box of belongings on your hip as you hand over your Pass and hit the dingy back stairs down to the car park.

Benedict didn't have the faintest idea what was happening to him or why. He drove up through north London in a daze and pulled in at Kenwood for a late lunch at the outdoor café overlooking the Heath. He couldn't go home yet, couldn't face Mary with all this. He walked for a while along the familiar paths where once they'd been happy, and stopped on the grassy bank where they'd huddled under a blanket together at a late open-air concert. It had been the 1812, fireworks exploding spectacularly above them. Life had been warm and all ahead. But now he was just numb and cold.

He sat in a corner at a rustic wooden table, coffee and salad baguette lying untouched in front of him. There was a fluttering somewhere up above in a nearby tree, and a small white feather floated gently down to land on his plate.

"It is a sign." The quiet, squeaky voice to one side made Benedict start from his reverie. He looked at the woman, small with sharp features and mousy hair, wrapped in a grey raincoat despite the sunshine. "I Am A Medium," she announced in capital letters, getting up from her table and edging forward with little steps to take the seat opposite him.

"Sorry?" he said feebly.

"The feather," she pointed to it, "it's a sign. There's an Angelic Presence with you." Benedict glanced from the offending article, stuck in mayonnaise, to the ground around them that was so festooned with feathers that this café must have been one of the holiest sites in Christendom. "I have to talk to you," she squeaked on. "My guide told me at breakfast this morning that there would be An Encounter."

"Your guide?" Benedict's side of the conversation was a bit limited.

"Yes. I have to give you the words of the Great Dark Cloud." Well, that bit seemed perfectly understandable. "You are in pain, am I not right? There have been troubles, and there will be many more…"

"Oh, thanks."

"… but you must not be downhearted for these troubles are blessings."

"I see." He didn't, of course, but he just wanted to get rid of her. The last thing he needed right now was some loony spouting gibberish.

"Remember your dream, Ben. The woman has betrayed you." That cold thing with legs started climbing up his spine again, and Benedict became very, very alert. "But this had to be, for there is another path you must walk. Yes, yes…when life kicks yo' in de balls yo' gotta turn round an' git yer ass in gear, innit. Oh!" She put a tiny hand up to her mouth, flushed with embarrassment.

"Gracious me, I do beg your pardon. You see, I'm only passing on now what your guide is telling me, my friend. I may have got some of the words a bit wrong, of course. Ah, let me see... a green dress, long black hair, rings – quite a lot of rings actually – yes, a very spiritual lady. Red Indian, naturally. They're the best, you know. So you see, Ben, you must pick yourself up, dust yourself down -" he prayed that she wasn't going to burst into song. "– and realise that Everything Has A Purpose."

She was off, fluttering away invisibly as Benedict sat rigid with shock. How had she known his name?

"Oh, by the way," she was suddenly back again, "there will be other signs soon. Look out for them, my dear."

Anyone observing Benedict during the next ten minutes might have been forgiven for wondering if he was in fact alive. On the outside, nothing moved. Not a muscle, barely a blink. As the afternoon started to turn chilly, the skin thickened on his coffee and a gang of sparrows that had been waiting patiently above now decided that it was safe to attack and were systematically disembowelling the baguette. There was no reaction.

But inside his head, Benedict's brain was in hyperdrive trying to process totally unfamiliar information. A bead of sweat appeared on his brow and he wiped it away, scattering the sparrows. One turkey short of a Christmas she might have been, but this insignificant woman had clearly known something and he was being warned of more to come. And more signs? Instinctively, Benedict looked upwards. It was simply an unfortunate coincidence, nothing more, that a bald and scruffy pigeon chose that moment to relieve itself.

Deciding that something rather stronger than coffee was called for, he headed up the A1 until the noise of London was far behind him, and pulled into the car park of The Gate. As he nursed his second single malt in a shadowed corner, Benedict began at last to relax. Or he would have, were it not for the conversation at the next table.

"...been at it for years, she had, right under 'is nose..."

"...planning it all, I bet. He walked right into it..."

"...you just don't know who to trust any more, do you?"

It was no good. He might just as well go home and get it all over with. Have it out, whatever it was. He knocked the whisky back in one and strode out with new determination.

Back at home, he wasn't in the least surprised to find the house empty and a note from Mary propped up against an old chipped mug on the kitchen table. She was out and wouldn't be back until tomorrow and she'd be glad if he'd pack some things and find somewhere else to stay by then. There was also some stuff about Neglect and Unreasonable Behaviour and taking the house in lieu of maintenance since he'd probably never get another decent job and certainly not in advertising anyway because Michael would see to it. Sitting there in the very quiet and very empty kitchen, Benedict realised that even the overheard conversation in the pub had been for him. It had all been planned. New lives sorted, old lives torn up. And every little detail of the day now took on momentous significance, maybe even that... what was it? He'd been following a slow black Porsche all the way home, and somehow now its registration number jumped into his mind's eye: DAN 622.

Without knowing or even caring why – he was long past the stage of reason, something or someone else was directing his brain – Benedict went to find the old battered Bible he'd been given as a boy at Sunday School and had kept just for the sake of it. He looked up the Book of Daniel, chapter six, verse twenty-two: thrown into the lions' den, Daniel had emerged unscathed, saved by an angel of God. And in that moment, Benedict knew he was going to be all right.

Somewhere far away, in another world, a long-haired young man clenched a fistful of rings and shouted "Yo!" in sheer delight.

Φ

Harry felt quietly satisfied. It had been a successful operation, undramatic, no loose ends, no-one unduly troubled (his wife had died a few years earlier – some sort of food poisoning). It had been a small unexpected flourish in an otherwise orderly life, that touch of style that the greatest commanders bring to their operations, whether they be blowing a supply bridge sky-high or merely committing suicide. But now Harry was himself sky-high and what was to be done about it?

The trouble was, having slipped through the NRC and strode onwards, he now couldn't quite get his bearings. To anyone who might have happened to be passing in that particular bit of Heaven just then, the colonel would have presented a peculiar sight. There was no doubt that he found himself standing in, on and next to absolutely nothing, with more nothing to be seen in every direction. He had not expected this (well, soldiers do not give a lot of thought to life-after-death). Nevertheless, he had spent most of his life accepting nonsensical things so he remained calm and gave the matter some thought. Clearly he had survived, so he must be in some sort of base camp while operational logistics were worked on by Higher Command. He contemplated this for what seemed like a very long time, until he began to wonder if indeed the afterlife really did just consist of billions of disembodied souls hanging around nowhere at all. This didn't seem reasonable. And that thought broke the spell.

"There you are, you old codger. What on earth are you doing there?"

"Whoever you are," he replied icily, "I should have thought that was obvious. I'm waiting." There was a chuckle in the nothingness.

"Ha! Same old Poojar!" The origins of the nickname may be glossed over for now. "Think of the 49th and look eight o'clock." A dim figure became visible just out of focus to one side. But Harry was used to seeing Smythe out of focus.

"Snorker, by Jove! What are you doing here? I thought you'd taken over half of Kent with that blonde farmer's wife with the enormous... you've lost weight."

"The bottom fell out of it. Too much for the old ticker. Anyway, what about you? You didn't give us much notice. I came to meet you but you weren't there...Some weedy chap from the Rescue Centre told me where to come. And here we are. You're looking surprisingly well, Poojar."

"In trim and up to form. And you look much younger, Snorker."

"Mmm, yes, one of those funny things here. You will too, pretty soon. Can't say I understand it but then you get used to not understanding anything in Heaven. There it is. Well, we can't hang about here all day, eh?"

"Why not?" Since they were now apparently in Eternity, it seemed to Harry that there was actually plenty of time for hanging about.

"Things to do, places to go, old boy. And the Witnesses are waiting for you."

"I'm not getting married am I? I thought this was Heaven?"

Smythe had never been one of Her Majesty's brightest sparks, and being dead had taken almost as much getting used to as being alive, but he did his level best to explain the Basic Principles as they floated off together. Things like it's-all-in-the-mind.

"I grant you it's a bit rum. Remember the 49th when chaps were always saying when were chaps going to do something about the food and other chaps said they'd think about it and nothing ever got done? Well, it's the opposite here."

"You mean the food's good?"

"No, you old codger. Do keep up. I mean you just think about something and it's done. Simple. So now we just have to think about getting off to meet these bods, and we'll be there in a couple of jiffies."

In fact, the journey probably took a good five or six jiffies since the old comrades couldn't help getting sidetracked by memories of seedy Hong Kong bars. But eventually Harry found himself deposited outside the yellow door of a late-Victorian mid-terrace house held together by wisteria, in a leafy suburban street. Smythe seemed anxious to be off, so he made appropriate noises and simply disappeared. This didn't worry Harry, since the Army afforded plenty of experience of appropriate noises and people suddenly not being around anymore.

On the other hand, these Witnesses did worry him. He wasn't an especially intelligent man – he wouldn't have spent so long in the Army if he had been – but he was quite capable of applying his mind fairly and squarely. True, he hadn't given a lot of thought to religion. It hadn't really come his way in the last thirty years or so, except when the chaplain came round to bless the mortars. One might just accept the idea of angels, delivering the occasional special message. But spies? Watching your every move? After all, a chap has to be self-sufficient, cook his own breakfast, and see himself through all sorts of other crises from tank battles in the desert to a touch of syphilis in the Persian Gulf. Security was one thing, but the idea of celestial fifth columns interfering with chaps' lives without chaps having any notion of it was bad form.

Moreover, it wasn't just these polemical considerations that disturbed Harry. It was the fact that these Witnesses were so…pathetic.

There were three of them, sitting in apparently terminal boredom on comfy chintz sofas in the front room. They did not have wings.

"We've been waiting ages," Gerry had complained.

"That is to say," interjected Dora, "we seem to have been waiting ages. The concept of time is of course an abstract construct upon the movement of physical bodies and there aren't any here, so there aren't any ages. But we do seem to have been waiting ages." Harry could tell that Dora was going to be trouble. He had remained respectfully at attention and wondered to himself why they hadn't come to fetch him if they were in such a hurry.

"Because you'd got yourself lost, you old fool." Harry had been taken aback, not by Kenneth's unfriendly answer so much as by the fact that he hadn't voiced the question.

"You'll have to get used to that," Gerry had continued. "You don't have to say anything because all your thoughts are quite open now. We are in a state-of-mind, after all. Of course, you can move your lips if it makes you feel better -"

"– though you really don't have any lips," added Dora, presumably intending to clarify things.

This turn of events didn't seem altogether fair to Harry. Was it not essentially human to be able to think all kinds of things in private that polite society might frown upon if expressed? Vocal chords were a most sensible arrangement; one could easily get into a lot of trouble without them. He was beginning to regret his situation.

"We hope you won't come to regret the situation, old boy." Kenneth had the laconic, thin and dry nasal tone of one who was entirely satisfied with his own position and had the firm conviction that nobody else should be. It was quite a remarkable sound for one who didn't actually have a nose. "I mean, you spent a good portion of your allotted span organising for people to be killed or maimed, and after you retired you just pottered about. Did you actually achieve anything in life? And your good lady wife wouldn't have left you for that grocer if you hadn't been such a crashing bore -"

"I say, steady on," protested Harry. "It was a pork butcher, actually. And I did try to -"

"No you didn't. Can you imagine what a thankless task we've had, trying to help you along when you never even gave us a thought? It's very dispiriting to have one's existence ignored. Personally, I don't even know why you're at Level One. If it were up to me... well, I suppose someone here loves you." It clearly wasn't Kenneth.

"I'm sorry, I'm sure, sir," Harry had said, somewhat chastened, and still assuming the Witnesses to be of higher rank than himself. "I just didn't know you were there... er, I mean, here..."

"Remember that time in the Falklands," Dora had insisted, "when you tripped over a cat and went arse over tip into a trench just as that shell exploded where you'd been standing? Who put the cat there, eh? Or when you got bronchitis just before the 37th were posted to Iraq? Barely half of them came back in one piece."

The colonel's head had been swimming now. If cats were to be considered instruments of Divine Intervention, the actuarial profession might as well shut up shop. More importantly, what were the rest of the 37th's Witnesses doing? Something didn't gel here. He could instantly think of a dozen or more times in his life when a spot of celestial interference would have been very welcome and had been conspicuously lacking. Heaven's entire campaign strategy seemed seriously flawed...

"Um, forgive me for asking," the thought struck him not for the first time, "but this *is* Heaven isn't it? I mean, there aren't any teachers' strikes or famines or Hollywood actresses here, are there?" He tried to chuckle light-heartedly but it came out like a mallard clearing its throat.

"You'd be surprised," Gerry had said.

The atmosphere had not improved during the rest of the interview, and eventually Dora had announced that it was time for him to visit the WC. This turned out to be the Welfare Centre, where Harry was supposed to rest and adjust, do something called Judgement and then get himself properly Processed. He had allowed himself to be led to what looked like a hospital room and be put to bed by a large and very hairy male nurse who was also clearly not an angel.

But what everyone had overlooked was the fact that Colonel Harold Arthur St John Markham DSO (ret.) (dec.) was an exceptional man. He didn't need to rest, and his mind was already adjusting fast. A lot had happened since he'd switched on the evening news, and on gaining new territory one must consolidate the position[2]. He conceded the Witnesses' point about being ignored; he had himself once been hopelessly infatuated with a delicate, sloe-eyed Malay beauty called something like Wang Pooh who wouldn't have anything to do with him. But it was entirely unfair for the rest of the onus for spiritual evolution to have been heaved onto his shoulders. Something Had To Be Done.

Having consolidated, one prepares one's defences. It wasn't that Harry felt in imminent danger of being catapulted back into his bath. But a chap would be totally vulnerable if every other chap could read a chap's thoughts all the time. He therefore conceived a devastatingly simple yet clever plan. Since one only had to think about something for it to happen, if Smythe was to be believed, he decided to imagine a small notebook, jot down his private ideas and then completely forget the book until such time as he needed to remember the ideas. It was a plan that could only have been devised by someone with vast military or political experience and training in the art of totally forgetting about important things.

He wrote the title 'Observations' and subdivided it into (a) Information, Earthly, insufficiency of; (b) Follow-up, Heavenly, inefficiency of; and (c) Attitudes, general, lax. There were a few remarks here such as "reliance on semantics", "lack of sympathy" and "Witnesses do not sit up straight". Then under the title of 'Requirements' he wrote (1) Communication, (2) Discipline (underlined), and (3) Planning.

One may not have a physical body in the afterlife, but Harry's eyes were definitely gleaming as he lay back and sank into a peaceful and dreamless sleep.

---

[2] He did first briefly consider the possibility that all his recent experiences were some ghastly hallucination, but dismissed it since it seemed extremely unlikely that any lysergic acid diethylamide or suchlike could have found its way into his bathwater.

Chapter Two ~ Mrs Gardner's Curse

The door of the little observation room didn't so much open as simply dissolve in sheer terror as Gabriel approached in all his majesty. A furious archangel really is something to be avoided if at all possible, which is why Anthony tiptoed several paces behind and flattened himself against the wall in a dark corner. Ranjit was dancing in the middle of the floor, singing along to Bob Marley with a huge grin on his face.

"Yo', Big G, how's it hangin? Gimme five, man."

For a brief moment, Gabriel considered doing just that. The music stopped itself, the lights flickered and even the computers seemed to hold their breath. This might just be a turning point in celestial history and it was as if consciousness itself was hesitating before deciding which way to jump.

"Have you any idea," Gabriel began very slowly and quietly in the way people do when they're about to explode, "what you have done?" Ranjit looked him straight back in the eyes, his smile frozen but his mood unquashed. He sensed that Gabriel was displeased about something but genuinely had no idea what.

"Nope, main man. Spit it out."

"Firstly, with no training and with absolutely no authority, you have activated the ECG and -"

"Woa there, slow down, bruv. The Easy What?"

"The Emergency Contact Generator," hissed Anthony from his shadows. "It's the ultimate Earth communication tool in case of apocalypse. Top Secret. Still experimental."

"I did that?" beamed Ranjit. "Well, the security was pants. My lil' sis could of -"

"– and you've single-handedly undermined the entire Plan. Every single PSI has been compromised. Every SG is up in arms demanding encrypted passwords. You've tripped every circuit-breaker at the BoSS, brought the TOE to its knees, and crashed the CAR. Moreover, the SoG wants my guts for garters." The atmosphere had turned a shimmering electric blue, paralysing everything in a fifty metre radius except RJ.

"Nah, sorry bruv, yo lost I back there. What's undie mining?" Gabriel stared in disbelief – and that's saying something – at this extraordinary figure who apparently didn't have enough brain cells to rub together and work out when he was in deep trouble.

"You're dead!" offered Anthony with a smirk.

"Yeah, well I knows dat, innit. I mean, dat is de whole point."

"De point?"

"'Course, cos we is all dead, innit? But we is still alive too, so everyfing's hanging. Nuffin to worry 'bout. But our dude down there -" he jabbed a finger at the computer which squeaked as if it was about to get the blame "– Benny-boy don't know dat. He jus' know he been turned over. Screwed. Lost every damn fing he care 'bout." RJ counted them off on his fingers: "He job, he future, he home, he wife, he money, he -" He ran out of fingers.

"So what?" Gabriel retorted. "That's life. It happens all the time. And the whole point, actually, is that you have to learn from it."

"Sez who, bruv?"

Anthony smiled to himself. He might actually get away with this, now that the boy was intent on signing his own Outer Darkness warrant.

"Sez who?" RJ repeated, walking right up face to face with one of the greatest archangels of history. "Sez all dey new-agey gurus an' do-goody social workers an' two-degrees teacher-men? Ent no-one ever told dey guys yo' can't learn *nuffin* when yo's shit-scared? Tell me, Big G, yo' ever bin shit-scared?" Gabriel considered privately how he'd felt a little while ago when he'd received SoG's hmail, but let it go.

"So you thought," he replied, "you'd just open a direct line from Heaven and wipe away thousands of years of evolution? So now the human spirit counts for nuffin – I mean, nothing?" Ranjit merely raised one eyebrow.

"Yo' is outta line, bruv. I ent done dat ting. All I done is let the poor dude know he ent alone."

Nothing moved. Not a twitch. No reaction. There was silence for what seemed an eternity. Gabriel abruptly turned on his heels to leave.

"You'll be hearing from me," he hissed. Then he caught sight of Anthony cowering in shock in the corner. "Anthony, I believe you've shown some interest in New Zealand?"

"Aah… well, I did wonder…"

"No problem. I'll see to it myself. There's plenty of room there for more sheep."

Φ

On the very much more distant Elementary Level, where no-one sleeps and no-one has bodily form, Elemental Tfozb nevertheless yawned and scratched.

"Oh dear," s/he muttered soulfully. "This isn't going to get the price of eggs down. I can just feel something in my bones." The others were not taking a blind bit of notice. One became used to not having much to do and nothing to do it with anyway, rather as a geriatric eventually convinces himself that sex is pointless. With only abstract thought to occupy them, most Elementals gratefully took whatever opportunity there was between Committees to snatch some oblivion. Call it meditation, perhaps. "Oh dear, oh dear..." s/he repeated. The ripple of frustration reached Sxzbu.

"I worry about you sometimes," s/he said. "Or I would... metaphorically speaking... you know what I mean."

"I do know what you mean," Tfozb grumbled. "Everyone here always knows what everyone means. That's another thing that's frustrating. Look, doesn't anybody else feel something going on somewhere?" The disturbance continued to spread, waking other Elementals from their reverie, and a hubbub of ideas broke out.

"What the - ?"

"I say, can't a chap meditate in peace here?"

"The time has come -"

"Excuse us, we think you're sitting on our -"

"We think therefore."

"Is it that Tfozb upsetting everyone again?" Nftth interjected.

"Leave her alone," objected Sxzbu, "s/he used to be a woman."

"Ah well, that's half the trouble, isn't it? It was never like this before Equality. They can give you all the training in the cosmos but the plain fact is that a woman just doesn't think the same as us. Heaven ran perfectly well for aeons before -"

"It's the inalienable right of all -"

"Oh, so now we're onto rights, are we? I thought it wouldn't be long -"

"– and in any case, how can it be my fault," countered Tfozb triumphantly, "when we're all of One Mind? Eh? When you get Collective Consciousness, nothing can be anyone's fault, can it? It's only logical and..."

"Settle down, you lot!" The sharp authoritative command immediately restored equanimity, and all senses sheepishly turned to the 3rd Spiritual Secretary. "Kindly remember," he continued patiently with the faintest note of something like sarcasm, "where you are. Your little intellectual dispute is causing an etheric ripple through the whole system. Even SS1 is not unaware of it, and Heaven knows he's got enough on his mind, don't you think?" There was a general murmur of apology as he disappeared.

"There, I told you, didn't I?" muttered Nftth. "If it wasn't for -"

"By the way." The 3rd Spiritual Secretary had suddenly reappeared. It was a favourite trick of his and never failed to catch them out. "I nearly forgot to tell you what I came for. The Planning Committee is meeting soon. Do be ready. And Nftth – no conditionals here, please."

A buzz of anticipation swept through the Elementary Level when he'd gone. The Planning Committee hadn't met for, well, centuries probably. Something *was* going on somewhere. Maybe This Was It. The New Relative General Plan so long hinted at in backrooms and dark corridors. Things were going to happen at last.

Actually, things already were. SS3 only wished he knew what. Of course, he knew about The Plan – but then, there was this disturbance. For a moment, he felt sorry for having spoken harshly to the Elementals. It wasn't their fault and they weren't causing the ripple, only becoming aware of it. But more than any other beings, they had to be kept calm if order was going to be restored.

The really worrying thing was that there seemed to be something happening on the lower levels that was reverberating through the system. Yet how could that be, when all causes start at the Elementary Level?

Φ

When Harry eventually woke up in the pale yellow, cheerless WC, the first thing that occurred to him was that he ought to try out these all-in-the-mind powers that Snorker had alluded to. Any campaign requires its commander to have total self-control.

With a considerable effort of sustained willpower, he imagined himself back on Earth and arrived just in time to see his own coffin being lowered reverently into the limey soil of St Agatha and All Souls graveyard in Buckley Rise. The day was grey and drizzly, and attendance was sparse but included a pale, medium dry Mrs Gardner on the arm of the Editor of The Gazette. Everything seemed in order.

Harry carefully imagined up a box of matches and set light to a pile of dry leaves swept up in the shelter of the church doorway. He then sat on them, reasoning that if he was dead then this should have no effect on him whatever. Unfortunately it did. On the other hand, no-one seemed to hear his yelp of pain. The experiment demonstrated one's ability to achieve all sorts of things by simply applying one's mind to them. He therefore amused himself for a while doing a silly walk around the grave and standing nose to nose with Mrs Gardner and calling her rude names. For all the notice that anyone took of him, this could all be an illusion after all.

But maybe death is just one big illusion.

Φ

Whatever the army of self-proclaimed mystics would have you believe, life on Earth is not awfully spiritual much of the time. People are often quite nasty to one another. The little matters of finding somewhere decent to live and getting enough money together to put food in one's mouth can be quite draining. Even when you know that somehow you're not alone, you still regularly come up against the solid brick wall of being human. You feel frightened and angry and lonely.

Benedict had felt all those things over the next few weeks. But as the mist of sheer incomprehension began to thin out, he realised with surprise that what he didn't feel was regret. He'd been pushed off the edge of a cliff. But he was still alive and, looking back, it hadn't been a very nice cliff anyway. He hadn't woken up every morning with the joy of another new day on the cliff. Perhaps he should have jumped.

For a while he had succumbed to the need-to-get-a-job instinct and spent many frustrating days at the computer searching for what was increasingly obviously unattainable. It wasn't just that, as Mary had promised, people were 'too busy' or didn't respond at all. The machine itself was also still playing up. It froze at inopportune moments. It presented him with websites that had nothing to do with the addresses he'd entered. When he did once get through to his old company's home page to find out what was going on, the computer switched itself off. An engineer confirmed, of course, that the machine was working perfectly.

At last, Benedict saw the pattern. Why hadn't he noticed it before? Every stray website had something to do with art – galleries and exhibitions. And when it froze again as he typed the letters 'AL', the dream came flooding back and he suddenly recognised the young woman.

Somewhere on Level One there was a sigh of relief. It had taken Ranjit three months and some pretty ground-breaking technological ingenuity to get the message across.

On his own more parochial level, Benedict decided one wet Thursday morning to take himself off to one of the exhibitions that had presented itself to him recently. There at Tate Britain, sitting giggling irreverently in front of a famous large canvas of swirling colours that might easily have been painted by a chimpanzee on heat, he found Alison.

"Hello again," he said quietly, sitting beside her. "Sorry it's taken a while to work things out."

"Doesn't matter," she smiled. "You're here now. Everything's clear."

On the other hand, just a few hundred yards away in her sister's Pimlico council flat, things weren't at all clear to the newly unemployed Evie Gardner.

"I don't know what to do, I'm sure," she said.

"'Course not, dear," agreed Gladys.

"I mean, it were all such a shock."

"'Course it were, dear."

"The colonel all white an' floating there. I didn't know what to do."

"'Course you didn't, dear."

Evie paused for a while to reflect on it all. She hadn't been able to get the image out of her mind.

"'E were intestate too, you know."

"Dirty bugger."

The old brass carriage clock on the mantelpiece clunked an apologetic chime for the half-hour as the two women settled back in the musty stillness of the front room and contemplated the chances of sherry in next week's Budget. The south-west London traffic was a muffled hum outside. Things creaked, and a shiver went down Evie's spine. In normal circumstances, she was not one of humanity's greatest examples of sensitivity, but recent circumstances had been anything but normal and she was feeling decidedly edgy. There was something in the air.

"Quite old are they, these flats?" she ventured hesitantly. "Funny noises? Things moving?"

"Well, there's the sideboard, yes dear," confirmed Gladys. "Always did 'ave one leg shorter than the others. I did 'ave it propped up on an old Bible but -"

"I don't mean the flippin' sideboard," said Evie irritably. She was having presentiments of some Great Truth trying to force its way through to her unconscious. "I mean... things. Spirits. The undead, 'auntings an' that." Gladys considered for a moment whether one could apply for a rent rebate on those grounds.

"No, you're imagining things, dear. It's the shock. The funeral an' that."

"Mmm, it were weird. Just like he were actually there, right next to me."

Evie's mind took itself off for a stroll in the middle distance. She hadn't been able to settle to anything these last few weeks, and Mr G hadn't exactly been supportive. She shouldn't have been surprised, for Stan hadn't made a significant contribution to her life (or anyone else's) for the best part of twenty years now.

"Yo'll `ave to gerranother job, then," he'd announced, having realised that the colonel's estate held no promise. The possibility of getting a job himself never even occurred to him. The dole was something one had earned. At forty-nine, disillusion settled over Evie like a lead homburg. True, she didn't have too many illusions about Stan. Once a fine figure of a young man, he'd taken to wearing cardigans within a year of their marriage and had grown fatter and balder by the day ever since. Children had just seemed out of the question. With a quiet little internal sob, Evie realised that life had passed her by and now she was alone. She got up from the chair, put on her old fawn mac and tied a blue scarf around her head.

"Think I'll go for a walk," she announced, "along the Embankment."

"All right, dear."

Φ

SS3 paced his softly-lit executive office with what might easily have been taken for impatience. There hadn't been a stir quite like this since that monk Copernicus had evaded all attempts on his life, finished his book on astronomy and then left the Church to face the Ptolemaic music in the sixteenth century. All right, so most of what he'd written was true, but there's a time and a place for truth. SS3 had been in the FEW then and the furore had nearly cost him his promotion. Only some concerted papal interference had kept things on an even keel for another century or so. And then you just can't allow for a nutter like Galileo, dropping things off the top of the Tower of Pisa to see what happens.

He made an effort to relax, straightened the Turner print on the far wall, sprayed the butterwort, and took a fresh white shirt from the filing cabinet. Due in no small measure to himself, he reasoned as he changed, the Interim Plan had run smoothly since those difficult days, so one little ripple wasn't going to upset him. There would be no panic. No leaping from higher levels or leaving one's clothes on the shores of a distant space-time continuum. All the same, he'd waited long enough for the Central Processes Unit to figure out the answer, so he decided to go and check on them.

Fuzru, the Chief Programmer, scratched his thinning pate, tapped the Escape key and shrugged.

"I blame the hardware, Duflc," he sighed, using SS3's familiar name. They were old friends from their NRC days. "I've put in every scrap of ripple like you told me, and programmed it to find the common factor. But we just keep getting a buzz on the machine. Now, there's this new model the research bods are working on, ninety-third generation stuff, makes this utterly obsolete." He waved a hand expansively at the banks of gleaming ROM along one side of the room. "It's no bigger than a gnat's -"

"What do you mean, 'a buzz'?" interrupted SS3. His friend chained the program and sat back. The cursor flashed, there were a couple of those irritating little beeps that software writers always put in to make sure you're awake, and the screen flashed its answer to Heaven's problem.

"BZ," it said.

"There you are," said Fuzru, "I told you – a buzz." SS3 very nearly clouted him round the head in exasperation.

"That's not a buzz, you… Elemental," he rejoined. "That's someone's initials. It's the answer. Get the code book out."

"Oh, right," Fuzru conceded sheepishly. "Er, which one? I mean, what day is it?"

"You're asking an SS3 what day it is? How the heck would I know?"

They thumbed through several gold-bound files stored in a dusty cupboard before finding what they needed.

"Ok, well it just says 'EG'," Fuzru announced, none the wiser. "Must be an example of something or other. Not enough information, see? You can't expect me to solve problems with old hardware and -"

"It's not an example," interrupted SS3 sharply. "EG is the answer. Get the Anal. boys onto it right now, will you." He disappeared.

"Yes sir, no sir, three spiritual secre -"

"And if they can't solve it," SS3 had just as suddenly reappeared, "I'm bringing in the SGB." For the briefest moment, the whole CPU froze.

Φ

"Yo'll not mek Brum!" Pru's Da had bellowed from behind the racing pages of the Express and Star. He was on the upstairs toilet, which always gave him a sense of authority. In fact he spent a good portion of every Saturday morning on the toilet. It was a sort of tradition. The Black Country is full of tradition.

As he thus delivered his judgement, the rest of the tiny house in Darlaston Road had been in uproar. Prudence herself was flying from room to room, gathering up odd esoteric possessions and stuffing them into a rucksack. Her Ma was trailing behind, wringing her hands and spraying tears like a leaky watering can, pleading with her to stay. The family dog, a cross between Cousin Daphne's disgraced poodle and something very large that could scale garden fences with breathtaking speed, was spinning in circles trying to avoid being trampled.

Prudence herself had been nineteen. She had six good O Levels and a burning desire to leave this house for good. She had not been a pretty girl, but she was clever enough to know that she deserved a lot better than five and a half days a week at Woolworth's. She was going to better herself. She was going to London.

"But why, chicken, why?" her Ma had wheedled.

"Why, Ma?" she had grabbed the little china horse that the boy in the next desk had given her at Infants, stroked it thoughtfully and turned to her mother. "Because I could have gone to college if he'd let me. Because I could have had a boyfriend if he'd let me. And mostly because I'm sick of him up there on his throne bleating every day about three-legged horses and Villa's lame centre-forwards."

"All the same, chickie, he is your Da. An' that counts for -" Her voice had trailed off as if she couldn't quite decide what it counted for.

"No, Ma," Prudence had faced her mother and spoken gently, as if to a child, "what he is is a mean old bastard who can't stand me having more brains than him. So I'm just doing what you've wanted to do for twenty years. London is where everything's happening now, so I'm going where it's at."

"Werritsat?" Her father had entered the room, pulling up his braces. "Yo' don't even know worritis."

Pru had replayed the scene in her head a hundred times or more since. It had been what drove her on. She had stayed with a friend's sister in Belsize Park, waited on tables in a local restaurant and served in bars, earning enough to pay her way and get her through evening classes. Her tutors had been astonished by the single-minded ambition of this girl from the sticks. She wasn't interested in fashion or boys, only in making the most of her talent for organisation and research. An Open University History degree had finally got her where she wanted to be.

Isn't it just the way of things, though, that when you get what you want it turns out not to be what you thought? She had believed that for a woman like her, the Civil Service would be where it's at. But she hadn't counted on glass ceilings. Year after year, she had watched as prettier young things, with the right education and the right connections, were promoted above her and above their own abilities. The girl from the suburbs had remained a very junior servant in Her Majesty's administration.

On her fiftieth birthday, Prudence took her lunch flask and sandwiches along to the bench on the Embankment and considered her life. Cheese and cucumber, with French mustard, as usual. A few hundred yards to her right was the hub of national government, the power-houses of policy and intrigue, the plush offices of mandarins who didn't even notice her existence. She had an insignificant job and a one-bedroom flat, with a little china horse on her bedside table, above a Chinese take-away in Bayswater. She had a small car, took holidays in Portugal, and had never knowingly been touched by a man within six inches of any erogenous zone. It wasn't where it's at. Inevitably, that last day in Darlaston Road flashed though her mind again, and she shuddered.

Yet Prudence was clever and discreet, and she had an extraordinary memory and ear for information. She knew things. Things that certain people wouldn't want other people to know. Maybe it was time for the chicken to come home to roost... She barely noticed the other woman, in fawn mac and blue headscarf, sit down on the bench beside her.

If Prudence felt cheated by life then she was going to feel even worse about death. Had not the gypsy in Hyde Park assured her that she had an exceptionally long lifeline (although admittedly that was before Pru had refused to buy any plastic angels from her)? But then, you never know when your body will strike back.

There must have been a particular moment, but no-one was holding a mirror to her nostril just then. She simply, suddenly, doubled up in excruciating pain and was dead. And it was almost as if the day hadn't noticed and Creation had forgotten to readjust its clothing... an irrelevant moment, the merest wobble of energy fields, and like everything else in Pru's life not a terribly significant thing.

She herself did notice of course. You're bound to think that something's up when you find yourself thirty feet above a London pavement, apparently sitting in a vat of loose semolina pudding. No evening class or wise parent had prepared her for this. But Prudence didn't panic. Having been a civil servant she had ample experience of things not being quite what they seem. She got the picture when she finally looked down, to see a small group of quietly murmuring people gathered around a bench and pointing at two figures on it. One of these was herself, mouth open, skirt blown up around her waist, a half-eaten sandwich in one hand.

She had spilled her tea. The other figure was Evie Gardner, who had fainted.

Across the road, Benedict and Alison emerged from the gallery smiling and shyly holding hands. As Mousey Medium had predicted many weeks before, in the darkest hours there is still hope. There is a purpose to every thing, every calamity, every turn of events beyond our control. Now they had found each other, these two, and they were beginning a whole new path together. In all human experience, there is hardly anything better, happier or more exciting, than this discovery. The rest of the world could go to hell.

So Alison's mind was entirely elsewhere when she stepped off the pavement, just as an ambulance tore past with brakes screeching. Across the road, Mrs Gardner came to just in time to see a young woman's body flying through the air to land in a crumpled heap of blood and broken bone in front of her.

Φ

In the small, suddenly deathly quiet office on Level One, Ranjit sat at his desk and stared through his tears with disbelief at the monitor. How could life be so totally cruel?

On the Embankment in London, Benedict sat on the pavement and stared through his tears with disbelief at the heavens. How could life be so totally cruel?

But somewhere on the very distant Elementary Level, a single soul sat on nothing at all and saw the momentary flicker of energy with understanding and, to all intents and purposes, relief. They were nearly in place.

Φ

"Oh yes?" said John Clarke politely, for at least the twenty-fifth time. He was a good listener. That is to say one could talk at him for hours without eliciting any comment, which is what most people require when they're talking about themselves. And that's the natural thing to do when you find yourself newly deceased and standing in a queue to get into the afterlife. NRC[4] Jones had still got no response from the Destiny Control Officer at the FEW, so after two cups of tea John Clarke had been sent to wait outside. He did so patiently, having no desire to be a nuisance.

Others were not so calm. Boris was doing his best to process as many as he could, but he was pretty much on his own now with his procedures up the spout. He wouldn't get anywhere near quota now, which meant another tricky Review interview to come. And there was distinct unrest developing in the masses.

"'Ere, what's going on up front there?" an angry voice drifted past.

"Come on, we haven't got all day, y'know."

"Have you lost our luggage, then?"

"My gran's expecting me. She'll be getting worried."

"So I'd saved up all year for Glastonbury…"

"Oh yes?"

"And you know what?"

"No?"

"It poured down for three days, it did. Total washout."

"Oh dear."

"All the little bonfires were sizzling out, tents blown away, choruses of Harry Krishna in between the sneezes. Peace 'n love? Give me a break."

"Oh dear."

"And you know what?"

"No?"

"No-one even noticed me 'til they were clearing up on the Tuesday."

"Oh dear."

"So there I was, laid out on… oh, looks like it's my turn. I'm off, then. Nice talking to you, mate."

"Goodbye, then."

A good way further back down the line and shuffling forward slowly, Prudence and Alison had struck up a sort of friendship. Finding themselves almost simultaneously in the semolina, so to speak, they had drifted off together. Though it would be more accurate to say that Pru, being cool and rational, had grabbed Alison's distraught soul as it catapulted past her and held on until she'd calmed down. At first they were both shocked, as much by finding themselves alive as by the dreadfulness of death. But there was at least comfort in sharing it and, the spirit being what it is, they moved on.

"How are you feeling now?" Pru asked the younger woman.

"Mmm, aching all over, like I've been hit by a… well, I'm all right, I guess. You?"

"Yes, a bit of a sore head, that's all. Aneurism, I think."

"It's not fair, is it?"

"No." Prudence paused thoughtfully. "But that's life, Ali."

"Don't you have any regrets, then? Don't you wish things had been different?"

"Oh my word, chicken, of course I do," Pru answered, feeling strangely maternal. "There were all kinds of things I missed out on. Though that was usually other people's fault." Darlaston Road popped into her mind again. "But I think I did my best, considering."

"I have. Regrets, I mean. Especially, right now, not taking religion more seriously." They both giggled.

"Well, a bit late for that, my girl. Well, what's the worst that can happen anyway?"

A little way up ahead of them, something very much like the worst that can happen was happening to John Clarke. Stachov and Hurski of the SGB were equally feared and renowned in the astral world for their uncompromising approach to trouble. They shot it. They were old school, a sin was a sin and a plague of frogs was a plague of frogs. None of this modern sociowhatsit civil rights stuff. The Nepalese chap had certainly received short shrift – a term of A Level then straight into the WC to contemplate his qualifications. Oh yes, any ripples in the etheric current and Stachov and Hurski could flatten them in no time. They were unique.

Or they had always been, until now. Perhaps they'd become complacent with success. Even dead legends can't top the ratings forever. And John Clarke was a different and formidable sort of trouble.

Ziggie had been quite right about the FEW getting on to the SGB as soon as the query went through. If Destiny Control had no records of a soul, and obviously couldn't admit that, then somewhere along the line there had been an almighty foul-up and some equally almighty sorting-out was called for. Moreover, the Anal. boys having got nowhere with Fuzru's EG, SS3 had had no option but to carry out his threat.

"We don't like mysteries," growled Stachov, putting his face up close to John Clarke's in the classical threatening pose. This was a pretty silly remark, since mystery was their entire raison d'etre. The trouble was, of course, they now had two mysteries to deal with at the same time, and that made them feel uncomfortable. The partners had decided to assume that the two problems were connected, since they weren't bright enough to deal with more than one at a time.

"So what's EG, then?" demanded Hurski for the fifth time. He metaphorically flexed his metacarpals belligerently and flicked imaginary dust from the lapels of his stonewashed denim jacket. They were in NRC[4]'s office, while Jones himself peered disconsolately through the two-way mirror at the agitated crowd outside.

John Clarke was genuinely trying to be helpful.

"Elves and Gnomes?" he offered. "The Elephants' Graveyard? Ethyl Glycerate?" Stachov considered for a moment. He had no idea what that last one was but it had a ring of plausibility about it. His partner glared at him.

"Now, come on, John," he decided to try wheedling. "What's all this about, eh? Let's get this over with so we can all go home, right? Who are you?"

"My name's John Cl -"

"Yes, yes, so you've said a hundred times." Stachov set off again up the short path he had been wearing in Jones' magenta carpet ever since they'd arrived. "But that's not enough is it? You're not just a name. Not just 14 Acacia Avenue…"

"Acacia Street, sir."

"All right, whatever. Street, then. But who are you really?"

"Well, I'm John Cl -"

"I think what the gentlemen are getting at," interrupted Jones, exasperated by the stupidity of it all, "is what sort of person have you been? Eh? We need to know where to send you on to from here, see?"

"Exactly," breathed Stachov. "Just what I said." He sat back heavily in Jones' chair and wished the stuffed carp in the glass cabinet would swallow this little man.

"I don't know, sir, I'm sure," said Clarke, puzzled. "I rather thought that you were going to tell me that."

"Us?" Jones gave what he hoped was a light-hearted little chuckle. "How could we do that? We don't keep files on everyone, you know." He shot a sidelong look at the SGB men to encourage them to join in the joke. They didn't get it.

"So what's it to be?" growled Hurski. "Up or down?"

"I'm afraid I really don't know what you mean…"

"Well, were you a good chap? Were you kind to cats? Invite the neighbours round? Buy a new poppy every November?"

"I'm afraid I really don't know what…"

"Did you have flowers in your garden? Take the bus to work?"

"I'm afraid I really do -"

"What about abortion? Nuclear weapons? Conservatives?"

"I'm afraid I -"

"Vegetarians? Stocks and shares? The CIA? Charlton Athletic?"

"I'm af -"

"WHO'S EG?"

"I'm very sorry, sir, I've no idea. Could it be an anagram?"

NRC[4] Jones reached for the Thought Module on his desk as the SGB men sat back exhausted.

"What do you make of him, Ziggie? Is he having us on?"

"Don't think so, guv," the disembodied voiced crackled back. "All the instruments are showing positive. Straight as a whisker. If you want my opinion, not that you ever take any notice of it, this is the first genuine bit of Zen we've had in ages. In fact -" The shrill rattle of the VIP Advance Notice bell by the door cut off Ziggie's opinions.

"Oh no, please, not right now," wailed Jones, thumbing through a pile of papers for his Special List. "I'd completely forgotten about the Masonic riot. It's only the flaming Prime Minister coming." The panic had communicated itself to Boris outside and he came in at a run.

"You yelled, sir?"

"Boris, you should have reminded me. The PM's almost here and he'll expect an escort. He'll be livid if he's kept waiting. Can't you shift that lot outside?"

"I'm doing my best, sir. It's not that easy when -"

"Just do it, NRC[3]. And get rid of Clarke, for heaven's sake."

"Er, well, what do you want me to do with him, sir?"

"Do? Why ask me? It doesn't matter if he doesn't exist, does it? Send him back for all I care – give him Clapham, five sisters and a Fiat, that'll teach him to mess us about." Jones' head was spinning with the impending crisis. His whole reputation hung on his tidy ship and personal touch. This could be ruin. His forehead itched with something definitely like sweat. Clarke was bundled out of the door as Stachov shot him a look that definitely said 'We haven't finished with you, sunshine'.

The jostling and complaints outside were becoming uglier by the moment, not helped at all by the sight of Jones trotting out of his office, hand outstretched, obsequious smile fixed in place.

"Settle down now, please. This isn't very British, is it?"

"What's going on, then?"

"Yeah, we've got our rights, y'know."

"And I've got private insurance, anyway, so -"

"Ooo look, it's 'im off of the telly."

And as if a switch had been flicked, ninety per cent of the goodly, decent, newly deceased working folk of England instantly forgot their own discomforts and craned their necks backwards to watch the celebrity, whoever he was, being escorted past them by a fawning NRC[4] Jones.

Prudence and Alison had almost reached the front of the queue anyway, and now they strolled over to the unguarded barrier. Everyone's attention was elsewhere.

"Not very well organised, is it, for Heaven?"
"I was thinking just the same."
"We could be here forever."
"Mmm."
"Shall we just go through then?"
"Let's."

Chapter Three ~ Meetings

The thing about dreams is that, however clear they seem to be, they never tell you the whole story. You might be getting information from your unconscious that it's decided you need to know, but it would be asking a bit much even of the unconscious to know the Whole Truth. In any case, the unconscious itself is not just one control room but a whole collection of separate offices – autonomous nerves, somatogenics, psyche and so on – that do not necessarily talk to each other. Rather like people, in fact. So how are you to know where the message is coming from?

Suppose you dream that the doorbell rings and the postman gives you a large parcel which turns out to be a painting of a beautiful young woman under a waterfall with fish jumping playfully about. But as you look at it, the water turns blood red and the woman morphs into a black lizard that emerges from the canvas towards you holding a knife. You wake up sweating and feeling sick. Obviously this is a warning (the bell). You are going to hear some news (the postman) and uncover a secret (getting the picture). A good situation is not what it seems (morphing), you're going to come under attack (the knife) and suffer serious injury (the blood).

Then you realise that the alarm clock has just gone off, that last night you attended a Reception where a pretty waitress had served you some sour red wine and dodgy canapés, that you are about to be sick and that you need to run for the toilet.

When Benedict had his dream, he could not have known of course that it had been engineered by a Level One Witness during the warm-up for an international football match. But even without archetype training, he had sort of understood from the dark, clammy fearfulness of the thing that this was a warning. Sure enough, his life had duly collapsed around his ears. So when the bad parts of a dream come true, it's reasonable to assume[3] that the good parts will too. These usually take a bit longer to materialise since the dust has to settle around the collapsed old order first, but eventually he had indeed made his way to the gallery and realised that Alison was his true life partner (though he'd missed the double meaning of the initials).

So why hadn't the dream warned him what was to happen next? Was that too much to ask? To have suffered so much, then found peace

---

[3] Actually, reason has nothing whatever to do with dreams. But that's a different book.

and happiness, then have it all snatched away, was so… incomprehensibly unfair. You might say that the unconscious, or in this case Anthony, hadn't known that bit. Or maybe the match had kicked off before Anthony could fit it all in. Or maybe there are some things that we just can't know, or are not being allowed to know. Or maybe life is sometimes just random.

In his north-west London bedsit, Benedict was in rapid decline and losing the will to live. He'd got the signs, he'd been promised that he wasn't alone, and now he was alone with not the teeniest sign in sight. This is when the human spirit is tested.

For several days, Benedict spent his time testing other sorts of spirits. So he was hardly in the right state of mind to notice any signs that might be coming his way.

This was incredibly frustrating for Ranjit. Having been of a certain social class himself, not to mention simply downright irresponsible, he understood perfectly well how attractive certain substances can be when one's life is down the pan. But he was working his little multicoloured socks off trying to reassure his dude that he had a friend, somewhere. It wasn't working.

For one thing, he had himself been left entirely alone for what seemed like ages, with no instructions and no training. Anthony had sulked quietly in the corner of the room for a while, completely ignoring the young man, and had then just disappeared. He'd seen neither hide nor hair nor shimmering golden aura of Gabriel either. RJ had set about exploring the technology at his disposal, but all the codes had been changed and the systems didn't connect up the way they had before. He had to spend all his time inventing new hacking techniques, only to find that what worked one moment suddenly failed the next.

It was as if RJ, and more importantly his guidee's PSI, that had seemed so crucial a while ago, had been completely forgotten about by The Powers That Be. Having been of a certain social class himself, not to mention on his own admission a bit of a prat, Ranjit was used to being ignored. His habitual response had always been to give up and drop out. But now, rather to his own surprise, he felt a strange and powerful determination to do something about all this. It was the rage and the sense of injustice. And, seeing the state that Benedict was in, it was compassion. This was new.

Φ

There are a lot of misconceptions about the afterlife. For one thing, there's practically no lying about on chaises longues contemplating pastoral scenes, and nor do the ears ring perpetually with inspirational symphonies. Of course, in one sense Heaven is by definition inspiring, but even a liquorice allsort loses its appeal after half an hour of chewing. Being newly dead is not unlike being newly born, wonderfully gratifying at first and all the sleep you want with nothing that has to be done until tomorrow. A baby has all the joy of new discoveries like pulling men's beards and sucking the cat and smashing the occasional ornament. After the best part of a year sitting hunched up in a wet balloon, suddenly there's colour and sound and movement. But soon you find that beards rarely come off and most cats taste the same. So it is with Heaven. Yes, there are some interesting discoveries about the mind and for a while you feel gratified and quite holy, but it soon wears off.

Then there are the people. Those contemplating death as a means of escaping from the insufferably boring fools they've been lumbered with on Earth, need to be warned of a flaw in their logic. When all the energy wobbles have settled down, you find yourself in pretty much the same surroundings you thought you'd left behind, and with much the same bunch of fools.[4]

Best not to worry. Best to assume that the people you're drawn together with, including the insufferable ones, are there for a reason. This helps one to feel more relaxed anyway.

For example, it's quite natural to worry about being recognised in a lap-dancing club by someone you know. But anyone who might recognise you would be there for the same reason as you, wouldn't they? In fact, one Thursday lunchtime at Annabelle's, Harry had indeed recognised someone who, shall we say, probably ought not to have been there. But a nod and a wink to each other were sufficient. Although their paths didn't normally cross very often, Harry not being a Catholic, the two men had held each other in greater esteem after that day, as if they had a bond. Such peeks up one another's sociocultural skirts can be quite enlightening and reassuring. One does not feel so alone in the world. Similarly, Heaven can be quite tolerable once you stop caring what other people think of you. If they think of you at all, then they're like you.

Suppose that an ordinary, decent person such as you were to visit a naturist beach on a hot and sunny afternoon. On the one hand you have the inexpressible sense of freedom in being at one with the sun and the flies, while on the other hand there's the lurking dread of your private parts being seen by someone you know who hasn't seen them before. But when

---

[4] This doesn't apply to the serious, dedicated career spirit, naturally. But they know what to expect anyway.

you do in fact, while hovering in the shallow water, meet your old headmaster or the stunning blonde widow from down the road, then fear evaporates and you welcome one another with the instinctive warmth of common souls doing the most natural thing in the world.[5]

Then, if you're not a naturist you may not enjoy the afterlife quite so much. As Harry had already discovered to his distaste, one's thoughts do tend to hang out for all to see.

Astonishingly, it was Prudence who actually had some experience of all this and so was adjusting to her new surroundings more easily. Her new friend was still upset, having found and then lost the love of her life within the space of an hour, so Pru was prattling on and taking the lead as they took their bearings.

Beyond the NRC barrier they had initially found themselves, like Harry, in something of a wilderness. But being a civil servant, with ample experience in making the facts fit one's own preconceptions, Pru gradually brought some familiar surroundings into focus. (Harry had not been able to do this because his whole experience of life had been to follow faithfully other people's preconceptions.)

The two women wandered arm in arm along Cheyne Walk and up to the Kings Road at World's End. To the right were boutiques and restaurants which seemed somewhat superfluous just now, so they headed left.

"Yes, well naturally I hadn't intended to go there," Prudence went on. "My boss invited me to go one Sunday afternoon, his country club he said, somewhere near Rickmansworth. I suppose I had a bit of a crush on him at the time. I was still young. And he had this fantastic XJ6 with leather seats.

"I assumed it would be frightfully upper crust with tea and salad sandwiches on the lawn. Maybe a junior minister or two. But I guessed something was wrong when we pulled up outside these big green gates and he had to ring three times in code to be let in. Oh look, there's a café – shall we?"

Gandalf's was a bit of a throwback to another, more innocent age. There were low tables, colourful cushions on the floor, a poster of Che Guevara on one wall and a few imitation potted palms. A selection of plastic Buddhas lined the window sill and the door was propped open with a crystal ball. The Kinks' Waterloo Sunset drifted scratchily out from the shadows. They settled themselves in a corner and ordered herbal teas.

---

[5] The embrace is, for the moment, best left metaphorical. One doesn't want to overdo things.

"Well, there was nothing I could do about it, was there?" Prudence continued. "I didn't know where I was. And I didn't know where to put myself. There were all these people prancing about without a stitch on, waving their towels and playing with their balls -"

"Your tea, ladies," said Adrian, setting down a tray.

"– and bats. Thank you. Young people, old people, all shapes and sizes, with great big -"

"Would you like some carrot cake?"

"– picnic baskets. No thanks. And then Clive, my boss, disappeared into the clubhouse and came wobbling out a few minutes later all pink and silly and showing me this great long -"

"Ice cream, perhaps?"

"– list of committee members I was supposed to meet. No thanks. And before I knew it, I was on the cleaning rota every third Sunday and had promised to straighten out his -"

"Chelsea bun?"

"– accounts. No thanks. Of course I never went back, just kept making excuses to Clive. I think I buried three grandmothers and a couple of uncles that year."

Alison laughed out loud for the first time since their arrival, tossed back her long hair and relaxed into her cushions. Pru was also feeling better than she could ever remember. It was dawning on her that not being a civil servant was a profound relief. She didn't have to hold her tongue and think of the future any more. New, warmer feelings assumed long buried within her were beginning to stretch their limbs, cough, and look forward to breakfast.

"What about a cheese and cumber sandwich, with French mustard?" she asked. Adrian smiled and bowed slightly. He was a lanky young man, in tight black trousers and a yellow tee-shirt with Ade printed on the front in gothic lettering. At his feet padded a large lump of dog with long and untidy grey hair, its parentage clearly owing something to a greyhound that couldn't run fast enough.

"I'm Adrian, by the way," he offered a limp hand to each of the women in turn, "Ade to my friends. Though I don't actually see many... well, we're a bit off the beaten track here. Or maybe it's my Kinks." He seemed to need to study his fingernails for a moment. "Um, you're new aren't you? You seem fresh, pardon my French."

"Do shut up, Adrian, you old poof, and get the ladies their food," boomed the military voice from a dark corner. Prudence and Alison started, having thought they were alone in the café.

"Oh, that's the major," explained Adrian with a flick of his head towards the voice. "Don't mind him. He's new, too. Having a bit of a moody are we, Harry? Come and join the ladies. I'll get you another g `n t shall I, on the house?"

"It's Colonel Markham to you, Adrian, if you don't mind." The immaculately uniformed figure loomed up into the light and considered the assembled company in some detail before advancing and heaving himself with a dull thud into a chair that hadn't been there a moment before. "And if there's one damn thing more boring than your damn silly joke about g `n t being on the house when you know damn well that every damn thing is always on the damn house," he grumbled, "it's the fact that none of the damn gins have the slightest damn effect. And stand up straight, man."

"Now, now, Colonel," Adrian rebuked him, "that's twenty pee in the swear box. No blasphemy here, thank you."

"And who's going to do a damn thing about it, eh?" Harry was indeed out of sorts. Since discharging himself from the WC he hadn't met a soul he could have a decent conversation with. None of his old comrades, including Snorker, were anywhere to be seen and he had no idea whatever how he'd come to be in London. He hated the place. Least of all could he imagine why he found himself coming back every day to this godforsaken excuse for a bar being served watery gin by this excuse for...

"It must be because you love us, Colonel," suggested Adrian. "We're your new regiment, eh dear?"

Harry glanced at the present company. They didn't seem like terribly promising recruits. But he was wrong there. He turned to Prudence, a mature woman still with a fine figure, who did at least sit up straight.

"I do apologise for my little outburst, my dear," he began politely. "I have been feeling rather... well, this," he waved a sharply creased arm around to indicate their surroundings, "is not exactly my cup of tea. But our young corkscrew here may be right after all. There must be some point to it, or we might as well shoot ourselves. Why don't you go on with your story?"

Prudence looked the man in the eyes. Her newly developing senses – or were they her old ones that hadn't been used in a long time? – felt that there was a fine mind, and maybe even a kind heart, beyond this gruff exterior.

"There's not a lot to tell," she shrugged. "I had a swim for a while. Nobody seemed to take much notice of me. Well, there isn't much to notice, to be frank. Clive went off to play with his -"

"I'll get that sandwich, shall I?"

"– friends. Yes please. Then I asked this wet chap who was walking past where the showers were and he pointed to the door he'd just come out of, so I said no, I mean the ladies', and he just grinned and pointed again to the same door. You know…" Her voice trailed off as her mind returned to that distant place of potentially life-changing moment and missed opportunity. "…it's a very strange experience, a mixed shower. There you are soaping yourself and you can't help peeking at other people's -"

"More tea?"

"– shampoo. Yes please. And you realise that everyone is really just the same underneath."

Φ

The New Relative General Plan ('Beyond the Millennium') had been kicked around in committee for aeons but there was still no agreement on the minutiae of its implementation. Come to that, even the minutes of the last Planning Committee meeting wouldn't have been agreed by now either if SS3 hadn't made an executive decision and told Tfozb to shut up.

You might think that the Elementary Level of the highly evolved is a haven of serenity and harmony where all are At One and in perfect accord. This is at least true in theory, and as long as there's nothing much to do. But as anyone who has ever served on the lowliest school fete tombola sub-committee will know, formlessness is not a quality that lends itself to decision-making. Having to thrash ideas about among those who consist of little more than idea themselves, is not an easy business. Thus, by virtue of being a disruptive element, Tfozb was perhaps actually the most useful member of Planning, and SS3 ignored the fact at his peril. With his vast experience of death, he should have realised that it is in the very nature of committees to make collective decisions which its individual members know perfectly well are downright silly, if not actually fatal. The lone dissenting voice is therefore often the most sane. Democracy is all very well as a sideshow for the masses but if there's something important to be decided then you can't beat straightforward totalitarianism with a side order of private deals behind the scenes.

The Third Spiritual Secretary may have seemed like just the frontman. But he couldn't let this lot mess things up. After all, this was the most important decision to be made in Heaven for two millennia. Second Comings only come once.

"I still say," insisted Tfozb for the umptieth time, "it has to be 2016 or 2017 at the latest." There was a collective murmur of exasperation around the enormous table.

"Not again. Is s/he still at it?"

"What's wrong with 2020? It's a nice round number and a multiple of seven."

"No, it's not."

"Isn't it? Well anyway, 2016 would ruin the Olympics."

"And the European Championships."

"It's supposed to be 1996 anyway. We did promise on that."

"Excuse me, you weren't even on the Committee in Daniel's day."

"No, but I've read the minutes. You specifically told him that Jerusalem would be relieved 1,260 years after Omar. 'Three and a half times', you said, and in Hebrew that's 1,260 which meant 1917. We did just that, on the dot. Then you told him – and John – 1,339 years to the Second Coming and that's 1996. I rest my case."

"Well, we've missed that."

"Oh, have we? When did -"

"The whole business of prophecy has gone to pot nowadays. Anyway, the calendar's all wrong now. You can't be expected to take these things literally."

"Why not?"

"So do you want an army of fire-breathing dragons from Magog to get wiped out on the Golan Heights by a fleet of white vessels from space?"

"If necessary."

"Well, tough. Too late. George got the last one, if you remember."

"Order, everyone, please," interjected SS3 tetchily. "Order. Come on, we're running out of time." There was a collective raising of eyebrow.

"Surely that's the least of our problems?" Sxzbu pointed out. "We can always bend a few years here and there, fiddle the odd incarnation. It's been done before."

"And s/he doesn't even have to be born, as such."

"Or conceived."

"No need for smut."

"Whatever." SS3 had always hoped for this job, but there were times when it didn't seem quite so enjoyable. "Look, there's all the preparation to get started on first anyway. We've got to sort out some earthquakes and droughts, brief a few prophets, organise the odd comet, all that. And it won't be easy with the computers playing up...oh, I mean..."

He shouldn't have mentioned that. There was a hubbub of disbelief and anxiety among the Elementals, and something akin to panic gathered pace as the meeting broke up sending a ripple throughout the system that wiped fifty billion dollars off Wall Street and took three Australian wickets in one over.

Φ

A disconsolate Ranjit sat hunched and motionless in the orange floral comfy chair vacated by Anthony. This had been his first proper job and now there was nothing to be done. But then, somewhere very deep within the dusty, disused back guest rooms of his mind, a small and pink Very Good Thought was born, seemingly from thin air if not actually a vacuum. It blinked, smiled at itself, stretched and discovered that it had legs. It began to move and explore its surroundings, searching for a way out. With a tiny cry of joy it slipped underneath several locked doors and began to run. Up the stairs, along twisty corridors, in through one door of a shadowy living room where the bulb had long since blown and out of another, the Very Good Thought accelerated and grew, faster and fatter and rosier by the moment. At last it emerged into the early light of semi-consciousness, skipping over synapses and slithering down neural pathways with unstoppable momentum until finally it burst out in all its freshness, vitality and beauty into what passed for RJ's brain.

"Yo' dude!" exclaimed its owner, slapping a fist to his forehead with such force that the Very Good Thought was nearly knocked out. "I is such an eeejit!"

With all his attention on Benedict's and his own sorry state, Ranjit had completely ignored Alison. He'd only got a C in maths, but he could at least recognise an equation when it stood panting and slightly stunned in front of him. RJ dead plus Alison dead equals RJ might be able to find Alison and put her back in touch with Benny-boy.

He leapt forward to the desk. With long braided hair swinging and fingers flashing across a keyboard, he might easily have been taken for a rock star.

Φ

Evie Gardner looked down over Watling Avenue from the first floor window above the florist's and wondered how on Earth it had come to this. She swirled the dry sherry slowly anticlockwise in the chipped glass, knocked it back in one, and took a long deep drag on the Raffles Light.

No, it wasn't any clearer. It was Saturday evening and the market had packed away, the street littered with paper wrappers, squashed plums and drunk traders hanging outside the pub. It was noisy and smelly and as far removed from the village life she had left so recently as anywhere could be. But whose was that life? She didn't even know anymore who she was. From quiet, boring, inoffensive housekeeper married to fat Stan in the backwoods of Hampshire, to dark angel of death haunting the streets of London. People were dropping like flies all around her lately. Well, three people. Of course it might just be a messy coincidence. Never the most sensitive or thoughtful of souls, Evie would have dismissed it all as such a few weeks ago. But now something insistent and terrible was nagging away at an inner mind she hadn't even known she had. Life had changed forever. Evie had changed forever. She was in the grip of something much bigger than herself.

"Guts," she had muttered for the tenth time. "Guts. In the street. Right in front of me. And a corpse on the bench."

"Yes, dear."

"I mean, why me? I didn't do nothing."

"No, dear." Gladys was neither the most intellectually acute nor the most supportive of sisters, but she was a good listener.

"And now I jus' don't know where I am, Glad."

"No, dear." A full five minutes had passed in silence, save for the creaking of the carriage clock and faint hum of traffic heading for Victoria.

"I can't go back."

"No, dear?"

"Home, I mean. I can't go back, I don't belong there no more. Dunno where I belong any more. I dunno where to stay."

"No, dear?"

"I don't suppose -"

"No, dear." They had each taken a sip, set down their glasses, and another five minutes passed. A thought finally worked its way through to Gladys' mouth.

"There's Betty's."

"What?"

"Betty's."

"Who's?"

"'Er off of Sainsbury's deli counter, remember? I went to bingo with 'er of a Thursday."

"I've never 'eard of Betty."

"No, dear? Well, she `ad a big win on the premium, took `erself off on a cruise, silly mare. `Er flat's empty. In Burnt Oak. You could stay there, dear."

"Oh. So how long's the cruise?"

"What? Oh, that were six months ago."

"But you said -"

"She only went an' got that bug, didn't she, soft cow. Leg In The Air, something in `er plumbing."

"Legionnaire's?"

"That's it. Isolation ward up Barnet General now. You could stay there, dear. Betty's not coming back. I got `er keys, dear."

It had been a week now, and Mrs Gardner was as lost as a budgie on Salisbury Plain. From rustic general store and mobile library in the true-blue shires, to pound shops and Afro-Caribbean vegetables she'd never heard of and at least five different colours of people. There had to be a reason behind all this, otherwise she would simply go loopy.

Sure enough, the very next morning when she ventured out down to the street for some milk, a stained and crumpled page from an old local newspaper blew along the pavement and wrapped itself unremittingly around her left leg. This is how angels sometimes communicate with one. When she had at last freed herself, Evie found herself reading a one-eighth block advertisement for the Spiritualist Church on Orange Hill Road.

Well, where else did she have to go?

Φ

Disabilities are sometimes obvious, like a missing leg or two. Things like an IQ of 50 or an allergy to frogs may be less visible. But one of the worst handicaps for a woman is to be born beautiful. The trouble is, you get so much attention from other people that you grow up believing yourself to be somehow special. This is a dangerous fallacy for anyone, along with believing that having your photograph taken wearing expensive clothes (or not wearing them) is somehow a worthwhile human activity. And worse than this, when you reach a certain age, men start acting like total numbskulls on the off chance that they might be able to touch your body and falling over each other to do every little thing for you from opening doors to buying you cars, so that never in your life do you learn to do anything for yourself.

Alison had not been born disabled. She was trim and intelligent, but her best qualities were a pleasant voice and an unremarkable, plain face. True, the eyes were clear and grey and deep, but few people ever got close enough to see them. As a result, she had grown up self-reliant and resourceful and with a good set of values. Young men had sniffed about of course – she had after all been female and breathing – but they hadn't stayed long, partly because she wasn't beautiful and partly because she was intelligent and had good values. She had wanted love, but had been prepared to wait.

She was the perfect office receptionist, calm and efficient, and completely unnoticed by the hundreds of people who passed by her desk each day, even by those who actually spoke to her and received directions. But she had noticed Benedict on her first day in the job, and the little jump of her heart had told her all she needed to know. It was just going to take patience and, not being beautiful, she had plenty of that.

"It's not fair!" she sobbed into her hankie. Meeting Prudence had helped her through the initial shock and then their attention had been focussed on finding their way. But now it was all catching up with her. "Three years! It took three years until he noticed me. And then another three months for him to realise that we belonged together. And then it lasted barely three-quarters of an hour…"

"Rough," agreed the dog. It raised itself slowly on uncommonly long legs, stretched, shook its main of wispy grey hair and loped over to their table to check for discarded pieces of cake. Adrian gave it a loving scratch under the chin.

"I miss him so much," Alison went on quietly. "Silly, isn't it? We hardly knew… But what's worse, I can't help thinking that he must be in a terrible state right now. The poor boy's suffered so much."

"Rough," said the dog. It was almost as if it understood every word. One huge, scraggy ear flopped over an eye as it cocked its head to the side and put on its best pleading expression as Pru raised her sandwich to her mouth.

"There there, good boy," sniffed Alison.

"She's a girl actually," said Adrian. "Strayed in off Kings Road one day and decided to stay. It's the carrot cake. I call her Bonzai."

"Eh?" Alison looked puzzled. "But she's so big."

"It's ironic, apparently," said the dog. Alison nearly fell off her chair and Pru froze rigid, sandwich in mid-air. Bonzai followed up with possibly the biggest understatement since Noah turned up his collar and said it looked a bit like rain. "Oh, suppose you didn't expect me able to speak, did you? I don't know why you surprised. We dogs spend most time with people so we bound to pick things up. Apart from stupid rubber bones, I mean." Pru was the first to recover.

"Yes, well I'm just really glad I'm vegetarian, that's all. So are there all sorts of animals in Heaven, then?"

"Whatever you like."

"And do they all speak English?"

"Naturally."

"Hmm, well no offence, Bonzai, but it does feel a bit odd talking to you." Prudence needn't have worried. Most people while alive spend a good deal of their time wittering away to their dogs, chrysanthemums and goldfish without any hope of reply, and yet are regarded as perfectly sane by society. Moreover, the British always witter in English wherever they are, on the assumption that were it not for the unfortunate circumstances of being born a chrysanthemum or French, everything and everyone would naturally be British. So when these impediments are removed by death, everyone will be found to speak English anyway. This actually turns out to be true.

There's a lot of irrational things to get used to, as Harry had already been struggling with. Take those Witnesses. There you are dead, and with hardly a by-your-leave they're giving you a hard time about being ignored and why hadn't you done this or that and did you imagine your immortal soul was safe just because you gave a tenner to Shelter at Christmas and by the way your tennis was rubbish too. So you think 'Hang on, I didn't ask to come here, you know' and they say 'Oh yes, you did and it serves you right'. Well, you can do without friends like that, can't you?[6]

On the other hand, things can be really confusing at first if you don't know how things work. Adrian had been too polite to tell Prudence and Alison that drinking tea and eating cheese sandwiches was utterly pointless, since they'd both left their digestive systems far behind on the Embankment. (In any case, he had a business to run which, things being as they are, wasn't doing very well.) Other things are even more troublesome, like travel being so easy, for example – no need for buses, no need for the eight-fifty from Croydon (and thankfully no need for Croydon). You just have to think about going somewhere and that's it. This can be a tricky thing to master. Suppose the kids say 'When can we go to the zoo?' and you say 'I'm thinking about it', then you'd already be gone and they'd be left behind.

So when Harry completely disappeared in mid-sentence from Gandalf's, the odd eyebrow was raised. Moments later he reappeared in exactly the same place, except that he was now upside-down on the chair

---

[6] So it's probably a good idea while alive to make friends with a few elderly and infirm people, so that when your turn comes there's a fair chance there'll be someone around that you're on speaking terms with who can show you the ropes and offer a bit of sympathy.

and pretty furious. Eyes screwed up in concentration, knees vibrating slightly with the effort, he tried again but didn't move.

"That's odd," he muttered. "It doesn't seem to work anymore. Something must be broken."

"Where did you want to go to, dear?" asked Adrian helpfully. Harry winced and looked at the young man as if he'd just crawled out of Bonzai's ear.

"If it's any of your business," he retorted pompously, "I just wished with all my heart to be with people like me."

"Well, lovey," said Adrian gently, "you'd better sit down and take the weight off your prejudices. It must be us." The colonel sheepishly did as he was told and Prudence turned to him excitedly.

"I say, sir, that disappearing was a wizard trick," she enthused. "How did you do it? Is it magic or something?"

"Oh no, my dear," he tried to sound modest, but couldn't help the glint in his eye. This woman was not a bad sort, fairly bright, in trim and up to form. And the first person to address him as 'sir' for a very long time. "All in the mind, you know. Frightfully complicated. I shouldn't worry your pretty head about it. Didn't understand it myself at first, but Freud explained it all quite well."

"You've read Freud too?" Her voice betrayed a small but definite admiration for the man. All right, he had just attempted to be extremely unsociable but as a civil servant she'd had ample experience of that.

"Oh no, my dear. He dropped in here for a schnapps one day recently on his way to the library. Looking for something on Jung, I believe."

"But surely," Pru was quick, "if anyone can drop in anywhere just by thinking about it, why didn't Freud just go and visit Jung?"

"They're not speaking."

The little group lapsed into thoughtful silence, being careful not to think about going anywhere else right now, each one in their own way vexed with the question of why they were all together here. Outside, there was a soft afternoon light and a gentle breeze. And then, giving them a cheery wave at the window was John Clarke.

"Oh bugger me!" hissed Adrian, not very spiritually, flattening Bonzai as he vaulted to his feet and in one movement clearing both the table and his customers into a back room with an astonishingly masterful gesture.

"What the -"

"But it's only Mr Clarke. He's a nice -"

"And you didn't see who was just behind him, did you?" explained Adrian. He pointed through a crack in the door. Several heavily built figures in trench coats and homburgs were sloping along the deserted pavement yards from a puzzled looking John Clarke, who was wondering where everyone had gone and was oblivious of others arriving.

"SGB patrol," whispered Adrian. "Best avoided if you know what's good for you. I've got a seventh sense for police."

As he spoke, the street outside was suddenly flooded by a searchlight and a voice crackled through a megaphone. This was all pointless, of course, but old habits die hard in Heaven.

"Stand right there, sonny, and don't move. You're nicked." The patrol jumped on the man, pinning him against the café door. "It's 'im all right," said one with a silver star on his lapel, studying a photograph, "'im as caused all the fuss at the NRC. Right, you scum. You've asked for it." Two men held Clarke up while another landed blow upon blow into his stomach and out the other side. "Think you can get away without records, eh? Well, what do you think about *that?*" A fat knee came up very sharply into the man's groin, and he sank to the pavement.

"I'm not really sure…" he moaned, before closing his eyes. The patrol left, laughing and high-fiving, and in a few moments the street was at peace again.

"Blimey!" said Alison. "You don't expect to see that sort of thing here."

"The SGB are a law unto themselves, dear. Believe me. I've had my share of harassment. They call it Spiritual Security."

"But the poor chap is completely harmless."

"Since when did that stop the police?"

The group slowly opened the back room door and ventured into the café, checking the street for surprise manoeuvres, before gathering around the prone man outside.

"Any 51gn5 of l1f3?" asked Alison, concerned.

"Wh4t d1d y0u 54y?"

"I just wondered if he was -"

"Dead? Well, of course he's dead. But he's all right," said Adrian. "Help me bring him inside. I'll make some fresh tea."

"Well, that settles it," announced Adrian, once they had all regained their composure and John Clarke had regained consciousness and his quiet smile of gratitude. "You lot need to disappear, and soon."

"Eh?"

"What?"

"?"

"Didn't the hoods say that John had no records?"

"That's right," said Pru, "he was at the NRC with us. They couldn't process him, whatever that means."

"And Harry, didn't you tell me the other day…"

"I discharged myself, yes. No processing."

"Nor me."

"Me too."

"So you know what this means, then? You're all fugitives. That must be why John turned up here, following you. So the SGB will be after you too before long." There was a deathly silence while they each took it in.

"Good grief!"

"Lummy!"

"Rough!"

Chapter Four ~ Seeds of Anarchy

It was no coincidence, Jungian or otherwise, that at the very same moment that Adrian reached his conclusion, the Central Processes Unit computer (ninety-third generation) worked out the next bit of ripple. The letters HA followed by PRU popped onto the screen.

"Now that," said Fuzru in relief, "I do understand. The second bit anyway." He presumed that the first bit was an exclamation of triumph. With a self-congratulatory smirk, he reached for the red Thought Transfer Module and dialled 3.

"What?"

"Duflc? CPU here. You sound depressed."

"Don't ask," groaned the Third Spiritual Secretary. "What have you got?"

"Ah, well, good news. I've got an answer on the latest program. See, I used a five-bit hexadecimal inverted Until loop with an atPercent assumption modem hooked into the -"

"Fuzru?"

"Yes?"

"Just get on with it, will you?"

"Oh, right. Sorry, I'm sure. Just thought that being an SS3 you might like to know about the latest techniques, optimal resource tracking, that sort of -"

"What's the flaming answer?"

"PRU. Has to be the Psychic Research Unit. There's your hiccup."

"Right. I'll send the SGB down there straight away." In view of their recent performance, it could be thought that this was SS3's second big mistake in a row.

Φ

The purpose of the Psychic Research Units has never been rigorously defined. Officially they are maintained by the Elementary R & D committee, but being dotted about at all points of the compass in Limbo, the lowest astral level, any actual control over them is pretty tenuous. In any case, only the most eccentric would choose to work under such shadowy and ill-defined conditions and in a field looked down upon by proper science.

Arthur Stone, the director of PRU (North-East), was indeed eccentric and had been left very much to his own devices for some time now. With a skeleton staff, an untidy and cramped workshop, but at least with more electricity than anyone could possibly use, he whiled away eternity tinkering with etheric multi-stage switchgear, dreaming up ever more elaborate protocols for the ultimate experiment.[7]

He was relaxing in his tiny office overlooking the workshop, a small and exceedingly scruffy man, feet up on the desk and bottle at his elbow, reading the paper. Nations were at each other's throats, social workers on strike, scandals in high places – so things must be even worse on Earth. Suddenly a small sound made him start but before he had even had a chance to hide the bottle Stachov and Hursky were at either side. They lifted him bodily from the chair and up against the wall, legs dangling.

"Vot in ze name of - ?" he began.

"We came in the back way," said a grinning Stachov.

"Hope you don't mind," grated Hurski.

"Mind? Mind? I didn't efen know zer voz a back vay!"

"We always manage to find one," said Stachov. "We, Professor – or should I call you Brother -" they chortled together, like marbles rattling in a can, "we are the SGB."

"You zink I don't know who you are? Ze SGB voz my idea!"

"Yeah, well." They dropped him. "Thought we'd pay a little visit, see. A social call. There's been… disturbances. Oh, by the way -" Stachov opened his clenched fist to reveal a small silver module with two wires hanging from it. He closed his fist again and there was a crunch as the ultra-grade derivative circuits disintegrated. "– your alarm system doesn't work. On your own today are you? Records say you have an assistant…"

"Ah, zat is Nigel. I sent him home early," said Stone, still in a heap on the floor. "Voman trouble. You know how it is." Stachov didn't and was never likely to. Hesitantly, Arthur picked himself up as if not expecting to remain vertical for long. "Zo, vot sort off disturbance?"

"Just a ripple." Hurski was wandering around the office, amusing himself by picking up bits and pieces and dropping them. This was the part of the job he was good at, straightforward bullying. "The odd buzz at the

---

[7] For the record, it should be explained that Arthur Stone was not his real name. It had been changed by Destiny Control on the grounds that knowledge of his previous identity as a Very Important Leader might seriously destabilise about a sixth of the Earth's surface. This also accounts for the fact that he'd been stuck near the back of beyond in PRU(NE).

CPU. The computer's pointing the finger at you. Thinks you know summat." Nonchalantly, he slipped in the bait. "EG?" Stone didn't bite.

"For example vot? Anyvay, vot do you expect from zat old machine? Now, I've been vorking on a new generation intramultiple thoughtbend hub vich -"

"Yeah, Professor, just what have you been working on, eh? See, we're very interested in your work." A subtle pause. "EG?"

"Vell, I voz just giving you an exa -"

"Never mind," sighed Stachov, his head starting to spin. Things had been so much easier in the old days. You knew where you were with card files and steel toecaps. Your villains had respect, your grasses were reliable. "Show us your bloody machines, Arthur."

"Ah, vunderful. Yes, I vill show you," enthused Stone, glad to change the subject. He led the way down some steps to the workshop where banks of equipment gibbered away to each other on benches like green monkeys composing poetry. He pressed a button and the weather forecast for the Channel Islands appeared on five different screens.

"Very clever," agreed Stachov, impressed.

"Zat's not it. See, ve are vorking on a vay of manipulating the cloud systems with a controlled permonuclear infusion ray. It's over Manchester at ze moment. Seemple! A few bad harvests and ze class system vill collapse!"

"Won't people starve?" asked Hurski, frowning.

"So? Zat's better zan being shot isn't it? And it's vorth it to create vorld piss. I can see zat ve got it wrong before, appealing to ze proletarian ideology off dialectical materialism. Ve should off just appealed to zer bellies. Ah, Heaffen is vunderful, ze mind is so clear."

The thugs were getting anxious to move on. Coming down here was giving them the bends and this lunatic seemed harmless enough, as lunatics go.

"Nothing else, then?" asked Stachov. "Unauthorised contracts? Coded messages?" The memory of the cross-correspondence experiments still rankled with the SGB. You can't have regulations broken willy-nilly. "Red lamps? Ectoplasm? Knockers?"

"Vot?"

"Table knocking. Seances, that sort of thing?" Arthur Stone visibly paled.

"Ve-e-ell...zer's ze old dear in Edgware viz ze balls."

"You what?"

"Ze crystal balls. A medium. She popped up on ze screen ven -"

"Show me."

Arthur shrugged, pressed some buttons and turned some dials.

"It vill be no good. Zese people haf no idea vot's going on. Keep sinking it's Auntie Vera coming through and asking how ze cat is and is heaffen pink." There was a crackle of static and a misty picture appeared on an ancient monitor in the corner to reveal what looked like a small community hall, shaded by heavy brocade curtains and with a few rows of plastic chairs set out. A few nondescript people were entering at the back and taking their seats, while on the stage at the other end sat the old dear. On a rickety card table in front of her was a crystal ball, which she pored over with intense concentration.

"Zer, like I told you. Zis is nothing. She'll be off in a moment viz 'You haff a vunderful Red Indian guide and a great spiritual mission' and zen zey'll all haff a cup off tea in ze back and gossip about zer neighbours."

"Hmm, who's the old bag in the mac?" asked Hurski out of idle curiosity. But he was feeling queasy and already turning for the door as Stone keyed in the identity sub-routine. After what seemed an age, two letters popped up in the bottom corner of the screen.

EG.

"Bloody hell!" whispered Stone, who was not actually as dim as he seemed. Wiping a distinct bead of sweat from his brow, he turned nervously to the others. "Is zis vot you -" But they'd already gone.

Φ

"Surely," Prudence mused, "brainy people like Freud who lived long ago must be higher up the heavenly spheres than people like us? Oh, sorry Colonel, no offence intended."

"None taken, my dear. And it's Harold, please."

"Oh, right… Harold. And I'm Pru." She lowered her eyes with a shy, almost girlish smile. Adrian was quick to spot the start of Something Meaningful, and quickly busied himself with a tea towel.

"For one thing," he chipped in, "brains have nothing to do with anything. And for another, heavenly spheres are a load of old Balearics, pardon my Spanish."

"So we can just go and find anyone we like, say, Caesar or Queen Victoria?" Having studied History, Prudence had always wanted to give a few characters a piece of her mind.

"As long as they don't mind being found," shrugged Adrian. "What's the attraction? I mean, do you have anything in common with Queen Victoria?" Pru considered the matter and decided to keep quiet.

"See, you only meet up with people if you have some sort of attraction. My old Dad put it quite well. When he died, there we were having a stand-up ding-dong in the hospital, same as ever, and he says to me 'Nancy,' he says, that's what he called me, 'Nancy, let this be a lesson to you. Being dead means never having to say another word to someone if you don't want to. I could be gone from here in a moment and you'll never see me again,' he said."

"What then?" asked Alison.

"He was and I haven't."

"Oh, that's sad."

"Rough."

"Not really, seeing as it was him who battered my Ronnie to death with a whisky bottle when he found out about him and me."

He turned towards Harry, expecting some sarcastic jibe, but the colonel had lapsed into a moody silence again. Not long ago he'd had a determined vision of achieving things in this new life, but it hadn't taken long to realise that Heaven is not a place for visions. Everything was so, well, slack. Take those apocalyptic ghouls who called themselves Witnesses. Fair enough, it can't be much fun spending one's eternal reward banging on like school teachers trying to get through to so many mindless souls who couldn't give a damn. But one still expected some spark of professional idealism.[8]

Frustration was welling up again in Harry's mind like porridge in a rubber balloon. Something would have to give soon, and it probably wouldn't be the porridge. Why was it always so that Those Who Know What To Do are always so far removed from What Needs To Be Done? Though with his experience of the Army, he shouldn't have been surprised by this.

He felt an odd sensation now. A soft tingle was spreading up his arm and something was mellowing deep within, as if a far distant memory was yawning and wiggling its toes. He came to from his reverie to find Prudence patting his hand and looking at him with genuine concern.

"What's the matter, Harry?" The porridge exploded. He sat back and sighed, surveying the others with an unmistakable dampness in his eye.

"I'm sorry," he said at length. "Look, you're all decent chaps -" this was quite a concession to Adrian, "- but what have we got in

---

[8] Incidentally, while on the subject, there is a widely-held belief that spirit guides cannot exist because sooner or later a few of their considerable number would surely have irrefutably got through to someone. But this is self-evidently false, akin to arguing that because Adrian only had one GCSE at grade D to his name he couldn't possibly have spent eleven years at school.

common? If Adrian's right, then what's the attraction? I mean, I'm a soldier and you're…" Adrian helped him out.

"Two women, a dog and a corkscrew?"

"Well, you're not a soldier now, are you, any more than I'm a civil servant or Adrian's a -"

"I'm still dog, though," muttered Bonzai, with obvious disappointment.

"I know what it is," said Alison quietly. They all turned to her. "I know what we've got in common. Nobody cares about us."

But she wasn't right. A strange figure was dancing in the doorway.

"Yo, dudes! Found yo! I is your main man, innit!"

Φ

Evie crept as unobtrusively as she could along the back row of chairs in the dimly lit community hall. There were only a few minutes to go yet the place held just a smattering of people mostly, she noticed with relief, middle-aged women like herself or rather older, wrapped in coats and headscarves and undemanding smiles. A brace of elderly and slightly smelly men dozed in front of her. A solitary, earnest looking student with notebook at the ready sat at the front. She had never in her life been to a Spiritualist service so had few expectations; all the same, the atmosphere was not impressive. It did not seem to be the sort of place where one might anticipate divine revelations.

The events of the last few weeks had shaken Mrs Gardner to the foundations of her mind, although admittedly that wasn't very deep. After a quiet suburban life of ordinary and decent self-seeking, the vision of death had begun to pursue her relentlessly, along with a nagging intuition that more was to come. Somehow, it all had something to do with *her*. Nor was there any respite from the vision in her sleep. One night she would be wandering through the tangled overgrowth of a dark graveyard, picking her way between purple sheep, when the ground would open and a jet of pure white water would lift her twenty feet in the air like a plastic ball balanced on a sealion's nose. The next night would find her naked and being chased along a motorway by a huge rabbit wearing a white shroud. Gladys had taken her to the doctor's but it hadn't done any good. The little yellow pills put her to sleep, which was the last thing she wanted, while the blue ones stirred up very odd sensations in her lower abdomen which seemed to intensify whenever she saw a poster advertising a Mel Gibson film.

Evie began to feel a bit lonely as well as out of place. This wasn't even a proper church. No reassuring stone pillars, no solemn altar and no stained glass, unless you counted the old, chipped vase on the front table with a few droopy daffodils in it. The old dear, Chairperson Mrs P, still hovered over her crystal ball. Evie was just rising to her feet to leave when a resounding crash of B flat minor from the portable organ to one side froze her in mid-hover. The rest of the sparse congregation stood obediently for the entrance of the evening's Speaker, which never came because he'd been sitting completely unnoticed to one side of the stage for a good half an hour already. He didn't move. There was a little confused shuffling and irritated mumbling as everyone sat down again.

Judas Skim continued to smile serenely, vacantly and utterly immobile in his chair, his shock of red hair the focus of every eye in the place.

"Shall I wake `im, Mrs P?" hissed the organist, her fingers poised over a chord unknown in any classical repertoire. The Chairperson shook her head impatiently.

"`Course not. He's meditating. In deep trance," she hissed back. "Surely you can see his Master's hovershadowing him?" The organist craned her neck for a better view of the celestial mantle about Skim's aura, but conceded that she probably wasn't evolved enough yet. In fact, he looked much like her Jack did after Sunday dinner at the pub, and the only thing overshadowing him was dyspepsia. Silence reigned.

Backstage, however, it was quite a different story. The Witness In Charge for this evening's proceedings was Jaimie, a craggy and good-natured Presbyterian, but struggling to control the jostling, arguing melee of friends and relations anxious to get through to the congregation. These were in turn outnumbered by a crowd of sheer hangers-on. It was always the same when Skim made an appearance, much as a knot of spectators always gathers at the scene of an accident. Skim was a good turn, guaranteed to outrage someone with his ill-chosen philosophical asides, and totally immoral side bets were being made in every corner as to who today's victim would be.

"Come on, now," pleaded Jaimie above the hubbub, "let the relatives through, please. They've had a long journey." His job was to select the messages and then pass them on using the special code of esoteric symbols and extrasensory impressions to the medium's guide. Tonight this was Laughing Meerkat, a Sioux whose parents had wanted a girl. His was a pretty thankless mission too, since Judas Skim rarely took a blind bit of notice of him and made it all up as he went along.

Today was worse than usual, since in all this confusion there seemed practically no chance of any sensible messages being either transmitted or received. Jaimie and Laughing Meerkat might just as well give up and disappear to the RC canteen down the road. From a certain point of view this wouldn't matter at all, since nothing very sensible ever does get transmitted. That's the nature of things, and the reason for the brisk trade at the RC. But you have to go through the motions.

Φ

Back in PRU(NE), Arthur Stone's assistant Nigel wrestled with reverse octal linkages and racked his brains for a way of hacking into Edgware. Stone himself had been a nervous wreck since the SGB's visit, which of course had been its purpose. But more than that, it was the ID readout that really worried him. What was so special about an old bag in a mac? It might be against regulations, not to mention the conditions of his grant, but Arthur Stone was now tracking Evie for all he was worth. Sooner or later the two thugs would be back, and if this woman was their ripple then he wanted to know why before they did. Call it an instinct for pure scientific research. Or self-preservation.

"It's no good, Art," whined Nigel. "There's too much interference, quite apart from the security lock on Camden and the Met Police shield. Funny sort of code, too. I've only seen one like it before – that chap in the Middle East, remember? Long hair. Spent a lot of time knee-deep in rivers."

"Hmm," Arthur stroked his beard. "I haf read about zat case. Had a strange PIN, as I recall." They thumbed through back numbers of the PRU's official journal, The Psycho, and scratched some calculations on the backs of envelopes, pausing only to interrupt the gibber of green monkeys from time to time with a new piece of routine. Finally, with a flash and a beep, they were in.

"Vell, shoot me," breathed Arthur, eyebrows disappearing into his hair. "Somezing *is* going on!"

Φ

John Clarke had wandered off again to who-knows-where and the fugitives made a collective decision to get away from Gandalf's and lose themselves before the police came back. But when Adrian suggested that they all went up the ARCE he got a mixed reception.

"Steady on, fellah," snorted Harry, throwing a protective arm around Pru's shoulder. "I mean, ladies present. Any more of your -"

"No," Adrian winced, covered in embarrassment, "I mean the Arts, Recreation and Cultural Exchange. Everyone goes there, they'll never find us in that crowd. Look, I'll close up the café and we can slip out through the back pass…I mean, the rear door. And to avoid any further misunderstandings, you'd better have this." He reached behind the counter and handed out a piece of paper which spontaneously duplicated itself as required. It was a Rough Guide to Heaven. "I knocked it up a while ago. It's probably not complete, of course, I just pieced it together from what people have said in the café."

He led them on a circuitous route through Parson's Green, travelling on foot to be sure of staying together. Bonzai was banished to the rear of the column to sniff out any unwelcome followers, while the colonel marched briskly at the front. A rejuvenated Alison skipped happily beside the over-excited Ranjit, repeatedly begging him for more information about Benedict while barely understanding a word he said, while Prudence had been appointed honorary Corporal and permitted to walk alongside their commander and engage in tactical discussion (much as discussion at a dinner party is tactical, self-interested and biochemical). She could not help admiring the man. He was in trim and apparently had a working heart. Yes, he was also a pompous twit with a world outlook as rigid as a ten-year old cement mixer, but any woman knows that such minor flaws can be re-educated. He was even beginning to look and feel strangely younger too, as his sense of purpose began to renew itself. There was strength in his limbs, hair on his head and he could see his feet without having to hold his belly in. He mused that Prudence, too, seemed to be shedding several years and her loss was certainly her gain; her figure was mature but slim, her eyes bright, her hips swaying ever so slightly and stirring something a bit confusing in Harry's consciousness.[9]

Military self-discipline stepped in and he began to study Adrian's map with a professional eye.

"So there are other planets, then?" he asked.

"Eh? Oh, you mean Orgonia," said Adrian. "No, that's Earth too. It's a parallel time continuum, some old experiment that didn't work very well. Apparently it's practically identical except there's no tax and Kidderminster is in the Premier League. I've never met anyone from there. Mind you," he conceded, "I've never met anyone from Rochdale either but people say it's there."

---

[9] Heaven has this effect on most people. You know the one about the chap who goes to the dentist for some false teeth and asks if he'll be able to swim in them and the dentist says 'Yes' and the man says 'Good, because I couldn't swim at all before'? Death is a bit like going to the dentist. Well, that may not be the best analogy. The point is that you soon get a new set of everything as well as teeth. Not that you can use everything, of course.

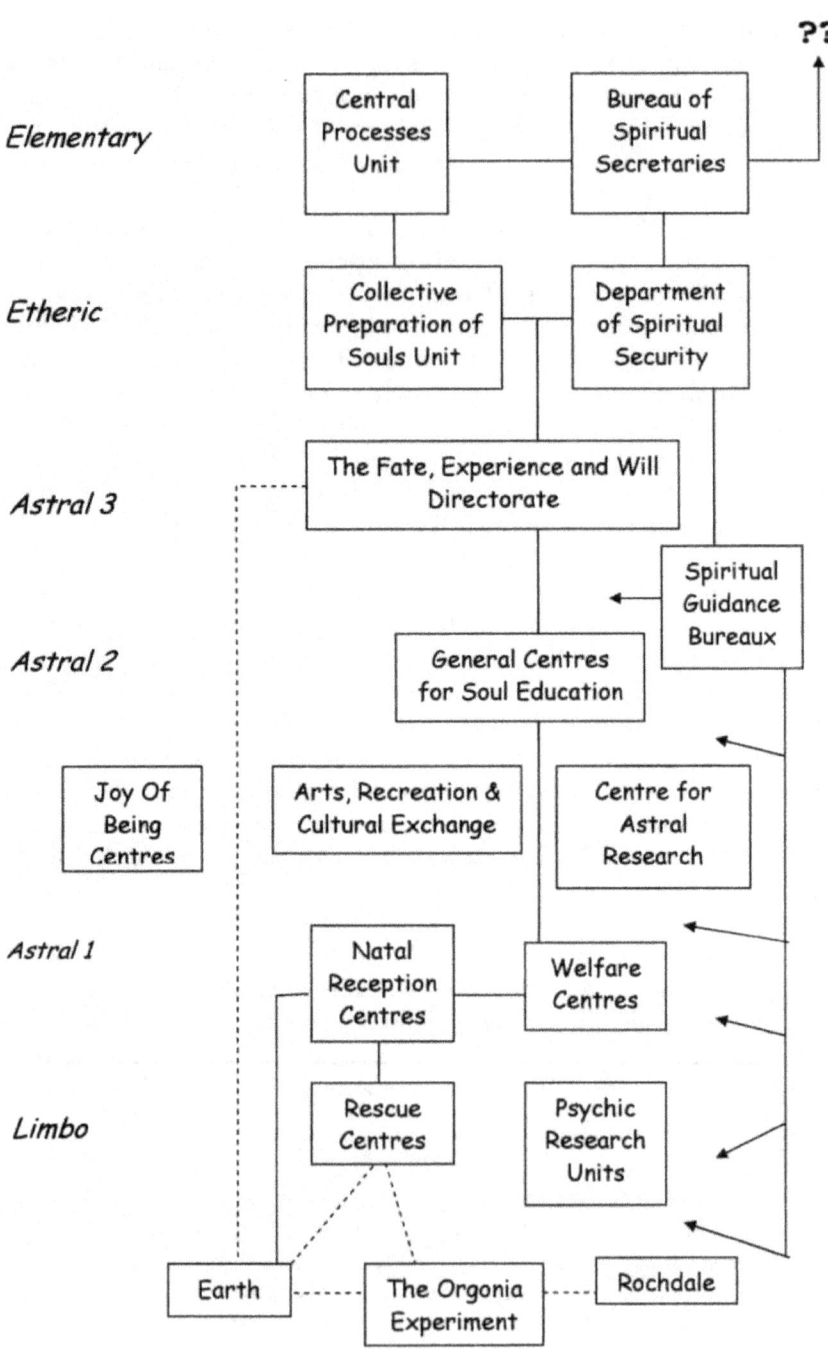

"Still, it seems well organised, really," Harry called back, striding ahead. It was in his nature to lead even if he hadn't the faintest idea where they were going. "Decent command structure. Plenty of technology."

"Well, that's the DoSS for you. They run the show. It might look good, but that doesn't mean that anything ever actually gets done."

"All the same," Harry halted peremptorily with a hand raised and they all tumbled into him like dominoes, "I think we can work with it. I must make a few notes." With a flourish, he thought up the pocket book in his other hand and studied its headings of Communication, Discipline (underlined) and Planning, adding a few remarks here and there before disappearing the book with surprisingly little effort. Prudence was again impressed by the trick. Not to be outdone, and getting to grips with the nature of things remarkably quickly, Ranjit capped it by producing a copy of the Kama Sutra, which would have been all the more impressive had page eighty-seven not been missing.

"You see," Harry went on, "a decent command structure is all very well but it's no good if it doesn't get through to the front line, the ordinary soul-in-the-street. This one obviously isn't working. For example, these Witness chappies are feeble – sorry, RJ, present company excepted -"

"That's cool, main man."

"– no drive, no determination, no..."

"Fibre?" suggested Prudence. Harry beamed with admiration.

"Exactly, my dear. Fibre. What a remarkable woman you are."

"Oh yeah," muttered Adrian, feeling somewhat sidelined, "you have to have fibre. You get the runs if you -"

"Adrian! I've warned you about smut."

They trudged on in silence for a while, passing through several junctions where all the lights seemed to be stuck on green and seeing hardly another soul on the way except for a ghostly number 31 bus heading towards Earls Court apparently without a driver. As they approached the enormous and imposing ARCE building in Knightsbridge, Adrian assumed tour guide mode.

"See, one thing there's no shortage of here is teachers. You can learn anything you want. There's free evening classes that go on practically all day. You can do psychometry, astronomy, binomial probability distribution – I'm doing genealogy, there's got to be a future in that. I know, RJ, why don't you learn the sitar?"

"Nah, bruv, yo' need sixteen fingers for dat, innit."

"All right, then, what about panpipes? Very popular nowadays. And there's sport -"

"Shooting?" Harry was suddenly interested.

"Yes, but you can't hit anything."

"Fishing?" he tried again.

"Can't catch anything."

"Hunting?"

"Won't find anything."

"What 'bout motorcycles, Ade?" chipped in RJ. "I allus wanted to be a mechnick man."

"Yeah, but it's only for Buddhists. Plenty of good music though – Led Zeppelin, Santana, Mahler…"

"Cliff Richard?" asked Prudence.

"'Fraid not. No jazz either of course. Mind, I'm only talking about our Level. There's probably other things higher up."[10]

When at last they reached the imposing solid oak doors of the building, they found them securely locked. An untidy, hand-written sign tied to the door handle announced that the Exchange was closed until further notice due to an Unforeseen Ripple. Adrian was definitely worried, and even Bonzai's hackles were up, her tail quivering between her legs.

"I don't like this at all," Adrian confided. "This has never happened before. There's something very odd going on. Have you noticed, we're practically in the city centre and there's nobody else around? You lot are definitely mixed up in something… and what's this Unforeseen Ripple? I bet it's something to do with that John Clarke."

"Hmm," agreed Harry. "He did seem like an odd cove." Another of those Great Understatements. Barely in human history can there have been a cove as odd as Clarke. It's certainly not every day that one baffles the NRC and the SGB while precipitating a celestial riot. The police were by now convinced that he had links with some antievangelical hit squad, and more patrols had been despatched to pull him in. But since the mind creates its own surroundings, where do you start looking for a vacuous one? They'd already gone back to Gandalf's but of course found it empty; however, the rottweiler had picked up a scent…

---

[10] Naturally, Heaven isn't entirely full of good folk bent upon improving themselves – that would be unbearable – but there is a lot of education going on. On the one hand the point is to develop the mind, and on the other to broaden one's perception. And on the third hand, the point is to learn that there really isn't any point to any of it. Adrian had discovered this when he enrolled on a basket-weaving course. He was well into the fifth lesson when he realised that not only, strictly speaking, was there nothing real and tangible to put in a basket, but also that there was no real and tangible basket either. Thereupon the basket had disappeared and he failed the course. But simultaneously he passed with Excellence a course in Metaphysics that he didn't even know he was taking.

"Hey, bruv," said Ranjit, without thinking it through, "why do' we go find the dude? See what's what? He am de key, innit?"

"Rather!" Harry enthused. This was right up his street, the old recce and pincer movement.

"Hang on," protested Adrian, "don't you think that might be a bit dangerous?"

"What are they going to do?" laughed Harry, bold as brass. "Shoot us?"

"All the same, I don't think Prudence and Alison -"

"Quite right. Good thinking, that man… er, Adrian. Dog, take charge here and get the lady chaps back to base." They exchanged salutes, and Prudence barely had time to think up a white hankie to wave before they were gone.

Φ

Tfozb put down her knitting and glared at the 3rd Spiritual Secretary.

"I told you so," s/he said. "You can't say I didn't warn you. But oh no, it was all 'Leave it to the computers' and 'Information technology is tomorrow's world'. And where's it got you now? There's a chip stuck in your ROM and the whole Age of Aquarius is up the spout." They were in SS3's executive space a little while after the debacle of the Planning Committee. Duflc shifted uneasily in his mock leather chair and studied the graffiti etched on the desk by its previous incumbents. They were in trouble, and some instinct – not to mention the weighty enquiries from above like a rain of elephants – told him that he'd better take Tfozb seriously.

"Come on, now," he wheedled, "it can't be that bad. Just some little hiccup somewhere. The CPU will soon sort it out."

"And that's another thing," s/he countered. "What use is all this technology when the computer only prints out a few letters at a time? This EG could be anything." He shrugged.

"That's how it is in a bureaucracy. Have you any idea how many forms the DoSS get through in an era? Anyway, the PRU printout was clear enough. Something will turn up."

"What sort of way is that to run a business? Honestly, when I was called I thought at least there'd be some efficiency and harmony among the Elementals." S/he took up her needles and attacked the next row fiercely. SS3 drew himself up and assumed his spiritual posture.

"You expect too much, Tfozb. Remember the teachings: "Thou shall expect nothing -""

"And nothing's what you'll get," s/he interrupted. "Knock and the world knocks with you. Platitudes, SS3. What are you going to do about The Plan? We can't back down now – they'll all blow themselves to pieces down there soon and then where shall we be? The NRCs can barely cope as it is. The RCs will be swamped, and half of the FEW will be redundant."

"There's always retraining. And we can put in a few more JOB centres to keep people occupied. Anyway, I agree, The Plan has to go ahead. It's been promised and the BoSS always keeps its word." This was what is known as an Executive Decision, the sort made in a flash without troubling more than a dozen grey cells upon realising that the light at the end of the tunnel is the approaching 7.43 from Glasgow. Tfozb dropped two more stitches in exasperation.

"So why didn't you support me in Committee, then?"

"You're tough. You can deal with them. Anyway, that's not how things are done."

He rose from his chair with a condescending smile and only the faintest twinge of conscience. Assuming a ministerial pose, hands clasped behind his back, he stared at the Thought Transfer Module and willed the Anal. boys to give him a break. There was a long silence broken only by the clicking of needles, and SS3 began to realise what it must have felt like during the French Revolution if you were on the wrong side.

"You know what your trouble is," Tfozb said at last. "You've got a mole." Duflc sat down again hurriedly and shuffled in his seat.

"I... er, well... how did you... look, some things are private, you know." S/he looked at him pityingly. He probably couldn't help being stupid.

"I mean, someone is trying to sabotage The Plan." As the unspeakable enormity of the statement sank in, SS3 let out an involuntary shriek and leapt up. By one of those odd coincidences, he banged his mole on the edge of the desk. The knitting flew out of Tfozb's hands and landed on the blotter. It was an odd shape for a scarf, with three legs and several large holes. "I suppose," s/he mused, "I could use it as a hanging plant-pot holder and say it's macramé."

SS3 slumped back behind his desk, having lost some of his authoritative presence.

"But who... and why... if not wherefore... with what possible...?" Tfozb sat upright with crossed arms as certain kinds of women do, and drew in a couple of chins.

"Well, clearly someone at the highest level," s/he said, as if the culprit's identity must be perfectly obvious to any passing caterpillar.

"Surely you mean the lowest level?" SS3 frowned.

"Not at all. Just ask yourself. They wouldn't have the means, or access to the technology, would they? Well?"

"I'm asking myself."

"And?"

"I haven't answered yet."

"Well, get on with it. And as for why...," s/he began, but hesitated, reason not being an Elemental's strongest attribute. After all, the Second Coming had always been taken for granted, an article of faith, a historical fact. Somebody had to sort Earth out. "Well," she went on, "answer yourself that one and then you'll know who."

Φ

"Zis is a big vun," Arthur confirmed to Nigel as they huddled, mesmerised in front of the small screen. "Viz Judas Skim in zis mood, anyzing can happen." He shook his head knowingly and they switched channels again, tracking Skim across north London. He'd led a comatose Evie Gardner out of the back door of the community hall to his old green Mini Traveller, and they were on their way to a secret address in NW3.

The service had, as expected, not been short of drama. Skim had sat frozen into his aura for a good fifteen minutes after Mrs P had announced him, moving not a muscle except for the infinitesimally slow sweep of his eyes across the congregation. His lips were fixed in the puerile, contented smile of The Saved, his fingers in the approved yoga loop, his white crease-proof Italian suit and ruddy complexion topped by that hair giving him the appearance of an advertisement for raspberry cornet ice cream. His spiritual tranquillity had, however, failed to communicate itself to a good proportion of his audience. They'd given up an hour's drinking time to get some holy wisdom and find out if Gran's arthritis had cleared up and whether Heaven was pink. There had been some complaints and the telekinesis of hymnbooks towards the stage. A small child had even crept up to deliver a sharp kick to Skim's shin, but with absolutely no effect. At this point several people reasoned that the medium was in fact dead and had left.

It was all to the huge delight of the throng backstage who were enjoying the proceedings immensely. When you're dead, there aren't too many opportunities for a really good laugh at someone else's expense and the undeserved butt of their humour was of course Jaimie. His was an unrewarding job at the best of times, though most weeks were routine enough. The odd warbled hymn, the mindless recital of a few prayers, five minutes of homespun nonsensical morality from Mrs P and then down to the serious business of Messages From Beyond. He had worked out a good system and was on friendly terms with most of the visiting Guides. Yes, they all knew that their evidence was as watertight as a toilet roll on the Titanic, but human nature is what it is. It was enough that an occasional seed of awareness was planted in a dull mind; whatever extraordinary and inedible fruit it might turn into was not his concern.

But today had not been routine. Psychic celebrities were always a pain and this particular one was as excruciating as they come. He had tried to warn Mrs P off but she was having none of it, stardust in her eyes and visions of a double-page spread in Readers' Digest, so now he was carrying the can of worms. He'd never hear the last of it. Still, in the event it was just as well that he and Laughing Meerkat had stuck it out.

The focus of the betting had switched to who would last out the longest between Skim and the dwindling congregation. The former had appeared to have it sewn up when an unexpected event backstage turned the tables and caused a minor economic collapse.

The figure that appeared at the back was at first felt rather than seen, and gradually a hush had descended as waves of onlookers parted like the Red Sea to let him through. Momentarily transfixed, Laughing Meerkat had then suddenly let out a whoop that would have chilled any remaining traces of bone marrow in the room to absolute zero, before tipping over prostrate onto his face like a felled tree. His single white feather had quivered slightly, as Jaimie looked in bewilderment from the collapsed brave to the new arrival, an Apache, his deep mahogany face etched with untold experience and shrouded by a flowing, brilliant yellow headdress. The eyes were cavernous. Arms folded within a white robe, he glided past Jaimie with a nod of acknowledgement, stepped over Skim's guide, and took up a position behind the medium's left shoulder.

Taking matters into her own hands, the organist had crashed her full weight down onto her special chord. But the fuse must have blown and the keys merely plinked emptily, the vibration shuddering back along her arms. Nonetheless, Judas Skim stood up. His address, if not entirely straightforward, was at least one of the briefest in Spiritualist history.

"Flowing to the ajna from the point of light upon the fifth harmonic of the seventh descending ray within the etheric Gobi plane, the eternal hierarchy of ascended masters commands me to vouchsafe this prophecy here tonight. The Messiah shall return to Earth within a year, within this city, and within the body of one here present."

He had sat down again. Unable to contain the energy, the stained glass vase cracked right down one side and emptied itself over his trousers. The audience realised there'd be no proper messages tonight and shuffled out complaining, the only satisfied one being the mother of a pregnant schoolgirl who reasoned it was safe to buy the blue wool now. Mrs P had hopped up and down like a demented gerbil in front of Skim, who had merely reverted to autopilot.

"Do something, Mr Skim, do something. We haven't had a hoffering yet."

The Apache had returned the way he had come, stepping over the still prone Laughing Meerkat, and gesturing over his shoulder as he whispered to Jaimie out of the corner of his mouth.

"Him cracked, that one."

A most unseemly fracas had broken out when he disappeared, as bets were cancelled and furious relatives demanded travel expenses and first go in next week's ballot. And as any sane and spiritually evolved souls would, the two guides had run for it.

Judas Skim had risen and, as dignified as one can be with wet trousers, walked to the back of the almost deserted hall to where Evie sat frozen in her chair. She knew. She had felt it. For heaven's sake, she had even seen the yellow feathers.

"You probably need a drink," he said. "Come on, I'll take you my place. Then we can discuss your training." Evie had allowed herself to be led away without protest, indeed still barely able to breathe. By the time they reached Skim's house, her head was spinning from the combined effect of naked psychic power and the botanically very interesting fungus that had eaten away half the Mini Traveller's wooden frame. She was at his mercy.

As the front door closed behind the pair, the picture on Arthur Stone's monitor crackled, heaved and finally broke up.

"Damn it," snorted Nigel, wrestling with his knobs. "Another security code!"

"Try Channel Fourteen," snapped an equally furious Stone. But it was Australian Rules football.

Φ

George, Mrs P's long-suffering husband, bakery assistant and part-time Orange Hill Road Community Hall caretaker, flicked off all the lights except for the front porch and jangled his keys searching for the last one. He sighed. It had apparently not been a successful evening. She'd come home in a foul mood muttering 'Judas!' over and over and had forgotten to get their usual cod and chips. Such was the spiritual life.

He was just about to close the door on it all, when he noticed the slightest of movements inside. A solitary figure still sat hunched up there to one side of the room, completely silent and oblivious to everything.

Benedict had come tonight, with the desperation of the grieving, wishing with all his heart to hear something from Alison. He didn't know why. He had never even thought about an afterlife. But he was doing and thinking about a lot of things these days that had meant nothing to him a short while ago. Someone in a pub had told him about someone's sister who knew someone whose mother went to the church and so here he was, feeling utterly stupid for having believed in this total shambles. He had sat quietly and unobserved, his mind focused on just one thing, on just one person, as chaos had reigned all around. And now he was alone again.

"Come on, mate," George said kindly. "Time to go 'ome." Benedict looked up at him uncomprehendingly, as if trying to make out the words of a foreign language. "Yeah, I know, mate. Shit, ennit?"

They shuffled out into the car park and George locked up. Benedict dried his eyes and took a couple of long, deep breaths of suburban air before he had to turn for the gate and the short walk back to his bedsit.

"Thanks, goodnight," he said to the other man, raising a hand in acknowledgement.

"'S all right, mate," said George. "Look, hope you don't mind... but jus' between us I gets messages too sometimes. Jus' a voice in my 'ed somehow. The missus won't 'ave it, of course, says I ent been trained. Well...Dunno what it means, but Arjee says Ali's ok. Ok?"

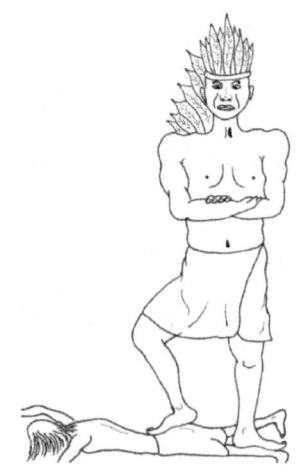

Chapter Five ~ Career Plans

Alison was indeed ok, but only just.

They had taken the more direct route back through Sloane Square, thinking that a spot of window shopping at some posh boutiques might be nice. A girl likes to try on a new image even when she's dead. It was a disappointing experience though, most of the shops being boarded up or derelict, and those that weren't displayed only rustic styles in tranquil mid-distance green or floaty gowns in garish episcopal purple. The fashion industry did not seem very lively, and Prudence had a thought that she might just do something about that now that she had plenty of time on her hands. She had never in her life worn anything remotely adventurous (one doesn't count the time when, at the age of four, she had rifled through her parents' wardrobe and appeared downstairs at their dinner party in crotchless lace panties and black leather balaclava, effective though this had been). But she was feeling a new sense of freedom now and the young girl inside that she had thought lost forever was emerging from under the bedclothes and demanding ice-cream.

Bonzai had not been at all impressed by such girlish fantasies. She had been entrusted with an important mission and was taking it seriously, slinking along the pavement, hairy body hugging the shop fronts, backtracking with eyes darting this way and that and huge ears vertical, sniffing for danger. They'd got as far as the antique market on Kings Road when it happened.

The girls were sauntering ahead arm in arm and chattering.

"Things really aren't so bad, are they?" said Alison. "I mean, it's true what I said before, that nobody cares about us. Not really. But now here we all are and we're all friends, aren't we? So *we* care about us. And RJ promised to try and get a message through to Benedict somehow, so…"

Bonzai froze, every wispy white hair standing on end. She looked like a hedgehog in a snowstorm. Then she flew into decisive action, racing in tight circles around the two girls to get their attention before rising on two feet to a majestic height and physically pushing them into the deserted market.

"Get out sight," she growled authoritatively, shepherding them towards a stall in the shadowy far corner, before taking up her own position, poised and alert, behind a wheelie bin near the pavement. Moments passed in silence, though Pru could have sworn she could hear her own heart thumping. Then the Rottweiler appeared round a corner, tongue slavering and huge teeth gleaming.

Very casually, as if merely passing the time of day, Bonzai stepped out and stood nose to nose with him. She looked him straight in the surprised eyes with an unflinching glare, her own teeth also bared but in a strange little smile.

"Hi Napoleon," she whispered. "You're going keep walking down the road, then take left and lead that scum over Albert Bridge. Ok?"

"Bonz? What you doing here?"

"Doesn't matter. What matters is I know about you and poodle in Notting Hill, right? So keep walking and don't come back. This my turf, right?"

"But hey, Bonz, I got job to do -"

"Rough."

Bonzai sidled backwards behind the bin and three pairs of eyes watched from the shadows as the SGB patrol passed the market and disappeared from view. Napoleon looked back over his shoulder just the once and opened his mouth to bark, then thought better of it. The poodle's owner was someone big in the CPSU. You don't mess with them, or if you do then you make very sure you're not found out. They can literally turn you into a dandelion.

Back at Gandalf's, Prudence and Alison took their minds off things for a while by inventing cocktails. They managed twenty-seven different shades of blue, yellow and red with matching striped cherries and revolving paper umbrellas, but they all tasted identical and not one of them had any effect. Bonzai, her duty done, helped herself to the last piece of carrot cake and sank into a proud and satisfied sleep in her back yard basket. The girls decided to explore the rooms upstairs so no-one noticed the young man enter the café.

It occurred to Prudence that perhaps they should find somewhere to live.

"I mean, I suppose people do still live in houses, don't they?" It was a fair point. Since their arrival they seemed to have spent most of their time either in the café or wandering the streets, without ever considering what to get for dinner, whether it was time to go home, how to get home anyway, or even what was on TV this evening. There didn't even seem to be much prospect of evening. They were just happily picking their way through the contents of various drawers, as one does when left alone at someone else's place, when a hysterical cry of dismay from below took them racing back downstairs. Adrian was bent over a body sprawled on the floor.

"A fine guard dog you are," he yelled out at Bonzai, who snored on, dreaming of sizzling pork sausages. Between them they heaved the stranger onto a table, now awash with the dregs of their experiments, and poured water over his head until he came to. His voice was not distinct.

"By jove, thasgoodstuff," he dribbled, peering at the empty glasses with respect through rolling eyes. "Canayavanother?"

"What in heaven's name did you put in them?" hissed Adrian, not amused. "That's supposed to be impossible. Deary me. This is the biggest thing since manna. It'll revolutionise the afterlife and I'll probably lose my licence."

Adrian explained that he'd only come back because Harry said he was in the way, and fussed about moodily with tea towels clearing up the mess. The girls busied themselves at the counter trying to recreate the effect, but neither of them could quite remember which colour combination was which. Each effort in turn was passed to the stranger for an opinion, and each glass was hurled over his shoulder in rejection, until finally a three-dimensional blue and pink chessboard effect topped off with a dash of pistachio ice-cream sent him toppling from his chair into an insensible heap.

Prudence turned him over delicately with one foot and they studied his contented features.

"Hmm, I've seen him before," said Adrian reflectively. "He's been in here a few times, aeons ago, never says a word." He reached down inside the man's jacket for some ID.

"You can't do that!" protested Pru, who hadn't quite lost her sense of propriety yet. But Adrian had already sat down heavily, wide eyes reading a small black pocket book identical to Harry's. Such an article should be entirely forgotten and not accessible to others, but memory is one of the first faculties to collapse under the effect of alcohol. Adrian whistled softly to himself and turned to study the long, limp figure snuffling quietly beneath the yellow table cloth Alison had thoughtfully tucked him up in.

"No wonder he never said a word," said Adrian, motioning the others to sit down as he read from the pocket book. "The name's Nigel Gibbs, does some sort of hush-hush work at a Psychic Research Centre up north. And that's not all. His boss is only -" he paused for effect, "- Arthur Stone!" It had no effect whatsoever, so he had to explain about Arthur's background. "Keep it to yourselves, though. Not a lot of people know. I only found out when I went ice-skating and bumped into Trotsky. You bump into all sorts of people skating."

"He's in Heaven too?" Prudence was incredulous.

"A lot of people are misunderstood, dear," remarked Adrian, looking hurt. "Anyway, looks like our Nige and Arthur have been naughty boys, up to something a bit dodgy on the side, according to this." Prudence took the book from him and pored over the appalling handwriting, eyes screwed up in concentration.

"You're right, Ade, some sort of industrial anarchy. Seems they're working on a method to destabilise governments by beaming some kind of ultrafrequency etheric energy through the senses. That would be practically undetectable. Politicians never use their sense. It's a sort of possession really, I suppose." Adrian laughed.

"Well, good for them. The world needs a shake-up."

"Are you a Marxist, then?" she asked accusingly.

"I am," he replied icily, "an oppressed minority."

"Sorry," she said sheepishly, tossing the book onto the table. "Oh dear, this is all getting a bit confusing. And upsetting. I wish Harry were back – he'd know what to do."

"You called?" said Harry calmly, taking a seat beside her.

Φ

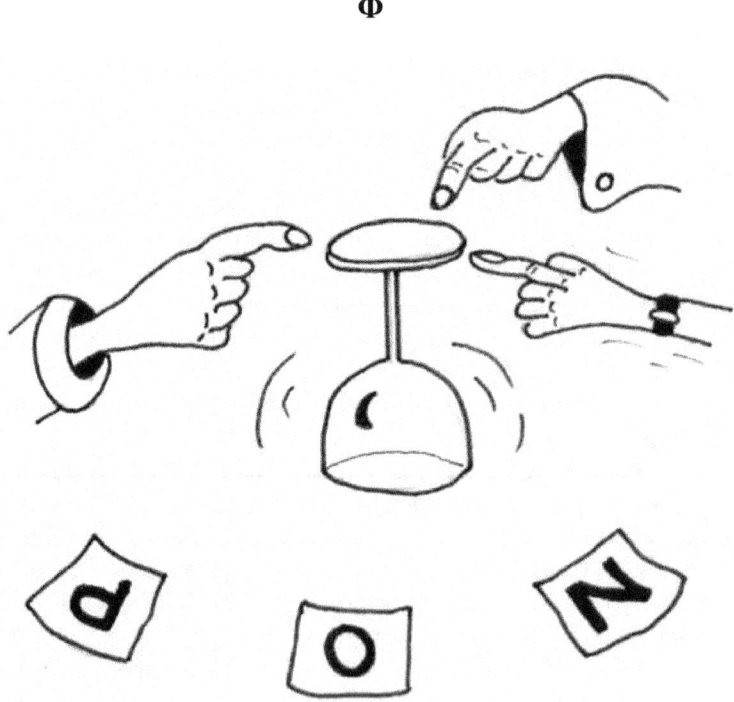

The acolytes had gathered in NW3 to await Judas Skim's return and were getting in a bit of Ouija practice in the meantime. Theological purists would probably consider these five an odd group to be in on potentially the biggest world event for two millennia. Not only were they very ordinary – two housewives, a subeditor, a fishmonger and a restaurateur – they were also to a man and woman remarkably stupid. Of course, it was for precisely these qualities that Skim had chosen them (the very least a prophet requires is blind obedience) one at a time from each of the five previous public appearances he'd made since coming out of the ecclesiastical closet. He'd needed one more to make the group the prescribed mystic seven.[11] Evie had seemed to fit the bill as well as anyone, being in any case the only member of the congregation left in the hall when he'd come round (except for a chap over to one side, but he was crying and you can't let emotion get in the way of divine providence). The fact that this had all been orchestrated by her guide Heap Yellow Feathers was utterly lost on him.

"You pushed!" accused Bill Shaddock, the resident sceptic (for balance). He glared through round, protruding eyes at the slip of a girl across the table. Slim and pretty, Pene tossed her long black hair defiantly.

"I never," she squeaked. "You're always doing this, Bill, upsetting the vibrations just when we're getting going. I wouldn't push, would I, Syl?"

"Never, dear," said her neighbour quietly, discreetly relaxing her own finger on the upturned wine glass. "No-one could call you pushy. Maybe fawning, shameless, a nymphomaniac, but not pushy, no." Sylvia Golightly's occasional outburst of rampant sarcasm was the product of a good French education (her father being something Diplomatic) and an excruciatingly boring marriage to a banker in Mill Hill. These weekly outings were her only outlet, apart from some part-time relief work at a massage parlour. Pene pouted and shuffled her bottom as she tugged at her black patent leather skirt. For its propensity to constantly ride up and get stuck, it must have been designed by lift engineers. Mario, directly across the table, dropped his pencil for the sixth time that evening.

"Well, what a thing to say," Bill gestured to the paper on which Mario had been recording their results. "Surely no responsible spirit would say that. It's… well, it's not nice." Winnie Khan (nee Louhdun) leaned across towards Bill to read the paper. Her eyebrows disappeared.

---

[11] The explanation of this has a lot to do with rays and harmonics and chakras and is better dealt with in a GCSE Physics text book.

"It's not just dubious," she agreed, "I'd say it was physically impossible. You certainly wouldn't get messages like that in Hertfordshire."

The room hung about them like a pink shroud, a single naked red bulb in the standard lamp giving the huddled group the appearance of a lobster card school. A very fine but ancient walnut grandfather clock wheezed in one corner. They tried again, and the glass dutifully careered across the polished dining table from one piece of paper to another while Mario struggled to record its progress. He was perhaps not the best choice for this task since his English was pretty much limited to 'lasagne', 'chips' and 'credit card'. But it didn't really matter since almost every message was an unbroken sequence of total gibberish that didn't even resemble Esperanto. The possibility that it was a psychic code had occurred to them once, and Winnie's husband Jim had run it through the Lloyd's computer. But all he'd managed to get out of it so far was an obscure reference to Cicero and a racing tip for Doncaster which, in the event, had gone lame at the second fence and burned his fingers badly. On the rare occasions when the wisdom was decipherable, the spiritual advice offered ranged from the extremely improbable to, like this evening's, the downright obscene.

The little band were not downhearted, however. It was after all their Master's will that during his public meetings they should assemble in NW3 to gather in the Light and the Love and the Power in preparation for his return. They trusted Judas Skim implicitly. Though quite how the vibrations were to be enhanced by the slanging matches that invariably ensued is not clear.

When Evie Gardner had eventually stumbled in at Skim's heels on this particular Wednesday, she was more than a little disorientated. Not long ago life had been straightforward, a matter of spray polish and shopping trolleys. Now she was in a dim north London parlour being introduced as the missing link in a metaphysical chain and asked to embrace five total strangers as her divine brothers and sisters. And there was no sign of the sherry she'd been promised.

The mutual embrace was a psychological touch Skim had picked up from an American evangelist who'd called at the door one day selling subscriptions. It was a sound idea. If the English could be persuaded to do that at least once a week, it was odds on that within a month their self-respect would be shattered and they could be persuaded of anything. Moreover it was a good opportunity to get his arms round Pene. The psychic energy that surged through him as her firm young body pressed against him generally kept him going for the whole evening. Clutched in

Bill's clammy embrace, however, Evie didn't get quite the same fix. Judas rescued her and dragged her back to the centre of the room.

"Behold," he intoned solemnly, raising her arm like a victorious boxer, "the mother!"

"Plissed to be meeting you, Mrs Skim," said Mario politely, offering a hand.

"Not *my* mother," hissed Judas, "*the* mother." Pene stepped forward, hands on hips and eyes blazing, and regarded with disdain the pathetic figure cowering before her in a calf-length floral print polyester dress, her curlers barely hidden beneath a chiffon headscarf.

"What?" she demanded. "You've been having it off with that?" Judas rolled his eyes in exasperation. It was so hard, sometimes, to get ordinary mortals to receive Essential Truths.

"As if I would," he said. Given the availability of Pene, this was also an Essential Truth. "Sit down, everyone, and I'll explain." There was a scramble for the only two comfortable chairs. "In the last few months I have been preparing you for the ultimate message. You were carefully chosen, handpicked one by one, and led up the...er, along the great path of esoteric knowledge, in sure and certain hope of Hierarchy's final command, that which will blow away the evils of the world in the soft universal wind of change. And tonight, in Orange Hill Road, it came to me."

"What, the wind?" asked Bill, who was having trouble following all this but did know all about wind. Winnie elbowed him violently in the ribs.

"The Message, you pillock. The Final Command of Hierarchy." She turned to Judas with a contented, expectant smile. As a landowner and leading socialite of the home counties, with her own modest stud farm and a husband at the hub of the world's insurance policy, she naturally anticipated a prominent role in the coming revolution. No-one else here was as remotely qualified.

"Tell us, Master. We are ready to take our places."

Φ

The woman that Skim had approached in the community hall had seemed vaguely familiar. Benedict knew he had seen her somewhere before, not too long ago, but that hardly mattered now. As he walked down Whitchurch Lane back to the grotty bedsit, there was a spring in his step and, for the first time in weeks, a broad smile on his face. A confirmed materialist, he had now had two encounters with mediums and a one hundred per cent hit rate. He would not have said that he was happy, of course – his life was in ruins, his heart broken, and George's message was not proof of anything. But somehow there was hope again. Alison was nowhere to be seen, yet the very idea that she was still thinking of him was immensely, irrationally, reassuring.

So what to do now? Perhaps he should just sit back and wait for this Arjee to get in touch again, but that was a bit too hit-and-miss. He'd had quite enough of things beyond his control happening to him over the last few months.

Benedict settled himself at the computer, a pile of cheese sandwiches and flask of coffee to one elbow, and began to research. First, it seemed reasonable to check out this Judas Skim since he'd been at the centre of the evening's drama. You can find almost anyone on the Internet, and Benedict had a lot more success than Arthur Stone had.

Φ

Harry was filled in on recent events and took it all in his stride as befits an officer, promising to mention Bonzai in despatches if there ever were any. Studying the pocket book for himself, the air of tranquil control lasted only as long as it took him to read Evie Gardner's name in it.

"Good Lord!" he spluttered. "Does a chap get no peace even when he's dead? The woman's haunting me." Adrian fixed him a drink, being very careful with the recipe.

"Well, lovey, you shouldn't be surprised. When people are important in your life they're bound to keep popping up."

"But that's just it," protested Harry. "I can hardly think of anyone *less* important than Mrs G. All she ever did was shovel the dust under the carpet and help herself to my sherry when she thought I wouldn't notice."

"Ah, sometimes it's hard to admit our true feelings, though. I mean, for example, call me a sentimental old fool but you keep coming back to my café, don't you, so that must mean that you -" Prudence had to hold Harry down.

"You're a sentimental old fool, Adrian," she said. "All the same, it is odd. This woman is clearly important somehow to Nigel -" she gave the still prone figure a small kick, "– and his research unit. Why would they be tracking her?" It was Alison who eventually spoke the words they were all thinking.

"Maybe they're using her to find you, Harry. Like Adrian said, people get drawn together when they have something in common."

"Hmm."

"Well…"

The colonel didn't much like this turn of the conversation. It sounded rather like they all thought he was the weak link in the group, making them vulnerable. So did they expect him to fall on his sword? It wouldn't work.

"It's just like that John Clarke, he keeps turning up too. Oh, did you manage to find him, Harold? Is he all right?" The man recovered his composure and assumed mission report mode.

"Not a pretty sight, my dear. We tracked an SGB patrol back to Bow Street and found him there. Interrogation, don't you know. Not exactly Geneva Convention either. Rum do, the cells all have sort of rubber walls so you keep bouncing around when they hit you."

"How did you get in? Didn't they see you?"

"Oh well," there was unmistakable pride in the voice, "one knows camouflage, you know. One merges into corners. It's all in the mind, see?"

"Can't quite see you as a rubber wall, Colonel. Want to demonstrate?" There was a touch of sarcasm in Adrian's voice.

"Well some chaps didn't hang around long enough to get involved, did they? As soon as Stachov got the hosepipe out, some chaps started yelping and nearly giving the game away, didn't they?"

"I know my limits, sir."

"Indeed. And that funny little Ranjit fellow wasn't a lot of help either, was he, jumping up and down and muttering about capitalist police states oppressing de disenfranchised, innit. Oh by the way, Alison my dear, he went off back to his office. Said something about calling the noose down to yo' dude. Said you'd understand. Damned if I do." She did, and she smiled. "But the really rum thing, my dear," he turned to Pru and found himself for some unfathomable reason putting his hand on hers, "was that this Clarke chap never squealed once. They didn't have the slightest effect on him. It was like they just couldn't touch him. Deuced courageous, if you ask me. Or damn fine training. Brilliant cover, too. No records, see; that's the thing about him."

"Sounds to me like an Elemental," Adrian offered, deciding to be constructive. "But how that's happened…" He couldn't offer any more.

Bonzai had loped back in a while ago, checked out the counter and the fridge, and settled herself in an untidy heap in the corner. She listened to it all, took it all in, and shook her shaggy head at the stupidity of humans. Finally, she could bear it no longer.

"Look, peoples," she began, stretching languidly into a more or less upright position, and looking from one to another with sad eyes and droopy tongue, "are you's all going to sitting about for eternity in this café and wonder what's going on and what is got to be done? Honestly. Hang around much longer and the filth is all over the place and it's no more sausages and cake for me. Or you. Ade is tell you this already."

"Go on, that dog," said Harry, intrigued. He was not in the habit of taking instructions from subordinates, but this one was a bit different.

"So that Clarkie chap he is got no records, right? That's problem. But you do got records – you bet life they got disks full of files on you lot, right?"

"S'pose."

"And that problem for SGB. So they going come for you later if no sooner. You got go."

"Bonzai's right," said Prudence. But she had also spotted another logical conclusion to be drawn. With a lifetime's experience of History and the Civil Service, she had ample experience of how vulnerable records can be. "But surely we could just alter their files too?" Harry almost gasped at the audacity of it. This was like, well, changing the truth. He was, admittedly, a bit naïve politically speaking.

"You'd need someone with darn good IT skills," pointed out Adrian.

"There's RJ."

"Not sure he's been here long enough for that. He's only on work experience after all. And the NRC uses special security codes, that sort of thing. How are you going to break them?"

"Um, hello," said a weak, sleepy voice with a slight tremor from under the table. "I'm, er, Nigel. I say, can I have a drink please?"

Φ

"That's settled then," announced SS3, dotting the final i, "The Plan is agreed." A hubbub of excited chatter broke out as the Planning Committee congratulated itself on its first major decision since the unfortunate business in Leningrad. They had reconvened only after assurances from Anal. that the systems were working perfectly and not only was John Clarke now in custody but a couple of very shifty Corsicans had been rounded up near Mount Etna. Weather systems could now be organised and the seeds of war that would usher in economic collapse could be sown. The acceleration of natural disasters would be the easy bit, the environment being in the state it was, and in any case a bit of a tug on a continental plate was childsplay for any PRU. The slide on Wall Street had already been halted just in time by a statement from the White House (to which SS3 had a direct line), although unfortunately nothing could be done about the Australian cricket team's collapse, despite five of the opposition mysteriously going down with food poisoning. Finally, with a mouthful of pride that would have choked a lesser man, SS3 had given Tfozb the Chair of the CPSU Millennium Sub-Committee.

"We'll have to move hallowish fast, then, to get it all done in time," said Nftth eagerly. S/he was the newest of the Elementals and still very keen, but hadn't quite grasped the timelessness of the unconscious yet. Sxzbu shot a withering glare across.

"That's so wet," s/he said. "Didn't you ever do relativity in the GCSE? It only takes a bit of a bend in the universe and we could probably put him down as far back as, what, 1950 at a guess."

"But aren't you just twisting events to fit the prophecy then?"

"So what? Everyone does it. Well, the other way round, anyway."

The 3rd Spiritual Secretary brought the meeting to order with a look of cool authority, and pressed on with the agenda. They just had to settle half a dozen matters of principle for the FEW to knock into shape. It was all going remarkably well, and as each item was ticked off unanimously he began to relax a little. There could even be a move up for him if he carried this off; after all, there'd be a vacancy.

Everything was back under control. Naturally, although little did the Committee know it, The Plan had already been in motion for some time; he just had to let the Elementals believe that they'd made the decision so they couldn't make a fuss later. The only tricky bit had been the prophets. Well, there were so many of them about nowadays and, as always happens when an industry expands, the quality had been seriously diluted. In normal circumstances, of course, it would have been Gabriel's responsibility. But he was on retreat. Stress, apparently. Eventually he'd farmed the job out to the Celestial Information Agency – their Apaches were pretty reliable and the tender was easily the lowest.

They'd swept along to the very last item of the agenda before the first objections, and a few eyebrows, were raised.

"I'm sorry, SS3," said Nftth hesitantly, "but are you quite sure this mother-person is suitable?" S/he had a deep suspicion of mothers, having been one in Abraham's day. "I'm sure Eleanor Glee is very nice -"

"A good, young all-American girl," affirmed SS3.

"– but actually she's just a bit-part actress in pornographic films."

"No, I'm sorry, I won't have that. Lily Pond Orgasm in Blue is a creative masterpiece of sensitively underplayed erotic spirituality. And the cucumber scene is a searing indictment of hypocritical small-town morality. She's a genuine star."

"But you only see her bottom."

"Indeed. Outstanding isn't it? Perfect child-bearing hips."

"That's as may be," interjected Tfozb, "but Nftth may have a point. I mean, I've taken the liberty of looking into her other qualifications... "

"Granted, the magazine pictures were unfortunate. But she needed the money, after coming out of the detention centre."

"Well, that's it, see? She does have a certain… reputation."

"There's plenty of precedent," countered SS3, anxious to wrap this up. "Check your Testaments. It's a thoroughly tried and tested method. I mean, you can't use a happy couple with a Renault hatchback, matching bath towels and a personal pension plan, can you? There's no anguish. Now, Eleanor has beauty, public profile, negligible IQ and she's absolutely ripe for Revelation. There's no question – the FEW ran thousands of records and she fits the bill. Right place, right time. Seven degrees east, moon in Scorpio."

"But nobody's going to believe in parthenogenesis at the Cannes Film Festival, surely?"

"Happens all the time."

What was also happening all too regularly now – due to what, ambition? – was SS3 overlooking certain things. Maybe this one was just a tiny quirk of Fate, one of those butterfly wings that changes the course of human history. Perhaps it was just inevitable, given all the circumstances. But you really would think he should have noticed Eleanor Glee's initials by now.

Φ

The subject of housing in Heaven can be quite vexing for anyone arriving from a mixed economy. You might expect, since all conceivable building materials are readily available and absolutely free, that here at last is a unique opportunity to create the home of your dreams, limited only by your imagination. Unfortunately most people are not very imaginative and, when it comes down to it, we like what we're used to. Moreover, since people of similar lack of imagination tend to live near each other, you find that vast tracts of the astral planes resemble rather seedy mid-Thirties council estates. And it's just as hard to get repairs done as if you were on a council estate. The paradox is that every one of these dwellings is in fact privately owned.[12]

---

[12] However, no-one pays a mortgage. This can be quite confusing for monetarists, and indeed a financial career is not the best preparation for the afterlife.

Moving house can also be problematic. Vacancies do occur from time to time as souls get themselves promoted up the planes and feel the need for something a bit more grand (or less grand, if it's a really good promotion). People get demoted too, sometimes beyond the need for housing at all. But there's complex legislation on the subject which states among other things that no property may be left unoccupied (and once something is created in etheric energy it cannot be demolished), so if you fancy something you have to get in fast and join the chain. Admittedly, the whole process is made easier by there being no estate agents in Heaven. A lot of people learn to avoid the rules by just uprooting themselves and their homes around them, finding a nice bit of space (there's plenty of that) to put it all down in, and then thinking up an extension. Granny flats, for example, do not require planning permission. But bear in mind that in Heaven grannies have grannies who have grannies ad infinitum, so if you're not careful your nice little retirement bungalow can turn into a tower block.

Adrian agreed with Bonzai that a home for the new friends was now not only a necessity but an urgent priority. The discovery of fugitives on his premises, not to mention a still that was both illegal and illogical, and he could certainly kiss goodbye to any angelic ambitions. Where to go? The creation of a neat row of semis in Parsons Green would surely attract unwelcome attention. But in any case, he now recalled, you have to have been fully processed and certificated before you were allowed to do-it-yourself. What was needed, he persuaded them, was a large old house on the point of being vacated and as far away as possible, and a landlord with a disinterest in paperwork.

"I've always fancied Guildford," suggested Prudence. "There's some nice cobbled streets and old bookshops. I wonder if the cathedral is still there."

"Let's go and find out," said Adrian, turning the 'Closed' sign over on the door and forcing another glass of Bishop's Brew, the new cocktail, down Nigel's throat. Bonzai carried him along on the way, teeth sunk into the loose skin on the back of his neck. They were going to need Nigel.

Finding Guildford is not as easy as you'd think. The M25 is permanently jammed with confused, Earthbound souls going round in circles, and the town is much smaller than its equivalent in Surrey since a good many of its erstwhile inhabitants had financial careers. Most familiar places do have their counterpart in Heaven. Guildford is quite pretty, and people like to recreate attractive and interesting places (which is why most of Wolverhampton does not have a counterpart). But it's little more than a village now, and the huge cathedral statue on Stag Hill that looms out of the mist and scares you half to death when you approach at night has been replaced by an altogether more modest chapel without even an altar. So the friends were half way to Southampton before realising that they'd missed it.

When they did arrive there was nothing to be had. They checked every shop window, and the old chap in the tourist Information Bureau merely shook his head and said that no-one ever leaves Guildford and why would they want to anyway. Prudence was beginning to feel a bit low, having set her heart on country life, when another of those funny coincidences occurred, as it were, in answer to a prayer. A lad on a bicycle, delivering the new edition of the Surrey Guardian, tossed it towards the porch of the house Pru was passing. It hit her square between the eyes, as if to say 'Read Me' (you may remember that Evie had a similar angelic communication in Burnt Oak). They found the property page: there was just one advertisement.

TOILET

In lge old hse fve slf-ctd flts
shr ktn & bth sml gdn stng tnt.
Mst mv du emergny.
Stn Ldg, Clndn Rd.

"I'm not sure I want to live in a loo, even if it is self-contained," objected Alison.

"Silly, that's a misprint," said Pru. "I think it's perfect." But Harry shook his head.

"I don't know, my dear. Don't much like the idea of sharing a kitten. They're a big responsibility, you know, always wandering off and getting themselves -"

"And the bathroom seems to be just a tent in the garden with wasps."

But they went anyway. The house in Clandon Road was indeed charming and the present occupants delighted to see them, anxious as they were to get away. Other people had already viewed the place but had been put off by the 'stng tnt', who turned out to be Sammy, an unusually aged artist who occupied the ground floor. He nodded politely to them as they passed on the stairs, long sable brush in one hand, wine glass in the other, and a pipe apparently glued to his lower molars and from which issued a revolting herbal smell.

"Its rly vry cmftl," the lady of the house assured them, her hands hovering over two suitcases. "Yll tk t?"

"Wll tk t," agreed Pru before anyone else could get a syllable in. Alison and Prudence took the first floor which also contained the kitchen, while Harry and Nigel, the latter albeit unconsciously, chose the second. The spare room became their meeting-place and was soon furnished with a selection of comfy chairs with garish throws. No-one was more pleased than Adrian, who promptly disappeared back to London promising to keep his ears open at Gandalf's. For her part, Bonzai promised to infiltrate the strays in Battersea Park and keep her considerably larger ears open too.

"Well, my dear," said Harry, tapping the plasterboard tentatively and eyeing the damp patch beneath one window, "I hope you've made the right decision. The old codger downstairs seems a bit rum, don't you think?" Pru laid a hand on his arm and beamed happily.

"I just know this is right," she said. "I can feel it. Trust me. And it will be nice to share with a painter, very cultural."

Downstairs in his studio, piled from floor to ceiling with full canvases and empty bottles, the old codger smiled to himself and drew on his pipe with satisfaction. The new neighbours seemed very promising.

"Right, settle down men... er, ladies. And get the prisoner sat up straight." Having thought up some wardrobes and chests of drawers, and then thought up some things to go in them, the commanding officer had summoned his squad to the spare room for a strategy conference. A flip-chart was set up at one end, a baton had appeared in one hand and his own small pocket book in the other, and he was in neatly pressed battle dress. "Now, as I see it, things are pretty slack in these parts and we can't have it. Whinging witnesses, inefficiency, blaming somebody else, Reception Centres in chaos, hidebound bureaucracy, bullying police...I don't need to go on, do I?" He hoped they'd agree because he couldn't think of anything else for the moment.

"Right."

"Indeed."

"Permission to speak, Colonel, sir?" Nigel stood up unsteadily and saluted. Harry beamed. He hadn't been saluted for a very long time.

"Ah, Gibbs. You've clearly been in the ranks, eh?"

"No, just the CCF at school. And a load of bullying fascist prats they were, too, prancing about with their toy guns and -"

"You had a question, son?"

"Well, yes. Where the hell am I? And who the hell are you lot? I don't seem to be able to remember much since I drank that pink stuff."

"All you need to know, Gibbs, is that you're in a safe house. You blew your cover, son. Sky high. And we have -" he patted his chest pocket, "- your black book." Nigel's face fell a couple of inches.

"Ah... then you know about -"

"The miners' strike? Tony Blair? Oh yes, and a lot more." The young man brushed the long, straggly hair from his eyes, scratched the designer stubble on his chin, and looked around the room uncertainly. They didn't look like thugs, and they hadn't turned him in. The loony in the khaki whistle and flute even said he was safe. Funny things were going on.

"Well, can I at least have another drink, then? It's rather good."

"Later. Maybe. If you cooperate."

"What? Me? Why do you need me? I'm nobody, just Art's dogsbody. I make the tea, type up the notes, put the cat out, program the... oh, I get it. The computers. You're blackmailing me, aren't you?" Prudence put a hand up to her mouth in mock alarm.

"You won't tell the police, will you?"

Nigel hung his head and shrugged. Being rather good with computers[13], and despite appearances, he was logical enough to realise when he was up to his ears in manure.

Φ

Judas Skim took a deep breath and started his big speech again.

"So... the soft stream flowed to my ajna from the point of light upon the fifth harmonic of -"

"The seventh Gobi wotsit, yes, we know all that," interrupted Sylvia impatiently. "Get on with it. Who's the bag in the hairnet?" Skim gave up.

"The mother of the Messiah," he said simply. A stunned silence filled the room as the words trickled down six sets of Eustachian canals and plopped into the attached brains. Mario broke the spell.

"Plissed to meeting you, Mrs Messiah," he said politely, offering another hand.

"Look, Skim," exploded Winnie, leaping from her chair and hovering over him like a vulture, all disappointment, rage and teeth. "What

---

[13]   Hadn't he himself invented the technically unwinnable subelectronic infragraphic Haunted Snoopy tennis game that was all the rage in the ARCE bars?

about me? I've got contacts, you know. And who's paid your rent for the last three months, eh?" Judas was unperturbed, holding his ground.

"Where your wealth is, there shall your heart be also," he recited.

"Never mind that," protested Sylvia in turn, "what about me? I was your first believer, don't forget."

"And the first shall be last." Not to be outdone, Bill was jumping up and down at the back of the queue.

"And where do I fit in, o Master, eh, tell me that? Couldn't I be the father?" He wasn't fussy.

"And you shall be a fisher of men."

With genuine consternation all over his innocent face, Mario, who had hardly understood a word of what was going on but could at least perceive that his chances of making Pope seemed to be disappearing fast, popped up in the middle of the throng with arms outstretched.

"Pliss, pliss, amici -" he pleaded, until a solid blow to the stomach felled him at the prophet's feet. Skim looked down at the writhing figure with pity.

"Blessed are the peace-makers." This of course only enraged all the others even more. Meanwhile, Evie had wandered out to the kitchen to put the kettle on and chanced instead on a bottle of vodka hidden behind the tins of beans in a cupboard. Suitably fortified, she now returned to the fray and, with a confidence that surprised even herself, made an announcement.

"I don't know why you're all so worked up, I'm sure. I mean, me? I'm over forty anyhow and my Stan `asn't... that is, we didn't...and I'd never... Well, it's not nice, is it? So this Messiah bloke'll jus' `ave to find someone else." Skim shook his head and fixed her with his best penetrating stare.

"There's nothing you can do about it, Evie," he said. "Hierarchy have spoken. Blessed are the meek, and there's nobody here meeker than you. As for Stan... well, I don't suppose he's necessary anyway."

Seeing his own chances disappear down the toilet of destiny, Bill pulled on his raincoat and cap.

"I'm off," he said. "I've heard quite enough for one night."

"Me too," agreed Sylvie. "Coming Win?" The three of them made for the door, closely followed by Evie. Winnie hesitated with her hand on the knob, congenitally unable ever to leave without having the last word.

"I must say, Mr Skim, I find your attitude very disappointing. I'm sorry but I shall have -"

"Blessed are the sorrowful, for they shall -" The door slammed shut with a cry of 'Judas!' on the other side.

Skim sank down into an armchair with his feet up on Mario's still gasping body, closed his eyes and considered his position. This was a prophet's lot, after all, not to be heard in his own home. There was nothing to be concerned about. The Message was delivered. Evie was on her way, like it or not. And new disciples grew on trees nowadays. And there was always Pene.

As if in answer to some unspoken command from the fifth harmonic of the universal stream, she rose quietly from the corner chair where she'd been sulking and stepped out of her shoes. Then she stepped out of her skirt. Skim heard the soft rustle of her thighs as she slowly approached. Slender fingers brushed away the buttons of her blouse as if they never existed, and the thin black cotton fell like an Arctic night from small, firm breasts. She stood before him, one foot either side of a now blissfully reposing Mario, and finished the quotation.

"– for they shall find consolation."

Chapter Six ~ Feet in the Door

Arthur Stone sat glumly in front of a monitor, chewing the nails off chocolate fingers. Not only had he lost Evie Gardner just as things were getting interesting, he'd also lost his assistant. Not that Nigel was interesting, but he really did know how to get these machines to do things they weren't designed to do. The best Arthur had been able to manage, apart from Gaelic football on Channel Five, was Mrs P in Edgware. As a result of her recent brush with celebrity, however frustrating, she was now advertising herself as a fully-fledged trance medium in a well-known monthly ('Dora: advice from beyond the veil. Sexual problems a speciality, nothing too small for me to handle.') and was rapidly gathering about herself a motley group of similar old dears anxious to have their faculties developed. For the most part, the circle was dedicated to the utterly trivial, such as the telekinetic tinkling of cowbells and the dematerialisation of as many fancy cakes as George had been able to snaffle from the bakery where he worked.

"Oooh, them's nice," Kath was saying, poking each cake with a podgy finger as if reserving them all for herself.

"Never mind them," said Fran, "look what I brung." She flourished a brown paper cone decorated with luminous green stars like a witch's hat.

"Worrisit? Ice-cream?"

"'S a trumpet. Honestly. It's for our little spirit friends to use when it floats up on the hectoplasm."

"Worrif none of `em can play the trumpet?"

"'S for speaking through, you daft `ape'orth. Anyway, all the dear departed are perfect musicians, stands to reason."

"My Alf were tone deaf."

"Well your Alf ent likely to be coming through, where `e is, eh?"

"Now look `ere, you old bat -"

"Children, it's time to start," interrupted Dora with a sweet fixed smile as she sliced viciously through a wad of chicken sandwiches for later. They trooped into the blacked-out back room, sat down with hands joined and launched into the customary three verses of She'll Be Coming Round the Mountain to raise the vibrations. Arthur watched and shook his head sadly. If this was the state of spiritual awareness on Earth then no wonder dialectical materialism was on the march again. Of course, he didn't mind that but nobody likes to win by default.

The silence was deafening for a good ten minutes, broken only by bursts of deep, sonorous breathing from George's direction. (Dora had suggested he should join in out of marital loyalty and on the grounds that there'd be no cod and chips later if he didn't.)

"Strange," said Dora, checking under the table, "we've usually got at least one leg up by now." Then the cuckoo clock squawked and the sleeping cat stretched, knocking over the cowbells.

"Goody," said Kath, clapping her hands as if at a West End show. "It's started." It was Dora's signal, anyway.

"Omptypomtydomp," she growled through clenched teeth, eyes shut tight in concentration. "Ergleweeb."

"Ooh, wake up, George," said Fran, shaking him. "I think it's your Aztec chief coming through." She addressed mid-air reverentially: "Are you with us, friend?"

"Omptyweeble," affirmed the friend.

"And does you `ave wise words for us this evening, friend?"

"Da doo ron ron. Weeb."

Arthur could bear it no longer. Rules may be rules but there's a limit. He flicked two switches, entered Dora's password, manoeuvred the cardboard trumpet over Kath's head and gave them five bars of Colonel Bogey at a hundred and twenty decibels. When Nigel then suddenly reappeared through the back way (which Arthur still didn't know he had), apparently followed by three heavies in uniform, Stone threw himself to the floor to save them the trouble.

"Get up, Art," sighed Nigel, reaching across to turn Dora off. "And we're in enough trouble without any of that." His boss gestured to the others.

"SGB?"

"Much worse."

"Vot in heffen is vorse than ze SGB?" He studied them more closely. Realising that two of the uniformed figures were women, a sudden terrible thought struck him. "My got, it's not ze Salvation Army is it?"

"Arthur, they know."

"Zey know ze Salvation Army?"

"We know all about your work, Stone."

"Ah, you are ze Meteorological Office, yes. Velcome, velc -"

"Your other work. Like the Finchley selection panel. The Champions League semi-final. And Evie Gardner." Arthur sank back onto a chair and turned white as a ghost. Life used to be so peaceful, one was left alone to get on with one's little subversions amid the quiet inane chatter of machines and Nigel, and now it was all getting complicated.

"You know zis EG?"

"In a manner of speaking," Harry nodded. "Forties, small and weasely, hairnet."

"Zat's her. Vy is she so important?"

"She turned up on the CPU computer when they were investigating a disturbance," Nigel explained to the others. "So the SGB came looking for her at PRU but they didn't -"

"Hang on, I'm Pru."

"No, we're PRU. Psychic Res -"

"No, it's my name. Prudence, see?" Nigel looked at her quizzically for a moment as the little cog wheels of his brain clicked into each other. Then without a word he sat down at a keyboard and began tapping, fingers blurred.

"A while ago," he said, without breaking the blur, "I was just hacking about for something to do, and found myself in the CPU mainframe. It just came to me. Obvious really, an inverted polyglotic inferal animism lock."

"Obvious," agreed the colonel.

"Well, like I said, their chap Fuzru was working on some sort of disturbance and came up with... here it is, this is what he's got so far. EG. Then HA and PRU, that's... no, wait, there's a bit more now..." There was a brilliant flash of aquamarine on the screen and a small duck waddled across carrying a banner bearing the letters AL.

"Oops, that would be me," said Alison.

"And I'd be HA," added Harry.

"And all off you," chipped in Arthur, barely able to disguise the triumph in his voice, "are in efen more trouble zan me. Vell done, Niggle, zat's vorth a rise." Nigel shrugged.

"What's ten per cent of nothing?" he muttered.

Harry's shoulders slumped momentarily as he realised that his squad was under attack and his grand strategy in imminent danger of collapse. The others looked equally dejected. Yet in every campaign there's a moment when a man loses his bottle, when he goes over the top and the first bullet hits. You can still pull it off. The colonel had seen it all before. Yes, the circumstances were a bit different now. Mafeking, Dunkirk and Goose Green were one thing, but could he be sure that God was on their side now? Well, it didn't matter, Harry decided. Right is right, whichever side God is on. And when faced with massive odds, the great and intelligent commanders know what to do. Retreat. (Of course, the more intelligent thing to do is not get involved in the first place, but it was too late for that.)

Nigel's next remark boosted the troops' morale.

"I shouldn't worry about it, though. CPU won't understand the readout. Fuzru's a twit. We were at college together, only he got ambitious. He's been on all the right courses, yes, but he's got no feel for the machines. No flair, see? As I speak, he'll be telling his boss about AL and they'll be sending an SGB taskforce off to the GCSE."

Φ

"…yes, sir, absolutely… couldn't agree more… uhu, yup…" The 3rd Spiritual Secretary leaned back comfortably with his feet on the desk and a foolish smile on his face, basking in the warm, bubbly, lavender scented knowledge that his superiors believed everything to be under control. He was so relaxed that his extremities positively tingled in tune with the gold Thought Transfer Module by his side. "…quite sure, sir, yes… ahead of the game, as always, sir. As you know, we picked up the Corsicans immediately…yes, a sackful of money… well, they would deny it, wouldn't they? Claimed it was some sort of protection… mmm, on their way to the laundry or something… Yup, well you know these foreigners, you can't make any sense of… what? Were you indeed? I didn't know… uhu, yes sir, I'll remember that… The other thing? No, that's being sorted as we speak… yep, a taskforce… you know what A Level students are like, some foolish prank…No, I don't think so… I'm pretty sure they don't have voles in Sicily… no, nor weasels…"

Φ

If you type 'Skim' into any reputable search engine you're likely to get about seven million, five hundred and seventy thousand links. And for 'Judas' it's more than thirteen million. Ranjit realised that Benedict might need a bit of a nudge in the right direction. Back in the little observation room he now called home – he'd worked out by now how to think up a bed for the corner and a poster of Sachin Tendulkar for the wall – he'd been making fine progress with the technology, especially as he was entirely unsupervised and could play to his heart's content. Buoyed up by his success at getting information through to his dude, RJ's spirits were high. The techniques were being refined all the time, and at last he knew that he'd found his life's work. All right, he was actually dead. But better late than never.

For his part, Benedict was just about coming to terms with the idea that the total destruction of his life had somehow been necessary, since he himself had not been destroyed. Destiny was not something he'd ever given much thought to (except when he'd created the award-winning campaign for a hair spray of that name, the one with the dowdy size eighteen model finding herself pursued by a Russian oligarch). But there was definitely something in the air now, and it wasn't just next door's overflowing drain. In the few moments spent with a kindly if rather strange caretaker, life had started to make some sort of sense again. And now it had an all-consuming purpose: to find Alison, wherever she may be.

But the computer seemed to be acting up again. His first search had unaccountably yielded a site dedicated to famous Indian cricketers; then he had inadvertently clicked on a link that linked to something else and had learned that Maharaja Ranjit Singh had been the ruler of Punjab, had died in 1839 after a reign of nearly forty years, and had left seven sons by several different wives. Oh well, you never know when these things will come in useful.

RJ hadn't yet quite grasped the principle that communication needs actually to mean something to the recipient. Nonetheless he managed to link Benedict through to some very interesting pages while his charge himself sat back with virtually no idea what the machine was doing. First, of course, was Skim's official website (no self-respecting prophet is without one these days), set up by Winnie's husband. It wasn't that he cared one hoot about his wife's interests, but the freehold of their property was in her name so it was a kind of insurance policy. The site was full of ajnas and harmonics and vague references to future unspecified great world events, and was terminally boring. But Benedict also found himself reading some older, very much more obscure references to Judas in the archives of provincial newspapers and the records of magistrates' courts. The man had a history, and not all of it was as pure white as his suits. He'd been born of privileged stock in the West Country, had been expelled from two quite good public schools, had been charged at various times with possession of both suspicious substances and imported literature of, shall we say, the explicit kind, and had spent a while in prison having married three times without apparently bothering to get divorced in between. It was inside that he had got religion, with unlimited access to libraries and nothing else to do, and reinvented himself. And he was beginning to attract some serious attention, not to mention sponsorship.

Now, a career as a New Age guru does not in itself require too many formal qualifications, merely the unfailing gullibility of sufficient people who wish the world to be different and a proportion of whom have spare money. On the other hand, Benedict mused, this particular career would very quickly meet the slings and arrows of outraged fortune, were

Skim's earlier life experiences to become more widely known. What the man needed, clearly, was a professional publicist.

Benedict set to work. Sandwiches passed. Coffee was replenished. By morning he had his own website: 'The Apache Agency ~ your image is our business'. It had apparently already received over nine million hits. After a few hours sleep and more coffee, he looked out his best dark suit and a sober tie to match the only clean shirt he could find, and tapped Skim's address into the satnav.

He was driven purely by instinct now, and by love.

Φ

Having abandoned her spiritual career with Judas Skim, Winnie Khan had hardly put the key in the Golf's ignition when she was assailed by those perennial doubts that come to every born-again agnostic in the darker moments of life. Suppose – just suppose – it was all true? Suppose you were just doing the washing up one day and the last trump sounded, and all the graves opened up and billions of the dusty faithful were trekking down The Broadway to their eternal reward, and there you were up to your elbows in suds and you just couldn't remember the third line of The Lord's Prayer or the Archbishop of Canterbury's name? It's a chilling prospect. And Winnie, whose husband was after all in insurance, went suddenly cold. They didn't have a policy for this.

"Er, Mrs Gardner? Evie dear? One moment... don't dash off."

Evie wasn't dashing anywhere. She'd got a sleeve of her plastic raincoat caught up in a curler, and was standing on the pavement under the late evening drizzle like a futuristic Quasimodo. Moreover, she had absolutely no idea where she was or how to get back to Watling Avenue. She regarded Winnie with suspicion. The toffee-nosed madam had been the first to complain. But she did have a car.

"Perhaps I can give you a lift, dear?" Winnie flashed an ingratiating smile. "I mean, let's not let a little disagreement spoil our new friendship. What do you say?" A few paces further on, Sylvia now stopped with ears twitching. She realised in a moment what was going on (as a part-time masseuse one learns to grasp things quickly). "I was probably a bit hasty back there," Winnie purred on. "The higher vibrations, you know, makes one edgy. I'm sure you know how it is. After all, we're both women of the world and -"

"But that's just it," interrupted Sylvia, retracing her steps to join them. "She isn't, is she? Do forgive me, Evie – may I call you Evie? – but it was all just so... unexpected. Your wonderful news, I mean."

"Exactly what I was about to say," added Winnie, glaring territorially. "Yes, wonderful. And when Judas introduced you, well, you looked so... so..."

"Radiant," Sylvia seized her chance. "Yes, and such a glowing aura about you, all pale blue and crimson and..." Struggling, she gazed in awe at Evie's curlers. "...and yellowish."

"Mystical," offered Winnie. "No other word for it."

Evie had been watching this exchange like a tennis umpire, and sensed that she had to do something. Apart from anything else, each woman had by now taken a firm grip on one of her arms as if staking their claim, and she was in danger of being split down the middle.

"Shall we go back in then?" she ventured. They looked at the small terraced house behind them. The parlour was in darkness and just a thin light trickled through a gap in the bedroom curtains upstairs. One could sense the power being generated.

"Perhaps not just now," suggested Sylvia. "Judas will be, er, meditating. Anyway," she added brightly, "you don't really need him now. You've got me."

"And me." Their grips tightened.

Evie summed up the situation. She was not stupid. This big city gave her the creeps, she was living out of a suitcase, her spiritual search had got completely out of hand, and most importantly she was almost broke. A hurried search of the colonel's study had only yielded a couple of hundred pounds and a case of Peruvian sherry she hadn't even been able to give away. So she could definitely recognise a couple of gift horses when they grabbed her arms.

"Right," she said. "Are there any pubs round here? I feel like a stout."

This was when Nigel picked up the trace again. It was something to do with the juxtaposition of Evie and alcohol.

"Zat's her!" said Arthur excitedly, pointing to a dark corner of the screen. "By ze potted plant. Next to ze Toby Jug."

"Phew, she's ugly," exclaimed Alison, peering intently at the screen. "Rolls of fat, big red nose and -"

"No, zat is ze Toby Jug."

"Oh, I see. Yes, straggly hair, red face and -"

"Zat is ze potted plant."

"Right. Well, she seems very normal after all."

"Agreed," said Stone, raising a cautionary finger. "But zis Skim, now zere's a real weirdo. Scares ze villies out off me."

"Some sort of prophet she's got mixed up with," explained Nigel to the others, tapping away at a different keyboard. "Earthquakes, elections, the Cheltenham Gold Cup – he's always right. 'Course, most of them are dead certs but people are beginning to believe in him. His latest thing is some sort of cosmic upheaval... something world-shaking, but I haven't found out what yet. Still, Mrs G seems to be in it up to her neck."

"What?" spluttered Harry. "But she's so... ordinary!"

"Zat's just it!" shouted Arthur, banging a shoe on the table and rattling the walls. "You plant somevun completely ordinary and ten years later ven zey get to vork no-vun suspects a zing. Belief me, I know about zis."

"Who are the other two with her?" asked Prudence. "They don't look too happy."

"Glad you asked that," said Nigel, leaning back with a smirk. "Tombstone and Stroker there aren't actually important, but I've been digging around their PFs with an empifluid eleven.dot search tool and turned up some juice."

"I vish peoples vould speak English round here."

"Ah, but you'll like this, Art."

"Nasty?"

"As nasty as it comes. The one on the right, pouring her drink into the pot plant, now, her hubbie Jim is in the City. 'Broker and Company Director', the file says. Born Middle East. And the one cracking her knuckles under the table, her Ron's down as 'Banker and Company Director'."

"So vot? Ze usual vestern capitalist toads."

"But I checked Company House. See for yourselves." He spun the monitor round and split the screen so that the two lists of directorships could be compared. They were identical. There was a token light engineering company, an offshore finance business and a couple of charities, and so on. But at the bottom of the pile was the WICH Corporation.

"Oh, they're good. I saved a fortune on a new cooker after their report came out," said Pru brightly. "Mind you, it did blow up later."

"Ze cookers are just a smokescreen. All zat stuff is a cover for moving big wooden crates in and out of varehouses."

"See, WICH stands for World Inter-Continental Hardware," added Nigel, "short for rockets, tanks, missiles and generally anything explosive. Including cookers. It's a multi-trillion pound business, and not exactly always legal."

"So," breathed Harry. "My Evie's got herself mixed up in Armageddon."

Φ

As she knocked back her third stout of the evening, Evie was quite unconscious of all this interest in her (and in another half an hour would be unconscious of everything else), as were her new friends.

At this moment, their husbands also happened to be together, laying siege to the pink gin at The Rising Sun in Mill Hill. Jim Khan, whose real Christian name was neither pronounceable nor Christian, was small and dark and deceptively meek in appearance, yet with the calm smile of one who never has to worry where his next Range Rover is coming from. His father had started out in oil, before ending up in concrete as a result of putting too much pressure on an American congressman. By contrast, Ronald Golightly's career progress had been tough. A grammar school boy, he had started out as a branch manager of the bank in Walham Green. However, his shrewd investment sense and double thumbscrew method of bookkeeping had rapidly taken him further, aided not a little by the fact that a senior member of the judiciary had taken to visiting his wife's place of work. He dwarfed the other man, hugely rounded and at forty-five already into his fourth chin.

They had met at a corporate dinner and soon discovered many mutual interests such as alcohol, warfare and a Japanese escort agency in Dean Street. Their interest in WICH was a logical progression for any normal capitalist toad who has reached a certain position. People with money naturally wish to both increase and protect it, thus requiring the services of banker and broker. And if international tensions and rumours of imminent conflagration increase, then all the more need to get as much money as possible and to guard it carefully, and not to ask too many questions. This logic has all the convenience of a teabag and just as many holes, since in the event of actual hostilities investments get frozen and claims refused. Therefore the only people who can ever become truly rich in the long run are bankers and brokers with directorships of armament companies.

"This monsignor chap worries me," Ron was saying. "You can usually safely ignore priests, especially the sort who go to folk clubs and ride mopeds. British eccentricity, you know, people laugh at them. But this peace campaign waller is getting himself taken seriously. Did you see the Telegraph today?"

"I know what you mean, old boy." Jim's cultured Oxford tone matched his dark grey pinstripe. "Of course, back home we don't have that problem. None of this guitars and mopeds – well, half the population have only got one hand anyway. But no, you people here never know what to believe in. All it takes is some jumped-up cleric talking about love and trust, and GDP's down five points."

"And did you see," added Ron, "at that march on Sunday they got almost as many people out as last week's telecom share issue? Damn hypocrites! If they're all so holy, why weren't they in church? I don't like it, Jim, I don't like it."

If there's one thing the Rons and Jims of the world don't like it's the threat of peace breaking out. They swallowed their drinks and stood to leave.

"And another thing," said Ron as they crossed the car park towards his Mercedes, "this chap Sylvia and Winnie have got themselves mixed up with. What's his name... Silvertop? Cream?"

"Skim."

"That's the one. Well, I'm not so sure he's as harmless as they make out. Ok, registered charity and all that, not a bad wheeze. But he's into this spiritual brotherhood stuff too, isn't he? We need to keep an eye on the girls, don't you think?"

At seven thirty the next morning, Jim Khan would have cause to agree wholeheartedly with his colleague's suspicion.

When Evie had eventually passed out in the pub, a bitter argument had ensued between her two new disciples as to who should have the privilege of removing the body for safekeeping. They drank Martinis for it until they both felt sick and the lot fell upon Winnie. Evie was dragged out to the Golf and spread as decorously as possible across the back seat. When Jim came down for breakfast on Thursday morning, he recoiled in horror at the awful apparition of a green Evie in curlers and borrowed dressing-gown trying to focus on her eggs through eyelids that appeared welded together with putty.

"Good morning, dear," said Winnie, who looked little better. She pecked him below the left ear. "This is Mrs Gardner – Evie. We met last night at my meeting. Would you like toast? Evie's going to be the mother of the Messiah. Isn't that nice?" Jim dribbled coffee down his fresh white shirt.

"Good God!"

"Yes, that's the one, dear. And just think, it will happen right here in our own humble little home. Well, she hasn't actually had the angelic visitation yet but it probably won't be -"

Jim had already gone. The car was barely into second gear when he was on the `phone to friends in very low places.

Φ

"Right, chaps," said the colonel, "the Strategy Revision meeting is called to order." They were back in Guildford with the spare room converted to a War Cabinet Office, with several fine Winchester carvers around a polished oak oval table. There were bookcases along the walls, a drinks cabinet and, at Harry's insistence, a wall-mounted Holiday Planner. At Alison's insistence, there was also an elegant bonsai tree on a corner shelf, in honour of their friend. Nigel's bedroom had in turn been converted into an Operations Centre with a wall full of gibbering machines, including direct hotlines to both Arthur Stone and Ranjit. Nigel wasn't going to need to sleep.

The unholy alliance that had been forged back in PRU(NE) had a lot going for it, not least that any one party could at a moment's notice shop any other party whereupon they would instantly be shopped themselves. As any married couple knows, the strongest and most durable unions are all founded on exactly this sort of thing. In any case, they all shared a common interest in subversion. Admittedly, for Arthur Stone it was less a matter of principle and more sheer force of habit, so he didn't mind what he subverted. And Nigel, not having any principles, would go along with anything on the promise of Bishop's Brew.

"It seems clear," Harry went on, "there's some big hoo-hah going down and top brass are in a funk because of some cock-up in the tubes, so the rozzers are yomping all over the shop in one hell of a stink and we're bang across the wires, what?"

"What?"

"What?"

Nigel stood quietly and went to retrieve a small paperback from a bookcase. Blowing the dust off it, he sat down again and pored over the pages with an intense frown. Prudence leaned over his shoulder to look.

"Biggles?"

"Yeah," murmured Nigel, distracted. "Not quite the same sociocultural ethos but a similar dialect, related through the Hesiodan School on the Orphistic wing. Ah, here we are, I think I've got it…yes, what Harry is trying to say is that the Elementals have embarked upon some sort of big plan but it's gone wrong and the SGB think that we've got something to do with it. Am I right so far, Colonel?" Harry waved his arms in frustration, which they all took for agreement.

"But we *are* involved," said Pru, still shivering from the shock of her name coming up on the computer. "All our names have turned up on their system. It must be only a matter of time…"

Of course, it couldn't at all be a matter of time as such. Nevertheless it was just at this very moment that the letters BENE bleeped onto Fuzru's screen. He sat back heavily in his chair with relief, now that the system had assured him all was well.

"You see," Prudence continued with undeniable logic, "it's actually worse than that. We're not just involved – we're part of the problem. It looks like someone -" she glanced around nervously, as if expecting the culprit to throw themselves on the floor in a heap of remorse and confession, "is using us. We're lumbered."

"Up the creek."

"In a kettle of fish."

"Over ze vellies."

"And up to the neck."

Harry sat down, bemused. Only a while ago he'd been in command, orchestrating the troops and on the point of delivering a counter-offensive strategy, if he could think of one in time. But now it was Prudence who held their attention.

"What do you suggest, my dear?" he said weakly, but gallantly.

"Well, I for one am not going to be a pawn in some underhand government operation," she said with conviction, having had quite enough of that sort of thing when she was alive. Gathering her courage about her like a fur coat against the sudden chill of the astral planes, she banged the table emphatically. "I say we all go to ground. Get new identities. Nigel – you can change all our files, can't you? New names, facts, jobs, everything." Arthur's face on the hotline screen beamed with pleasure. He was warming to this one, even if she was a woman.

"Yes, I can do it," objected Nigel, "but the CPU master server will be onto it in a flash. That's what it's for after all, to pick up disturbances."

"Maybe so, but according to you the machines are a lot brighter than their programmers. If they're that incompetent we stand a good chance of twigging what's going on before they're onto us. Right, Harold?" Harry started from his moody silence and sat up straight.

"Quite so, my dear, quite so. More or less what I was going to say myself."

"I thought so." She smiled sweetly at him, with affection. They were turning into a team. Then she stood up and tossed her hair, something she hadn't done for at least thirty years. It felt good, so she did it again.

"But I must warn you," said Nigel, "it can be quite a shock, reading your own Personal File. Unless you're Swedish."

They gathered round his most powerful machine as Nigel got to work. It didn't take long.

"Here you are. Prudence Clearwater, deceased. This is your life." She gasped as her own image, full face and profile, appeared on the screen. Above her head it read 'Security Access Only. DoSS PF Clearwater, Prudence Emily. 190261UK70132/B/IR'.

"Is there no part of the system you can't get into?" asked Harry with respect, but beginning to have the odd doubt about his own file.

"It's pretty straightforward," shrugged Nigel. "The design hasn't changed much since ENIAC really. Shall we go on, Pru?" She gulped. Yes, it had been her idea but then a lot of ideas lose their appeal once they become reality. More than anyone, it had been she who had cemented the group together, kept Harry and Adrian from each other's throats, found them a place to live and now galvanised them into action. But friendship is one thing. Opening the wardrobe door and rattling the skeleton is another. Then she felt Harry's protective hand fall gently on her shoulder, and she nodded. Anyway, after the green gates of Rickmansworth, baring your soul could hardly be worse.

In the event she needn't have worried, for what appeared on the screen entirely confirmed their suspicions of Heaven's inefficiency.

> Mother: 193241UK64801/A
> neurotic, cowed
> Father: ? (check)
> Vulgar, council official
> No siblings
> Black Country
> IQ 115, Virgo rising
> Fate: routine mental, stage 4e
> (good History, poor Maths)
> Experience: civil service, definitely no men
> Will: frustrated
> Prime: 5' 6", 34B
> Method: aneurism, about 50 enough
> Witnesses: D Rosenthal & Co

She sat back, both relieved and somewhat affronted.

"It's not much, is it?" she said.

"I shouldn't worry," offered Nigel. "A lot of men don't like big boobs."

"I don't think that's what the lady meant, young feller," Harry bristled. "It doesn't seem much of a record for a human life full of hopes and fears and joy and suffering."

"You're right," she said, "and it's not complete anyway, or accurate. My Dad was a gardener and I got a B in Maths."

"That is pretty poor," Nigel pointed out.

"Well," she said defiantly, "make it an A* then. And while you're at it, you can put 20 on my IQ and three inches on my bust." By the time he'd finished she hardly recognised herself on the screen, which was the whole point. It was a glowing testimony and a nice suburban middle-class background. All that remained was to insert the data into NRC records and she was legitimate. Prudence Clearwater, revived, gave Nigel a kiss and passed round pink and green cocktails with banana cubes for everyone.

It didn't take long to transform the others either. Harry turned out to have no entry at all under 'Purpose', so in a fit of pique he demanded that Nigel wipe the entire record and reinvent him as a headmaster with an M.Phil. and a sexy young mistress. Alison was remodelled along the lines of an East European gymnast and assigned to the same fictitious Witness Agency as the others. It was a perfect cover for her. No-one would expect her to say anything and the discrepancies of physique could be put down to steroids.

Φ

Boris settled back in his new, padded swivel chair with his hands behind his head, and looked about the office with satisfaction. It was all his now – the mahogany veneer desk with red anglepoise lamp and Welsh slate paper weight, the zinc effect filing cabinet, the latest Thought Transfer Module with twin memory and automatic dial function, and the twelve square metres of blue Axminster. His reward. He strolled around, winked at the photograph of his mother on the wall, and paused before the two-way mirror to check the floodlit path towards the tunnel. All was quiet, just a trickle of arrivals, a chance to relax before the 3 a.m. rush.

The new NRC[4] exercised his authority and flicked a switch.

"Ziggie? Have the applicants all arrived yet?"

"Yes, guv, three of them. And a right bunch of miserab -"

"Thank you, Ziggie. I'll be ready shortly." He sat down to make a few notes for the NRC[3] interviews and a cup of tea appeared at his elbow. This was the life.

To be perfectly honest, there hadn't been a lot of interest when his old job had been advertised. The NRC was vital point-of-entry work, but not glamorous, and word had got round about the circumstances of Jones' departure[14]. In the good old days, souls would have been so delighted to find themselves still upright that they'd volunteer for almost any job as a gesture of gratitude. But nowadays everyone had done workshops and cranial sacral therapy and watched BBC2 so they had higher expectations. Having made it a few rungs up the spiritual ladder they weren't content to hang about, as it were, on the scaffolding. Boris was determined that his regime would be psychologically enlightened, and the welcome offered to each deceased would be sympathetic and respectful. He might even hand out some information brochures, with maps and moral guidelines. He flicked the switch again.

"Ziggie? Send in the first one, please." There was a pause, then a quiet feminine knock at the door and Alison entered. Boris checked the PF readout and beckoned her forward.

"Ah yes, Miss Krappskaya isn't it? Alla, do come in, think up a chair. I can see that your record is impressive... Moscow Institute... Diploma in Physical Education... oh, and the European Championships... fourth place, what bad luck... then Reception experience in the chemical industry, good, very relevant, and volunteered to test the new... if only more people were so altruistic. And finally... oh dear, a javelin, eh? You'd think they'd be more careful, wouldn't you?"

Alison was finding it hard not to laugh out loud. Not only had Nigel done an excellent job on the Personal File, but she was actually beginning to assume the new persona. Being someone else was an extraordinary experience, much to be recommended, and in any case she'd always secretly wanted to be an actress. She felt her confidence growing, smiling quietly and nodding politely as Boris droned on about security and sensibility and something called the New Efficient Empathy approach.

"You see," he continued, "it can be quite uncomfortable here at times, what with the low vibrations near Earth. We do get affected by material form, you know." He glanced down at her physical profile on the

---

[14] He could hardly expect to keep his job. Not only had an official barrier been damaged, but several souls had gone through unregistered. Most had been found but two seemed to have been lost forever. Statistically this was not significant, but it appeared that someone in a high place had decreed that a single lost soul was one too many. Jones had suffered the fate of any senior administrator faced with disgrace, and had been promoted to the newly-created post of NRC[5] i/c VIP Reception & Guidance, which gave him the considerable kudos of holding perhaps the most complicated title in Heaven.

PF and gulped. The finely muscled body had gone through some changes. What sacrifices she had made for her sport, for her country. Still, she was attractive enough and he liked a bit of paradox in a woman. He'd done an ARCE course on paradox.

The interview was going extremely well, not least because Alison hadn't been required to say a word yet. But then Ziggie buzzed.

"Guv? There's an OBE coming."

"What?" Panic welled up in Boris for a moment. He'd never been much good with the famous ones. "Get Jones on the red -"

"Nah, guv, not that sort. Out of Body Experience, cardiac arrest job gone wrong. Not due for another month. Mind you, `ardly seems worth botherin' just for a month if you asks me. See, there's too much fatty -"

"That will be all, thanks," said Boris, turning him off and calming down. "See," he explained to Alison, "the chap's clinically dead on the operating table but he's not supposed to be here yet. So we just gently explain it to him, turn him round, and off he drifts back down to his body. Easy. Of course, the surgeon will get all the credit and be treated like a hero but then we don't look for rewards here in Heaven, do we? He'll soon be back anyway. Let me see -" he consulted the notes, "– yes, a pot of hyacinths in twenty-six days.

"Look, Miss Krappskaya, why don't you deal with him? Sort of on-the-job trial run, eh? Just put this white shroud on..." Alison was suddenly nervous as they went out and strolled a little way down the path. Eery memories began to stir within her, and there seemed to be a nip in the air. A distant solitary figure could be seen approaching slowly, glancing bemusedly from side to side, the undignified hospital gown still flapping about his knees.

"Off you go, then," encouraged Boris. "Friendly smile. Efficient empathy." Alison moved forward. The man looked up and stopped, and saw the white figure with arms outstretched.

"Aaaaaarrrrrgggggh!" He turned and ran back the way he'd come.[15]

"Hmm, it wasn't quite what I had in mind," said Boris, back in the office, "but certainly efficient. We probably need to work on the empathy. Now, now, don't worry about a thing." He had noticed a tear in her eye, but not that she was heaving with suppressed giggles. "Tell you what, I'll

---

[15] As a matter of interest, he re-entered his body with such force that he fell off the operating table and fractured his skull. His wife was subsequently able to claim huge damages, with which she bought a controlling share in a chain of manicure boutiques.

114

give you a demonstration. Let's see…" He consulted the Planner. "Ah, yes, that's interesting. There's a last-minute entry coming through, a government agent no less, to be assigned straight on to the FEW. Confidentially," he dropped his voice to a whisper, "there's a bit of a flap on up there, so they're obviously calling in some top staff." Right on cue, there was a knock on the door and Pru entered.

"NRC[4]?" she said briskly. "Clearwater. I believe I'm expected. In rather a hurry if you don't mind." Boris bowed.

"Certainly, madam. Of course. Please just step this way, my secretary will escort you. I'll deal with the paperwork personally, it's just a formality. Do have a good journey." And that was it. Boris waved politely from his office door as Pru disappeared, then looked around for the other applicants. They seemed to have disappeared too. "Well, Miss Krappskaya," he said, "when can you start?"

Out of sight but not out of mind, Harry breathed a sigh of relief. The troops were in position. Now he could turn his attention to Phase Two. A Special Assistance Squad was going to be formed.

Chapter Seven ~ Luck of the Devil

Jim Khan had not been idle in the week that had passed since Evie's arrival in Hertfordshire. Over lunch with Ron at a discreet bistro in Greek Street he was summing up the situation. The corner tables were so deeply shadowed that one could barely see one's plate. This was as well, since the place was noted more for its discretion than for the origin of its steaks.

"To people like you and me," he said, sotto voce, "the whole thing is preposterous."

"Poppycock," agreed Ron through a mouthful of claret. "But then-"

"Precisely. It's just the sort of thing that certain people want to believe. If word got out… well, I don't have to tell you what it would do to WICH shares. The markets are nervous enough. And when the Australians lose by an innings…" Ron shook his head sorrowfully.

"We live in troubled times, Jim. So, where's the bag now?"

"Back at Gaddesden. I've arranged a little excursion for her this afternoon in Ashridge Forest. She likes the countryside and the birds and so on."

"Very touching. Accidental?"

"Naturally. People just don't realise how dangerous wild deer can be when they're rutting."

This was not all that Jim had arranged that week. Arriving home on Thursday afternoon, he had been charm itself. Making Evie comfortably relaxed, which only required a glass of sherry and two of Winnie's migraine tablets, he had persuaded her to write to Stan and Gladys assuring them of her safety without, of course, giving her whereabouts. He had taken these letters to London to post for her and, having made a note of the addresses, had shredded them. Unlikely as it may have been, there was now little chance of Stan Gardner fathering any children with his wife, divine or otherwise. Jim also arranged for Evie's things to be collected from Watling Avenue, and burned.

Meanwhile, Judas Skim seemed to have gone to earth. The house was under constant watch but the curtains were drawn and the place in darkness except for a pale light upstairs. Apart from the exit on the second day of a small, middle-aged Italian man with a foolish smile on his face, there had been no visible activity.

As the two city men left the bistro, making sure they'd be remembered by leaving a large tip and a waitress on the floor surrounded by broken crockery, Evie was padding happily along a leafy pathway in Ashridge Forest, thermos and sandwiches under one arm, unaware of the two pairs of eyes following her. She was feeling so much better for her country break. Life was pleasant again. Winnie and Jim were pleasant. Winnie's migraine tablets with sherry were very pleasant. As for the future, she barely gave it a thought. This was probably as well, since there were those who did not intend her to have one.

Sadiq Khan, who owned of one of the pairs of eyes, stole ahead to the next clearing and slipped the rope bridle off the huge, dark stag, who owned the other pair. Its nose wrinkled and its withers shook as it immediately caught the scent of the pheromone liberally sprayed on Evie's clothing by Jim earlier. Its muscled flanks heaved joyfully as it hurled itself through the overhanging branches in its determination to copulate with her.

Evie was not used to such enthusiastic advances. But by some primeval instinct and with lightning reactions, she threw herself to the ground and the massive beast sailed harmlessly right over her. It came to a sudden halt a few yards further on, blinded by passion and failing to negotiate a substantial oak. The forest reverberated with the impact, sending a cloud of wood pigeons into the air.

Evie scrambled to her feet just as the animal shook itself free and turned for another attempt. But again the instinct took over and this time a young birch took the brunt, snapping off cleanly a foot above the ground. Ten minutes later, after eight similarly fruitless passes, Sadiq Khan wandered sadly back to his Aston Martin. The woman was a witch. Or divinely protected. While she herself lay intact in a muddy clearing, a large proportion of Ashridge Forest lay devastated around her, although perhaps not as devastated as the stag which had sunk to the ground confused and exhausted.

This would probably be enough for one day. But when Evie had pulled herself together and tottered back to Gaddesden, she was met at the gate by a speechless Winnie, waving The Times under her nose. She pointed to an Announcement.

> ### Stanley Gardner
> Relatives of the late Mr
> Gardner of Buckley Rise are
> invited to contact Mssrs
> Grabbit and Steel, Solicitors,
> whereupon they may receive
> news to their advantage.

Already numb, Evie merely shrugged.

"Judas said as things could be arranged. Higher Archie told 'im."

But it had not been Judas who had arranged for Sadiq Khan to hold Stanley down beneath the cold waters of the Tay. And by what cruel twist of fate was it that, only a couple of hours earlier, Stan had posted off the pools coupon that turned up every one of that Saturday's eight draws? It was, or would have been, his first win in twenty-five years but the eight hundred and seventy thousand pounds was hardly any compensation.

Φ

Czosn, of the FEW, was a dour Czech who, in common with the rest of his erstwhile compatriots, deeply resented any interference in his work and never wore a tie. As a mathematician of some standing (publications include Elementary Statistics, Even More Elementary Statistics, and Blindingly Obvious Statistics), he saw no need for an assistant, least of all a woman. On hearing of Pru's appointment he had even checked his own Personal File, but Nigel had thought of that too. Not only did his Fate now apparently decree collaboration, but Experience was also deficient in feminine involvement while the Will to do something about it was on a positively exponential gradient.

This surprised him. He certainly wasn't conscious of the latter and it is common knowledge that Central Europeans are among the most sexually active on the planet – something to do with continuous invasion by foreigners and excess body hair. This is why so many of them rise to high rank in Heaven, having got most of that sort of thing out of their systems early. Nevertheless he conceded that Fate did have an organic autonomy function and such strange twists can occur with a probability of – he did a quick mental calculation – about two point seven one eight by ten to the power minus nineteen. He shrugged and decided to be civil.

Pru took a seat and squirmed a little nervously. She had been briefed about the man and knew this wasn't going to be easy, especially with only a B in maths. But with her ample experience of the Civil Service, she at least knew how to pull the wool over people's eyes. And she had the further advantages now of having lost several years and gained three inches anatomically.

"So," began Czosn, narrowing his eyes until they all but disappeared, "what do you think you can bring to our work here?" Prudence thought fast.

"Well, an element of quality to begin with." Wrong answer.

"You mean my work's no good?"

"Oh, not at all. I'm sorry," she felt herself blushing. "There's no question of the veracity of your technique, no, quite brilliant if I may say so. Your Eigen matrix percentile correlation Deviance Method remains absolutely unique, unparalleled even." Had she got all that the right way round?

"But?"

"Now, this is not a criticism," which always means 'this is a criticism', "but some of the human lives you have directed, although technically efficient, have perhaps lacked experiential validity." Here at least she could speak from knowledge.

"I see. You think a woman's touch…?"

"Something like that. And of course with this special project coming up soon -"

"What do you know about that?" He leaned forward suspiciously, thin lips drawn back so far his face seemed to split in two. Off guard, Pru made a stab in the dark.

"Well, the EG project. It's going to need delicate handling, isn't it?" Bullseye. Czosn had to admit privately that he was worried about it. It was the biggest job of his career and, while it may be unique and unparalleled, the Deviance Method had not yet been perfected. It could be useful to have someone else to blame if it all went wrong. He stood for a moment and padded around the office, giving Pru the opportunity to shrink her blouse to a size eight and remove a button. The effect was subtle but nonetheless effective. When Czosn turned back, his eyes riveted themselves to her milky soft cleavage, and there now seemed a decent probability that he could get on with this woman after all.

"Come on," he said, "I'll show you the factory." She laughed, but he wasn't joking. The long, low-ceilinged hall was windowless and dull grey (to avoid the interference of personality). Some hundred or so operatives, all with mathematical doctorates, sat at identical desks facing one end where a huge VDU screen occupied the wall, staring back like a green, one-eyed monster. With the obligatory bleep, a name and number flashed at the top followed by a sketchy summary of previous life histories in high-level code.

"A soul comes up for incarnation at the end of its tour," explained Czosn. "Sometimes even voluntarily. My assistants do the preliminary valuations – how much seventy-two years in Iceland is worth, that sort of thing. The result comes on line here. See…" He pointed to the text appearing like a teleprinter on the hovering monster. "This guy was Jose Wellbottom. 193438UK201P. Mother was a Spanish countess fleeing the Civil War who got lost and ended up in Huddersfield. He gets the bonus points for poverty and a silly name, but they seem to have been quite happy so he loses out there. Disappointing, but you can never be precise about happiness. So it looks like he got an early recall – well, there would have been no point going on with it. And just look at those previous incarnations: Egyptian queen, Inca priest, wardrobe assistant at the Moulin Rouge… barely five thousand points between them. What does this guy want, jam on it?"

Jose's Inverse Proportion Experience Quotient of 87% flashed up, and instantly 87 sets of dodecahedral dice were rolled on the tables.[16] Results were fed into keyboards as more operatives near the front tossed strange coins with holes in them and consulted arcane Chinese reference books.

"Here we are," said the director with satisfaction a few moments later as the prognosis was displayed before them. "Much better next time. Libya will be in chaos by then and he'll have to live on wild berries and cactus, probably get cholera too.

"Of course," he continued as he led the way back to his office, "it's open to negotiation, and he'll be offered GCSE refresher courses. We're not completely heartless."

"But if you don't mind me saying so," which always means 'I don't much care whether you mind me saying so', "it's all a bit austere isn't it? The factory, I mean." She accepted a glass of plum juice. "The conditions are bound to affect the dice."

"Certainly, that's the point. If you can't get psychokinesis here where can you get it?"

"But that's what I was saying about experiential validity," she persisted. "It could be much more… colourful, the results more meaningful, if you had some windows with a view, a powder blue carpet, pots of geraniums, rearranged the desks into a - " Czosn held up a hand to stop her, frowning.

"What's a geranium?"

Φ

The Christmas trade at the Ratcatcher's Arms was unusually brisk. A deep carpet of drifting snow was piled up along the hedgerows by the north-easterly that swept through Buckley Rise. Nobody had quite known where the emergency gravel stockpile was located and the council snow

---

[16] This relates to the fact that there are only twelve kinds of life, as anyone with a passing interest in astrology knows.

plough still lay at a seventy degree angle where it had been inadvertently directed into the village pond. If the weather kept up, everyone could look forward to another fortnight's holiday.

Deep furrows of footprints converged from all directions on the pub. In the car park, a variety of dogs tied to rotting wooden benches sat huddled together for warmth trying loyally to look as if they didn't mind, yet turning hopeful faces to the door each time the Herald Angels' songs reached a deafening and discordant climax.

In the smoky chaos of the saloon, the landlord, Sid Crocker, was certainly not complaining. The fruit machines in the corner were jangling their fifty-pounds-clear-a-day chorus, and the NSPC charity boxes on the tables were full to overflowing. Of course, no-one ever noticed the missing initial any more than they knew Nathaniel Sidney Piers Crocker's full name. He felt suddenly generous and emptied another packet of free peanuts into the saucers on the bar, before taking the tray of shorts over to the poker school in the corner and collecting his ten per cent of the pot.

It had been a good year all round, for the village had not been short of local mysteries to dissect over a few jars. The colonel had started the ball rolling – something slipped into the bath water, it was said – not to mention the mysterious spontaneous combustion of the church porch at his funeral. Then hardly had the tongues paused when that Mrs Gardner, who'd been found in flagrante delicto with the naked body and a bottle of sherry, had disappeared off to the big city without a by-your-leave, poor old Stan left abandoned and destitute and so heartbroken that he'd taken himself off to get drowned in Strathclyde. And now the brazen hussy had come back, dressed to the nines with a bouffant hairdo, throwing money around like confetti. Although naturally it would have been churlish to refuse the free drinks she offered.

Evie herself sat glumly but with stoic determination on her own by the fire. Money was supposed to make you happy. Hers was certainly making everyone else in the bar happy. But she found herself an outcast in her own home. All right, maybe the peroxide and the calf-length Brazilian ocelot were a tiny bit over the top, but why shouldn't she treat herself after all she'd been through?

Peace and goodwill. Thankful tidings. Chirpy red robins and holy infants. Stuff the lot. The house was up for sale, the euros were in the snakeskin bag, and she was off. She checked the Cartier one last time and got up, as a fifth and very original verse of Silent Night shook the mock Tudor beams and another couple of glasses shattered on the floor. The trouble with this village was that it had no class. With an almost vicious flourish, Evie heaved open the outer doors just as the gleaming ice-blue helicopter settled in the car park, its flashing blades hurling an avalanche of powdery snow, old crisp packets and dogs past her into the bar.

The colour drained from his cheeks, Sid raised a finger in protest but remained frozen to the spot as Evie, pausing only to toss him a tenner, pulled on her green wellies and tripped almost gracefully out to the waiting aircraft. A handsome young man in black uniform and peaked cap jumped to the ground, saluted smartly, and held the door open for her. On the step she turned, flashed her gold bridgework briefly, and was gone. Sid broke open more peanuts.

By contrast, the festivities in Clandon Road were a far more low-key affair. Arthur did rather disapprove of the whole thing as a bourgeois opiate but his misgivings had been overridden by the promise of Bishop's Brew. And it wasn't as if they hadn't tried. Token gifts of truffle chocolates and rude socks had been exchanged. Brightly coloured wrapping paper was strewn on the floor with synthetic ribbon in heaps like purple spaghetti, while on every computer monitor little festive graphic Christmas trees flashed cheerfully. Tinsel and balloons festooned the windows, and home-made cards fluttered like flying geese on a string above their heads. Even a half-eaten iced fruit cake sat on a workbench among the circuit boards and soldering irons.

But Arthur, Nigel and Ranjit sat morosely on the new green velour sofa (Arthur's present to the house). There were several reasons for their deflation, the most obvious of which was that there was no-one else at the party. Harry was consumed with the task of licking his new SAS squad into shape and had cancelled all leave; Christmas being as it is the season of heightened domestic tension and traffic pile-ups, Alison was doing overtime at the NRC; and Pru had sent word that the FEW Directorate was on alert for the new secret project and every hand was being turned to designing thirteen-sided dice and symmetrical geraniums.

Her absence also meant there would be no Bishop's Brew after all, since only she knew the recipe. This had hit Nigel particularly badly. He had been working hard recently and carrying a lot of responsibility. So naturally he had looked forward, like anyone else, to putting his feet up in a drunken stupor for a while and taking in a couple of Scandinavian films on Channel seventy-one.

Admittedly, though, the other reason for their depression was largely his own fault. It had seemed like a good idea at the time to wipe Ranjit's PF completely. The ultimate cover, since that which does not exist cannot be detected. But just as Alison and Pru had gained new confidence with their enhanced identities, by a reverse process Ranjit had begun to lose whatever touch with reality he'd had. He had become listless and could not see the point in anything. In this respect he had made a huge if paradoxical step forward in his spiritual development, but he was too listless to notice. Having some experience of identity crises, Arthur had observed that there was really nothing to grumble about since anyone with a virgin mind and a computer keyboard can assume any identity whatever. One might even consider him the luckiest chap not alive. He could be a Hollywood director, the world snooker champion or a performing sealion; the possibilities, and the free fish, would be endless.

In his lethargy, Ranjit couldn't come up with a single idea except the wish to return to his old self, which was the one identity logically impossible to create. It had been Nigel's idea to choose Santa Claus, in an attempt to jolly along the proceedings. He simply hacked into Destiny Control for Nicholas, Saint, 347TY612A and cloned the essential features. It had even worked quite well for a while, and Ranjit was getting into character with a lot of thigh-slapping, bell-ringing and bouncing Arthur on his knee.

But then the totally unexpected and calamitous blow had struck out of the blue. With one computer still tuned to the FEW, Nigel was idly flicking through the subetheric waves to see what Fuzru was up to when there was a whimpering bleep and every screen flashed with static followed by an ominously spreading crimson blot strangely reminiscent of blood. The flashing trees went up in smoke. Like a berserk octopus, Nigel threw himself at the keyboards trying everything he knew until the very prints were worn off his fingertips and he had to admit defeat.

The explanation was as simple as it was terrifying. In one deft stroke synchronised with breathtaking precision, every single security code in the system had been changed. Such an event had never occurred in their experience and it could only mean that either Something Big – as Big as Somethings can get – was about to happen, or that the DoSS was on to them. The latter seemed unlikely, since the DoSS had hardly ever actually been on to anything. All the same, cold shivers with many little legs began to crawl up the metaphorical spines of Arthur Stone and his assistant. Ranjit remained oblivious to the turn of events at first. Santa Claus being essentially merry, he continued to lope around the room uttering deep ho-ho-hos until a dull blow on the head from a flying monitor brought him up short. And the realisation that he was now stuck as Santa for the duration did nothing to lift his spirits.

Φ

General Sir Charles Forsyth-Furbright peered out from behind the safety of the Officers' Mess curtains and shuddered at what he saw. Not so long ago, the unit had been quite peaceful. Just a bit of map reading and uniform pressing to pass, as it were, the time. There was the odd lecture from a peripatetic Guide on the sociocultural aspirations of foreigners. But then this Colonel Markham chap had arrived and now it was all morning reveille, route marches and combat training in full gear. The card schools had been banned, there was a completely new menu in the Naafi with actually decent grub, and swearboxes in the Mess. Worst of all, Markham was giving daily pep talks and had been heard talking to the men in a friendly tone about efficiency, self-respect and morality.

The effect had been astonishing. In the old days, such a chap would have been laughed back to wherever he'd come from if not drummed out of the service with loss of pension rights. But the men were lapping it up like stray toms in a dairy and throwing themselves into the training like there was no tomorrow (which there wasn't). He might be unorthodox, but this colonel had a gift. The men liked him. They liked their unit's new name too. The Special Assistance Squad had a ring of importance about it. Forsyth-Furbright closed the curtains and shuddered.

"Sah?" said Sgt Willie 'Plonker' Glum hesitantly. He was standing with Harry casting a critical eye over the squad's efforts on the assault course water jump.

"Yes, Sergeant?"

"Well, sah, me an' the lads was wonderin' about -"

"Get up, Parker, you ninny!" roared Harry to a bedraggled private picking weeds from his ears. "How many times do I have to tell you that water doesn't exist? It only seems wet. Reality, man, reality. Believe in yourself and you'll fly over. There... is... no... water."

"Beg pardon, sir," squeaked Parker lamely, "but if it don't exist then what's this weed doing up my -"

"Parker!" shouted Plonker Glum. "Don't hargue with a hofficer. No shitake risotto for you tonight."

"Aw, Sarge, that's my favourite."

"On your way, Parker," barked Harry. "Over you go. Remember – reality." He turned back to Glum. "You were saying, Sergeant?"

"Yes, sah, well, sah, we was wonderin'...Like, the trainin's great, sah, no complaints. Even the trombones, keeps the spirits up though I say so has one who is not very musical. And we're getting' the hang of the jungle hexercises, camouflage an' that. As you say, sah, softly softly catchee monkey." In fact, Sergeant Glum hadn't the faintest idea what the purpose of it all might be. There seemed little opportunity for a military band playing music hall favourites. And he'd been in Heaven for aeons without ever coming across anything resembling a monkey, except perhaps Private Davey who had long hairy arms and a taste for banana soufflé. But the hofficer knew best.

"Spit it out, man." Harry knew perfectly well what was on the men's minds, but was determined that chaps had to speak up for themselves. There would be free will, self-respect and character in his squad. You never knew when the officer was going to buy one so a chap had to think for himself.

"Well, sah, weapons."

"What about them?"

"We ain't got none, sah."

"Of course you ain't got... er, haven't got any, Sergeant. What use would they be, eh? You can't kill people in Heaven, can you? Think, man."

"Well, no, sah, point taken, sah. Hall the same, sah..." This was tricky. Being able to kill someone is pretty fundamental to a soldier's mindset. "Spose we come hup against the henemy, sah?" He didn't have the faintest idea what sort of enemy they could come up against either.

Harry stroked his chin thoughtfully. It was a pretty fair point, and one that he himself hadn't quite thought through yet. But as he remembered watching the SGB in action and their effect, or lack of it, on the extraordinary John Clarke, the solution suddenly came to him.

"Sergeant Glum, you have a damn fine point there. Consider yourself decorated."

"Thank you, sah!" Glum beamed proudly, puffed out his chest, and was about to march off to inspect the snake pit when Harry pulled him up.

"On the other hand, Sergeant, the reason that you're a sergeant and I'm a colonel is that there is a perfectly good answer that you could have thought of but didn't." He kept to himself the fact that he'd only just thought of it. "You see, Glum," he continued, as the other man's chest resumed normal proportions, "you've missed the essential point of our training."

"Er, which is, sah?"

"Which is belief, Sergeant. You just have to hold a gun and believe hard enough that you can kill the enemy."

"Beg pardon, sah, but didn't you jus' say has `ow you can't kill hanyone `oo's already dead, sah?"

"Well, no-o-o... But you can make him *believe* he's been hit. You can make him believe he's hurt. See? You can addle his mind."

"So…," Glum nodded energetically, as if to encourage the thought along the tunnels of his brain, "it's hall a front, sah?"

"Like everything else here, Sergeant. It's the front line."

Harry watched him disappear and listened with satisfaction as the insults and exhortations gradually receded. Then he wasted no time in thinking up his pocket book and jotting down some tentative designs for weapons and assault gear, as horrifying and menacing as he could make them, borrowing heavily from a science fiction film he'd once seen. After all, people would expect to see futuristic ray guns, shiny black plastic android masks and silver Hover Glide Vehicles swooping down to the strains of Beethoven's Ninth.

But lost in his imagination, Harry entirely failed to notice the distant, lone figure in fake-fur jacket and wide-brimmed hat pulled down over the eyes, half-hidden in a clump of willows just beyond the perimeter fence. The eyes followed him as he made his way jauntily back to his quarters to work on his new ideas, humming the tenor part to himself. If he had only glanced up for a moment, he would surely have recognised the woman, not to mention the distinct aroma of pork sausage.

Φ

Winnie Khan strode furiously down the Rue des Teinturiers past the ancient, inert mill wheels, the medieval charm of her surroundings completely lost on her. This really was too much. Mrs Gardner may be the most important woman on Earth, but all the same it had been an act of pure selfless charity on her own part offering to chaperone her on her voyage of cultural discovery. She'd left her home and family at this the most festive time of year to offer Evie her companionship and financial expertise. And for what? First the woman had insisted on visiting practically every monastery between Calais and Clermont-Ferrand to ask if they had a Brother Jacques who'd overslept, and now they'd come all this way to gawp at a ridiculous bridge in Avignon. She hadn't even been disappointed to find only four of its twenty-two arches still standing, putting it down to all the dancing that must have gone on. The total of this woman's education could be contained in half a dozen nursery rhymes.

Winnie wouldn't even have begrudged the thirty thousand pounds that had already gone if only they'd spent it in comfort. True, there was the helicopter and its uniformed young man who'd been very obliging both on and off duty. But now, hanging grimly onto her skirt as the Mistral roared down the Rhone valley threatening to deposit them in the River Sorgue,

Winnie could think of any number of other places she'd rather be. Top of her list was Cannes, where one met a good class of ex-pats in January.

This prospect didn't appeal at all to Evie, who'd had quite enough of the English for the time being, thank you. Nor was she enchanted by Winnie's monologue about gentle sage-green hues and the scent of resin in the air as one wandered at leisure through the juniper and myrtle of the pine forests to inspect far-flung exquisite Romanesque remains before repairing to the begonias and palms of the elegant boulevards fringed with gardens of British turf, all of which had been culled from an old edition of Fodor's and painstakingly committed to memory. In the event, it was a casual mention that the Municipal Casino was open from November to May that did the trick. For years, Evie had studied the Ratcatcher poker school at a distance and was eager to try her hand. What was money for?

By coincidence, a hundred and fifty miles away in Juan-les-Pins, the very same question was running through the mind of the Comte de Pennis. Not having any money, he knew exactly what the answer was. Forlornly, he chased the croutons in his bouillabaisse with a fork and gazed out at the cold, grey sea. At least you got decent portions at the Potager, which was as well when you could only afford one meal a day. It had been his worst season for years. The only son of skilled village artisans specialising in hand-beaten tin baths, he had left the northern hills of Italy when the bottom dropped out of the business to seek his fortune on the Riviera. A title, a hired dinner suit and dark, rugged good looks had soon brought him a very decent income from rich and lonely widows with more self-indulgence than sense. There was even the occasional blonde, lithesome young niece to be had to break the turpitude and stir the bones (although he had learned by painful experience to avoid German girls, whose effect was exactly the opposite).

But now, nearing sixty and with thinning hair, times were getting hard. Perhaps he was losing his touch, or was it just that all the widows (not to mention the gendarmes) knew him by now? It had been his custom to repair to Juan-les-Pins once the brash, noisy young things of the summer had departed, leaving the resort as redundant as the crisp packets that littered the beach. The hotel was comfortable and modest, yet a decent enough address from which to manage his investments and plan the next season. But this year, unless something pretty spectacular turned up, he'd be packing his bags within a month and heading east to make plaster models of leaning towers. He paid the bill and with hands thrust deep into empty pockets took himself down the Avenue Esterel as usual to comb the beach.

He hadn't found anything interesting in thirty years, but all the same he carried out the ritual faithfully with a gambler's instinct. This evening like every other, he emptied the contents of the large plastic sack onto the floor of his room at the Eden to sift through them. The collection did not seem promising at first sight: three empty Seven-Up cans, a torn string vest, an empty sauce bottle with no message inside, one used condom, the English label from a jar of egg something-or-other so weathered that only the first two letters were legible, and a large paper bag. There was also a small dead fish of uncertain species with a white feather stuck in its mouth.

Having dedicated his adult life to hedonistic materialism rather than to esoteric symbolism, these discoveries meant nothing to the comte and he set about tossing them into the waste bin. But then his fingers closed on the clammy scales of the fish and felt something hard. In moments he had slit the belly with his penknife to reveal the tarnished but nonetheless pulse-racing gold eternity ring. Later that night, his eyes gleamed behind the jewel glass as he finished polishing the ring and inspected it with minute and expert care. Nine carat with seven zirconium stones, worth a couple of hundred euros at best. But the comte was not in the least disheartened. This was A Sign. Not only that, he also suddenly remembered that this was his mother's Saint's Day. Something was surely coming his way. He put out his dinner suit for cleaning, told Reception to prepare his bill, and got ready for bed with excited anticipation and a mental note to light a candle somewhere tomorrow.

Φ

SS3 hadn't got where he was today without being a bit ruthless. As the New Relative General Plan gathered momentum, nothing – but absolutely nothing – could be allowed to go wrong. Interfering with history is a tricky business. Get it wrong and you've got Dark Ages on your hands and you have to start all over again. Yes, the ripples in the system seemed to have died out but that very fact was, to him, highly suspicious.

What had Fuzru actually been picking up? The Psychic Research Units seemed to be functioning normally, which is to say their directors were all behaving as eccentrically as usual. There was still some doubt about the HA readout, so he'd had all the Hare Krishna followers to be found beaten up a bit just to be on the safe side. When after a long silence the CPU computer had blurted out SOD5 and announced that it had finished, SS3 decided to take matters into his own hands. He pulled on a woolly hat and greatcoat – even the Etheric plane can seem chilly for one used to the rarefied and conditioned atmosphere of the BoSS – and made his way personally to police headquarters. His poor humour was not improved by being made to wait outside since no-one would believe who he was and took him for a tramp. Eventually he just froze the guards with a look of pure authority, made his way in and removed the coat to reveal his formal robes and medal of office, and ordered the release of John Clarke.

A fierce argument ensued with the head of the DoSS. The SGB so rarely actually caught anyone suspicious that they were not about to let them go willy-nilly. SS3 patiently explained the plan over and over until its subtlety seeped into the other's consciousness. Since like attracts like is just about the only immutable law of physics there is, sooner or later John Clarke would lead them to his fellow conspirators. Top agents would be assigned to follow him closely yet with the utmost discretion. Alright, since there weren't any top agents it would have to be Stachov and Hurski.

Finally, SS3 had personally supervised the switching of all the computer security codes. As it happens, this had brought not only the Guildford safe house but the whole of the rest of the astral planes to their knees for a while since SS3 had omitted to warn anyone of his intention. Still, he was confident that the final preparations for the incarnation could now proceed. The idea was simple and ingenious. It was just a pity, for Heaven's sake, that it was carried out by complete idiots.

Ranjit was the first to be trapped. Unable to bear the gloom of the party any longer, he decided to make the most of his new identity and bring a little traditional cheer to the crowds thronging Oxford Street in London. This was unsuccessful as he was simply trampled by the rush to be first in the queue for next day's sales. Instead, he decided to have something long and refreshing among friends at Gandalf's. It was just an extraordinary coincidence that Saint Nicholas had had exactly the same idea at just the same time.

It was not long before an indignant and jealous fracas developed with red hats, tufts of white beard and gaily wrapped Taiwanese novelties being hurled in all directions. Adrian, not realising who his clients were, called the police.

As the warring fathers were being ushered in at Bow Street, John Clarke was being thrown out. Inexplicably, he immediately recognised Ranjit and stepped forward to shake his hand.

Φ

Benedict had retraced his journey to Judas Skim's house each morning for six days. There had been no response to the doorbell, although an occasional low moan might be heard from upstairs, and he sat patiently outside in his car for an hour each time, but the curtains had remained resolutely closed. Watching eyes in the shadows across the street, however, had carefully noted his arrivals and departures, and the registration of his car.

But on the seventh day, the curtains moved and there was light. A young woman, rather dishevelled but with a knowing smile on her face, had tottered out of the front door and swayed uncertainly away down the street. Benedict allowed a decent time to elapse for clothing and coffee to be put on, and then rang the bell again.

He introduced himself as Michael Benn, CEO of the Apache Agency, and handed over a brochure hot off the printer and full of glowing if fictitious testimonials from satisfied customers (who had at least been real clients of his previous employment). Skim looked dreadful. He seemed to have aged a decade in the last week, all life energy spent.

"I think I might be able to help you in your work," suggested Benedict. Then, as Skim started to shut the door in his face, "because you really wouldn't like your holiday in the Scrubs to become widely known, would you?"

Judas Skim was at a low point, his career as a world-renowned prophet having hit a brick wall that he hadn't foreseen. All his carefully orchestrated plans over these last few months now hung by a thread, largely because the prescribed mystical seven were down to just two. Moreover, having found the Holy Mother in Edgware he'd managed to lose her again. Yes, he had to concede, some professional PR work would not go amiss, not to mention some straightforward detective work. Benedict invited him to check the provenance of his website on the Internet, and within another hour had all he needed, including a deal. All his old skills had come flooding back to him, he mused, as he headed back to Hertfordshire on Evie's trail. So perhaps there had been a purpose to it all.

Φ

But Evie and Winnie were by now flying high above the squat and shuttered old farmhouses of the Maritime Alps. The wind was blowing itself out and Winnie was relaxing. Having persuaded Evie to hand over half her money ("for insurance"), all seemed set fair for a nice, long, relaxing holiday even if the silly bag did blow her share in a week at the casino. Le Suquet tower came into view at last and, after one sweep of the marina just for effect, within half an hour they were unpacking in the unashamed palatial luxury of the Carlton. In the lobby, Sadiq Khan waited patiently behind a newspaper.

Next to him, though both were for now quite unaware of their mutual destiny, sat the Comte de Pennis. In fact, the pair sat like this for several days until each realised that the other had occupied the same chair all this time and that his eyes were following the same pair of English ladies each time they crossed the foyer. Noticing each other for the first time, the two men immediately recognised the aura of dark machination beyond the other's blank, polite gaze. Accordingly, they set about plotting a joint venture.

There were some initial difficulties with this. The most fundamental was that one man wanted Evie dead as soon as possible while the other needed her alive, at least until she could be relieved of her fortune. Another problem was that the women were never seen apart (and Sadiq's brother had not yet asked him to dispose of Winnie), and never far from what passed as crowds for this time of year. A coalition plan was eventually forged, in which Khan lent de Pennis his small yacht in return for the comte's small Smith and Wesson pistol. The money would be split fifty-fifty.

"You will `ave to be patient," counselled de Pennis. "L'amour must take `er time, and after all -" he shrugged sadly, "- it takes me a little longer than it used to."

"Just do whatever's necessary, old boy," said Khan. "Remember, I'm the one taking the risks. And believe me, this old bag isn't easy." The debacle of Ashridge Forest still rankled.

It was in fact quite some time before the comte could make his move, as February ushered in the annual Mimosa Festival which set off his hay fever. To his fellow conspirator's disgust, he put the yacht out to sea and refused to step ashore again until the belching of the tree-frogs among the bougainvillea and prickly pear heralded the arrival of spring.

Meanwhile, far from blowing her share within a week, the silly bag was taking Cannes by storm. Having discovered a remarkable aptitude for the Texas Hold `em Method, she'd even taken Amarillo Slump Prestwick (one-time winner of the Las Vegas International) to the cleaners. The Municipal Casino considered banning her. But this small, weasely and eccentric Englishwoman brought in so much peripheral trade in the shape of incredulous hangers-on, for all of whom she bought drinks, that the management realised they were making a healthy profit despite habitually losing to her. She was the toast of the town, with a private drier at the hotel hairdresser's and a reserved table overlooking the harbour at the Bistingo in the Palais des Festivals. It was here one evening, as she struggled to unwrap the vine leaves on her banon, that she confided her inner thoughts to Winnie.

"Y'know, Win," she began pensively, "I'm `aving a whale of a time, I really am. But when I think back, eh… poor ol' Stan…" Winnie laid a consoling, ring-infested hand on her arm.

"Do you miss him, my dear?"

"What, Stan? That miserable ol' bugger? `Course not. All the same…" Her voice trailed off into the distant land of far memories where life had been full of hopes and dreams of romance, wealth and adventure. Well, she had two out of three now, but it wasn't enough. "…`e were the only man I ever knew."

The new waiter with the strangely familiar Arabic features hovered at Winnie's elbow and poured the smooth, clear Chateau Grillet. Gazing out over the still water beneath a waxing moon, neither woman noticed the grains of white powder slipped into the glass, instantly dissolving.

"I know what you mean, my dear," agreed Winnie solemnly, recalling the day when she'd realised that dogs and horses were better company than men. She drained her glass in one draught. "Yes, I remember when my Jim was just a yeurrrggh…" Puzzled, Evie peered at her companion, who seemed to be closely inspecting the curd cheese on her plate.

After the ambulance had gone and she had graciously accepted the management's apology and free bottle of champagne, Evie settled back to contemplate the prospect of a whole evening without her minder. Her head instinctively filled with foolish thoughts of Latin lovers and wild romance. She didn't have to wait long. Handing her the small bouquet and a wicker bowl of crystallised fruit, the waiter gestured towards a suave, elegant gentleman with dark features across the room. Evie couldn't help smiling as she experienced again for a brief moment the effect of the doctor's little blue pills and advertisements for Mel Gibson films. Across the crowded restaurant, her eyes met de Pennis' and the rest is history.

Φ

Adrian was totally distraught. Pacing the second floor landing of Sutton Lodge in Guildford, he was so beside himself with guilt that he was wearing two tracks in the carpet. At last Ranjit arrived, hissed "Don't say a ho-ho word!" and limped straight past him. Adrian did his best to apologise but Ranjit's mood was distinctly unseasonable, and it was left as usual to Pru to calm things down.

Ranjit had had the narrowest of escapes. Being recognised by John Clarke, he'd been hauled off to an isolation cell and interrogated mercilessly despite his plaintive protest that surely everyone recognises Santa Claus. When Adrian arrived with the news, Arthur had got to work with uncommon efficiency, contacting an old friend in the DoSS who'd been passed over for promotion eleven times due to 'irregularities' in his PF and was only too willing to spill what he knew about the new security codes. There was enough there for Nigel to work on, and just in time. He broke into the files and made the necessary alterations moments before the Bow Street duty officer checked them. Ranjit was apparently genuine and the other chap turned out to be a nineteenth century Bolshevik cashing in on capitalism.

Of course, although Ranjit was now free, this also meant that he was the sole heir to the title and destiny of Father Christmas. This could mean sewing plastic eyes onto cuddly toys for eleven months of the year in Arctic conditions and dealing with sackfuls of threatening letters from grasping children, not to mention the mad dash up and down the world's chimneys. But Pru, on a flying visit, had some good news. Snooping about quietly at the FEW she had stumbled upon piles of cardboard boxes in a dusty basement, which contained card-index Personal Files discarded when the systems were computerised. If Harry's squad could get them out, there was a chance they might find Ranjit's so that Nigel could restore him to his former self. It would mean the irrevocable demise of Santa Claus but, as Nigel pointed out, that would serve all the greedy little buggers right.

The rest of the news wasn't so good. For no apparent reason, John Clarke had made straight for Gandalf's when he was released, followed by two very obvious SGB agents in grey, belted raincoats and black homburgs. Adrian saw them coming and hid upstairs, but the police had frogmarched everyone else off. Incensed by the injustice, Bonzai had made quite a fuss and got herself arrested for insulting behaviour and obscene language.

"Oh no," said Pru, "what's going to happen to her?"

"She'll be all right. It's not the first time, after all. A night in the kennels and a few kicks up the backside with a size twelve."

"Rough," said Nigel.

Chapter Eight ~ The Inconceivable

The fugitives shared a quiet game of whist and considered their position. So far they'd been extremely lucky, almost as if some unknown hand were helping them. But how long would this last? The release of John Clarke had been a brilliant ploy and surely he would catch up with them sooner or later. Did they have to live forever in fear of a knock at the door?

There was a knock at the door.

Shamefaced and uncharacteristically dejected, there stood Harry flanked by two strangers. One was a small, stooping man with darting eyes. The other was a plump woman, in a fake fur jacket and wide-brimmed hat, and with an odd perfume. Harry lifted an eyebrow towards her.

"Barbara," he explained. "My wife. And that," he lifted the other eyebrow, "is her private detective. Seems they tracked me down and followed me here. Sorry. I never imagined she'd... Anyway, apparently they know our plans somehow. You know what wives are like – they always know what you're thinking before you've even thought of it." In point of fact none of the others had the remotest experience of wives, but they got the idea. Barbara swept past them into the room, stood with hand on hip like a Reuben model, and surveyed the slightly shabby surroundings still littered with Christmas debris.

"This the best y' could do, Poojar?" she scoffed. "Not awfully impressive. And I s'pose this -" she scrutinised Prudence from head to toe, "is y' fancy bit? Strange, she doesn't look like y' usual tart." Prudence flinched but held her ground silently. Having been a civil servant, she had ample experience of obnoxious people.

If Barbara Markham was aiming for the Miss Astral Popularity title she hadn't made a good start. The friends sat glumly together as the detective took out a small leatherette notebook and began reciting in a nasal monotone the fruits of his researches. He knew almost everything.

"So what do you want?" asked Harry, shoulders hunched.

"What do I want?" retorted his wife. "I want what's mine, Poojar, what's mine. Y' owe me. I gave y' the best twenty years of my life -"

"If they were your best -" Harry began, but thought better of it.

" – cooking y' disgusting meals and washing y' disgusting underwear and entertaining y' disgusting friends. And I s'pose y' thought I didn't know about Wang Pooh? And I stood by y'."

"No you didn't," Harry pointed out, "you went off with that butcher."

"Only because y' made my life a misery."

"You never said," mumbled Harry, thinking that people often seem to leave it rather late to point out Essential Truths.

"We get the point, Mrs Markham," interjected Pru, unable to allow the tirade to continue. "What exactly is it that you want? It's not as if you can inherit anything. The general rule for that is that you have to outlive someone. So what do you want?"

"I want Harry."

"What?"

"Eh?"

"Ho ho ho."

"That's right, I want my Poojar back." She inspected her nails and assumed an air of superiority, as if she held all the cards, which she did.

"But after all those things you just said about him -"

"I wouldn't expect y' to understand, my dear. Y' too young. See, a mature woman learns to accept a lot of suffering, and -"

"I say," interrupted Adrian, jumping to his feet with eyes gleaming, "we've been most awfully rude, dear lady, haven't even offered you a drink. Do take a seat and I'll be mother."

With Barbara and her detective safely tied up under the table and dead to the afterlife, the friends slumped onto the new sofa in relief and congratulated Adrian on his quick thinking. Their troubles were not yet over of course. How to dispose of their prisoners, since the disposal of anything eternal presents a thorny philosophical challenge? Pru held Harry's hand comfortingly; the breakdown of a marriage twice over is always an unhappy business. But he cheered up when she told him of her discovery at the FEW. It would be an excellent training exercise for his new squad.

"It's funny," observed Adrian to Harry, "but we were only just saying before you arrived how nervous we were of a knock at the door."

There was another knock at the door.

Without either waiting for an answer or bothering to open the door, Sammy appeared. Briar stuck to his teeth and glass in his left hand, he dribbled down his smock in agitation as he spoke.

"I say, awfully sorry to disturb you good people." His slow voice was educated and his smile gentle as he stepped forward, expressing no surprise at the bodies heaped under the table. His soft tone eased their tension. "Only it's rather important. Normally I wouldn't dream of interfering... sitting tenants can be such a nuisance, eh? Especially old codgers like me, hah? You're probably all very tired and -"

"What is it, pops?" asked Nigel. "Run out of turps?"

"Ah, no... no, that's not a problem I ever...see, the thing is... well, I thought you should probably know that a chap called John Clarke is coming up Clandon Road followed by two rather obvious SGB chaps in grey raincoats and - "

Their tension stopped easing and went into overdrive. As one, they shot off the sofa and raced around in ever-decreasing and pointless circles until suddenly halted by Sammy's command.

"Stop!" The soft voice had extraordinary authority. "Look, as I said I don't like to interfere, but the circumstances are quite urgent. But we can deal with it quite simply, if you wouldn't mind coming down to the studio. Now." It was an order. "Oh yes, bring the two bodies, will you? And take all your clothes off."

When John Clarke and his escort, who had by now given up all pretence at subterfuge, arrived at Sutton Lodge they were met at the door with a flourish by Sammy, decked out in Flemish ruff and long cape, palette in hand. Stachov and Hurski pushed him roughly aside and marched triumphantly into the studio only to halt in their tracks, stunned by the life-size tableau before their eyes.

Ranjit, draped in black, stood motionless gritting his teeth with the strain as he supported the naked but still lifeless body of Barbara on one knee. Prudence hung around his neck by one arm. The colonel was more in character, dressed in full armour and flowing red cloak, standing proudly astride two horses (Arthur and Nigel in rampant costume, the other very dormant and played gamely by Adrian and the detective) while holding Pru's left leg. She had at first objected to this undignified pose on the grounds that despite her enhanced bosom she was nowhere near genuine Rubenesque proportions. But it would have taken a boorish expert to notice, and the SGB men were not experts in Baroque art or anything else.

"It's the Rape of the Daughters of Leucippus," explained Sammy to a transfixed Stachov. He edged past the man to his easel and filled in a little more colour on Ranjit's whiskers to disguise their Christmassy appearance. "A neo-Impressionist version, quite ambitious I think. Now, what can I do for you gentlemen? Only I am rather busy..."

Hurski, having some trouble controlling his tongue, eventually turned to Clarke who was still standing meekly in the doorway. He had of course recognised most of the group and was a trifle surprised to find one of them apparently ravishing another, but he was too polite to bother them when they were clearly preoccupied.

"Like this sort of muck, do you?" scowled Hurski to him.

"Well, I'm not really sure..."

"So why drag us all the way to Guildford?"

"I… er, that is…"

"Oh, I often get strangers drop in," observed Sammy calmly. "Art lovers, you know. It's usually the false modesty of my Judgement of Paris or they've got me mixed up with Botticelli. You see, his Primavera muses do bear a passing resemblance to -" But Stachov and Hurski were not in the mood for critique. There was the sound of some gratuitous ransacking on the first floor, then the front door slammed as they left in disgust and empty-handed. The tableau collapsed.

"Vell done, old codger," said Arthur, slapping him delightedly on the back and dislodging the pipe. "Zat voz brilliant! But how did you know zey were coming?" Sammy merely shrugged and smiled.

Harry helped a shaky Prudence upstairs, his cloak about her shoulders, and they surveyed the wreckage of her room.

"Something's got to be done about Heaven, and soon," he barked. "This is rank bad form." He stroked her hair protectively.

"It doesn't matter," she murmured, nestling up to his manly and metallic chest. "It's only things. They're easily replaced. You were wonderful back there, Harry."

"I say, steady on, girl."

"Masterful," she continued. "It was a pleasure to be ravished." She turned her face to his, lips parted and eyes closing. The cloak slipped to the floor.

There was a knock at the door.

"Am I interrupting?" asked John Clarke.

Φ

Just off Dean Street and a world away from the City, Ron Golightly flopped back in the verbena-scented jacuzzi like a great white whale in a glass of lemonade. It had been a terrible morning at the bank. The dice of Fate were clearly loaded. He resolved not to move a muscle nor a tendon for the next half an hour – the bubbles would just have to find their own way round him. Sharing the same bath and stubborn opinion was Jim Khan, his already sultry face nearly black with gloom. The world was going mad, if not actually breaking up. In the last month alone there had been a hurricane in Hurley, a tornado in Torquay, and in Shittlehope in Durham they had recorded earth tremors at 4.1 on the Richter Scale. Holland had won the cricket World Cup. Governments throughout the civilised world were wracked with scandal and taking the markets down with them. Jim hadn't made a killing for weeks and was feeling quite suicidal.

Normally the pair would have been cheered by other news of escalating sectarian violence. But the Chinese arms industry was having a sales drive and their Mad March Special Offers on rocket launchers had completely undercut the WICH Corporation. Then to cap it all, Judas Skim had turned up again.

Finding himself at a loose end over a frugal breakfast of scorched eggs (his wife being at the other end of Europe protecting her investments) Jim had idly turned on the TV news to find Skim suddenly a media celebrity. Despite his men's surveillance in NW3, someone had clearly been working for Judas and smuggled in a Yorkshire TV crew to do an interview with the prophet for their upcoming series on natural disaster. They got more than they'd expected. Splashed across every channel, the sickly smile and ruddy complexion was sitting up in bed proclaiming the imminent arrival of the new world Saviour. He spoke lyrically of a new age of peace and universal love, a prediction only enhanced by the extra pair of feet visible at the end of the duvet, and followed up with the day's horoscope and a 100 to 8 tip for the first race at Newmarket. For all his connections, Jim had been unable to nobble the horse which duly cantered home by five lengths. Now the whole country was dusting off its prayer books and another five hundred points had been wiped off the FTSI.

There had been only one possible consolation for Ron and Jim, one experience that is never devalued and never disappoints. Yoko and Kyusha, the new girl, went gracefully and silently about their work, lathering the cares of the world from the men's tormented bodies. There is something truly selfless about the Japanese woman.

Unknown to Jim, his wife was also in torment. In the hospital isolation ward she lay fully alert yet completely paralysed, unable to do a thing about the slim young orderly arranging her bedding or the urges he stirred. It is a scientifically proven fact that it is the presence of nubile young bodies tightly enclosed in starched white uniforms that effect medical recovery, rather than any chemical substances (which are administered purely for the health of the pharmaceutical industry). But the effect depends upon the patient's ability to respond. In cases such as Winnie's the effect was merely to scramble the hormones, and she was sinking fast into confusion and hallucination. For example, the doctor who had just entered her room with a syringe and a sly smile bore an uncanny resemblance to that waiter at the Bistingo.

Barely a mile away on the dark golden evening sands below the palms of the Boulevard La Croisette, Evie was hallucinating too. The last few days had been a dream of paradise, she was floating on air, nervous as a kitten, and several other things only heard of in songs. It had never been like this with Stan. The comte had style, charm and clean fingernails. He knew what a lady needed – to be roused gently at midday with a yellow rose, to spend the afternoon in the hair salon, followed by a couple of bottles of Guinness with dinner before hitting the casino. She was a new woman.

For his part, de Pennis was working his socks off as never before. The stakes were high. He'd seen enough to know that the weasel-faced woman was loaded to the ears, but it wasn't easy to romance such a creature if one has any self-respect. With a finger crooked minimally in hers as they strolled at the water's edge, the shimmering reflection of a full moon at their feet, he glanced at her contented profile and knew that he couldn't keep this up much longer. Despite the instinct born of thirty years of lechery that she wasn't quite ready for the taking, he resolved that it had to be tonight. It had already been too long. He summoned up his strength and most successful lines.

"Eeevie, mon amour," he breathed, taking her shoulders lightly in his hands and trying not to notice the green highlights in her stiff, lacquered hair, "aah, `ow I lurv gazeeng eento yurr eyes. Can eet be I see ma self zere?" She giggled, sending a shiver down his spine.

"Ooo, Count, you say such luverly things. `Ere, where shall we go for nosh, then?"

"Tonight eet eez special, non? Zee moonlight, zee springtime, et l'amour. I weel tek you to zee Oasis at La Napoule. Eet eez ze best restaurant een all France. We weel `ave zee oysters een zee garlic sauce -"

"Ooo, them makes you randy do' they?"

"– an' we weel `ave zee Senancole, c'est une liqueur sans pareil, made from zee `erbs een zee monasteries of Provence. Eet eez just a few kilometres along zee coast, so we weel go in ze yacht, oui?"

"Oui oui. I never bin in a real yacht. But we'll be back in time for the baccarat won't we?"

"Bien sur, ma leetle lady lurk. Et après per'aps…?" She giggled again and slapped him in the chest.

"Ooo, Count, you Frenchies an' yer aprays!"

Φ

Once Sammy had blown his cover there was nothing for it but to fill them in on the rest. Having cleared up and calmed down, they gathered together again in the studio, more modestly attired, and waited patiently while he struggled unsuccessfully to light his pipe.

"Awfully sorry about all that disturbance," he began, giving up on the matches and just imagining the fire instead. "You good people have had quite a bit of bother lately, eh, one way and another."

"I'll say," they all said.

"I wouldn't normally interfere, of course... I mean, one doesn't like to... look, the fact is I'm not who I seem to be."

"Well, anyone can see you're no artist," observed Nigel, leafing through a stack of canvases and frowning at a cubist still life upside down.

"Actually, I am," said Sammy, evidently hurt, "or I was. About fifteenth century, I think." He looked hopeful. "Maybe you've seen my Apollo and Marsyas, in the L... " They were shaking their heads. "Ah well. I've done a few other things too, a bit of philosophy here, some politics there, one gets about a bit over the years, you know. The last time was by far the best, racing Bentleys at Le Mans. Now there's a machine for you. No synchromesh of course but I recall one night, pouring with rain on a blind corner and -"

"Do get on with it, old chap," chided Harry gently.

"Ah, sorry, yes. What an old codger, eh? I'm getting a bit -"

"Absent-minded?"

"Senile?"

"– off the point. Look, I'll just show you how I knew Clarke was coming, shall I?" He crossed to an easel and pulled off the dirty cloth covering it. The canvas was blank except for a slowly flashing green cursor in the top left corner. Sammy took a brush, dabbing quickly at the squidges of paint on his palette, and instantly an image of Guildford High Street appeared on the canvas. Stachov and Hurski could be seen clearly, trudging forlornly away over the glistening cobbles.

"Stone me!" exclaimed Arthur, grabbing a brush himself. "It's a TV. Let's see vot else is on." It was badminton on Channel Four.

"It's a computer," Sammy corrected him, "and rather advanced, though I say so myself. Amazing what you can do with a little imagination, and of course art is the highest form of spiritual creativity..." He gestured towards another pile of canvases in the corner.

"Oh my!" exclaimed Pru, holding one up and then passing them round like holiday snaps. "They're linked in to all the places we've... look, there's the café, Arthur's lab, and there's Ali at the NRC, and... oh, who's this one?"

"Ah, Brigitte Bardot actually. Well, a chap has to relax sometimes."

"So you've been spying on us, have you?" accused Harry, drawing himself up militarily.

"Ah… keeping an eye on things, I prefer to say."

"Spying," repeated Harry, indignant. "Look here, old bean. I'm sure we're grateful for your help just now, but this is too much. Heaven seems to be jam packed with ruddy snoopers. A chap has to have some priva -"

"Do sit down," said Sam sternly. To his surprise, Harry found himself sitting down again and quite unable to move. "You see," the old man continued pleasantly, "there are things afoot, big things. I have… certain information. But I can't do anything about it on my own because… well, I'm quite well known in certain parts."

"The SGB didn't recognise you," Nigel pointed out.

"Well they're policemen aren't they? Anyway, if I interfere I'll just get thrown out of Heaven – it's happened before, you know. That's where you come in, see? No-one knows you. No-one much cares. No records, new identities. That's why I brought you here."

"What?"

"Surely -"

"But -"

"Ho ho how?"

"I'll explain all that, later," Sammy answered, casually knocking his pipe out on a bust of Venus. "But right now, we have to move. I thought this place would be safe, with the M25 permanently jammed, but they've found us once and they'll be back. Don't worry, I know another safe house. Nice Jewish area."

They didn't argue and didn't even bother to pack. The circuitous route passed through Dorking and, to confuse any pursuers, through the Departure Lounge at Gatwick Airport, before skirting Tooting to pick up the District Line. The Underground seemed a good way of staying very close together (and was after all appropriate for a band of fugitives and a mole). Adrian got off at Fulham Broadway and John Clarke was thrown off at Ladbroke Grove, wandering away quite happily. Barbara Markham and her small, stooping employee had been brought along too, propped up between them with unobtrusive drips of Bishop's Brew attached underneath their coats.

"I'm sorry about them," Sammy had said. "My fault. I never thought she'd be so persistent."

"Well, you've obviously never been married, either," grunted Harry. "And now I suppose I'm never going to be rid of her."

They switched lines twice and one station after another lurched and rattled past, but no-one paid them the slightest attention. It isn't done on the Tube.

"I know," Pru said suddenly, as they pulled out of Dollis Hill, where Arthur got off to catch the direct connection back to the Psychic Research Centre. "How do you get rid of someone on Earth, permanently?" Harry raised an eyebrow, having some experience of this at least.

"You see 'em off, my dear. Turn their toes up. Put the lights out. Send them to the great biscuit factory in the sky."

"Exactly," enthused Pru. "Send them into the next world. So let's do that with Barbara and her dic."

"Well, I dunno if you'd noticed, Pru, but we're already in it."

"Oh, you're all so dense," she was getting a bit irritated, "I mean send them back where they came from. It must be possible, and we'd be doing them a favour really, since they're going sooner or later."

"Brilliant!" exclaimed Nigel. This was genuine subversion. They all turned to Sammy, who was stroking the dribble on his chin thoughtfully.

"Hmm, not that easy. Takes a lot of preparation and special security codes."

"It can't be that complicated. I mean, a bottle of vodka and five minutes in the back seat of a Vauxhall, and there's a population explosion."

"Yeah, Vauxhall has a lot to answer for."

"The tricky thing," continued Sammy thoughtfully, "is that it's always voluntary. And the parents have to be consulted -"

"I'm sure mine weren't," observed Pru with feeling. "And I never agreed to -"

"Oh yes, you did," interrupted Sam with equal feeling, as if he knew. Wembley Park rocked by. "Mind you," and his eyes sparkled as the idea formed, "there is another method. Rarely used and a bit risky, but I'm told it works."

"What's that?"

"SEx."

"Eh?"

"Ho ho ho."

"Steady on, old chap, ladies present."

"I mean Soul Exchange. The only problem is that you have to find someone on Earth willing to do a swap... More or less willing, anyway."

Φ

Benedict was fired with enthusiasm. He knew he was on the right trail, even if he didn't have any idea where it might lead. This Evie was the key. Find her and somehow there'd be a link to Alison. But unfortunately, the esoteric guidance that had brought him thus far seemed to have entirely dried up now. Whenever he turned on his laptop and keyed in a random website, instead of cryptic clues all he got was a flashing graphic Christmas tree. And it was already March.

On the other hand, Judas Skim was now on every front page thanks to Benedict. He even appeared on a popular late-night TV chat show, causing a general atmosphere of fear and guilt to spread inexorably through the country.

"The man's lost it," said a shaken interviewer as he stumbled back to the green room. "His prophesies fill me with dread, since he's never been wrong."

"I know," said his producer. "My head's splitting."[17]

Still, the people of Hertfordshire, in particular, were being uncharacteristically honest and only too willing to tell him what they knew about the weasely woman who had come into money and disappeared off to the Riviera with their neighbour. Benedict headed for Stansted.

Φ

Harry, Prudence and Nigel did feel a lot safer in the Stanmore house. It was not an area that anyone could easily get into, even if they found it. On almost every street corner stood slim young men in smart suits, jacket pockets bulging, with short dark hair, talking quietly into portable Thought Transfer Modules. But Sammy had merely glanced at them in his inimitable way as the group passed, and the watchers melted back into the shadows. It was an exclusive area. The shops contained absolutely nothing of any possible use to anyone, and from the delicatessens wafted a sad aroma of rye bread and TVP salt beef.

In a few moments of intense concentration, Sammy had teleported his entire studio and their electronic equipment from Guildford. Harry and Pru shared the largest room; it seemed like the right thing to do, now that their growing feelings for each other, and everything else, had been exposed. But they were only just settling in when Sammy reappeared and led them to the studio. He pointed to a half-finished Adoration of the Shepherds, dribbling down his smock in agitation.

"Can you see it?" The sheep were wandering about aimlessly. "You must get back to the FEW, Prudence. And you, Harry. Fast. It's started, I can feel it, and the whole system's moving. They're counting down. You need to get hold of those records, I don't know, turn the place

---

17 Sophocles' 'Antigone', King Creon's penultimate scene.

over, do something to delay it. Please! You'll understand when you get there." He didn't sound like an old codger any more, and the electric blue of his now visible aura was pulsing with energy. They didn't ask any questions.

"And don't worry about the SEx," he called after them. "I'll do it while you're away. I think I know someone who deserves it."

"Are you sure you can do it on your own?" asked Nigel, hopefully.

"I think so. There's always the library up the road. And if I need any help I've got a, ah, friend who lives nearby."

"Yeah? Some sort of artist, I'm guessing."

"That's right. Giselle. A wonderfully sensitive dancer. You should see her rumba."

"Don't suppose I'll get a chance," grumbled Nigel. "Come on, RJ. Let's go after the others. They might need some help." Ranjit shrugged and got up. It was either this or squeezing down chimneys for eternity.

Prudence and Harry were on their way up ahead, innocent as children and utterly unconscious of the enormity of what they were letting themselves in for. That, as Sammy would point out much later, was the whole point. Once people have experience of skiing off the tops of mountains and crashing through thin ice, they tend to be wary of cold weather. Sometimes it's best not to know.

Czosn watched their progress on his office screen with a mixture of interest and amusement. His new assistant had after all proved helpful and efficient; even SS3 had commented, when he popped in to inspect the arrangements for the ceremony, how nice the potted plants were. Czosn had encouraged Prudence to go off on a spot of leave to get her out of the way so he was a little puzzled to see her returning so soon and with such a motley crew in tow. No matter. They wouldn't get past the guards.

For the first time in his professional career, he had changed his Slavonic pale blue shirt and shapeless woollen jacket for a grey suit with all the trimmings, topped off by a double-Windsor knot in the narrow black tie one always has in the wardrobe just in case. His bull neck bulged over the collar like a pie case with too much bicarbonate, giving him the odd sensation of being slowly strangled. Still, special occasions demand personal sacrifice. A final check of his fly, a small glass of alcohol-free slivovice (such a travesty), and he closed the office door behind him.

At the pinnacle of his career, Czosn set off to create Man. He strode purposefully along the dim back passages of the FEW Directorate, acknowledging the guards' brisk salutes, waited patiently in the aura scanner and at last entered the hidden lift. Usually quite unemotional, he couldn't help the slight thrill as he touched in his etheric ID-print, pressed L, and began to glide swiftly down, down, down.

He had seen the Reincarnation Ante-Chambers in action many times of course. They were cool and functional, organised and efficient, like himself. Their very existence gave one reassurance on the arduous journey of the soul where, however well-prepared and honourable one's intentions, there is always the unexpected, the sudden fog of uncertainty, the insidious overheating of human desire in the heart. If things break down, the RA-C could get you back on track.

Most of the others were already assembled, Chamber One overflowing with a host of the holy and righteous merged in a shimmering mass of spirituality. Everyone who was anyone wanted to be in on this, to speed the Special One on his vital and dangerous mission.[18] Something to tell the grandchildren, and their grandchildren. There would not be a lot of work done in the CPSU or DoSS today. The room pulsed with the excitement of a derby fixture and still the crowd arrived by every lift, emerging into the brightness only to be swallowed up in the single Mind of the spectators. There was always room for more, for even here perfection was beyond reach. Regular reincarnation sessions were not like this. Despite the paradoxical fact of both promotion and relegation being at stake simultaneously, they were routine affairs played out in a flat atmosphere. Even now, along the corridor, Chambers Two and Three were at work as usual with a skeleton staff. Sometimes the occasion might be a bit more special, the energy more penetrating and intimate, and one could get oneself involved. But one always longed for more, every climax followed by the yearning for another, a greater satisfaction. And then perhaps once in a lifetime might come the biggest that there is – a world final, a cosmic event, the moving of the Earth. One will do anything to be there.

Yet Czosn, high as a kite himself as he pushed through to his place at the control panel, couldn't help feeling some small nagging unease. He was of course a professional fatalist. However much one gets caught up in the passion of the moment, on the edge of self-control, one's mind knows that perfection is unattainable. Everyone knows it, most people accept it and settle for the best there is. Human happiness depends on acceptance. But when your job is the creation of lives, you can't help feeling the space between What Is and What Might Be more keenly. Czosn sat back in the softly padded chamois upholstery of his operations chair,

---

[18] Despite Tfozb's objections, masculinity had again been preferred, the world being how it is.

where many a sheep and goat had been separated, and ran his fingers lightly over the shiny platinum-effect controls. He flexed his thoughts and settled them onto the keyboard. What was it? This might be the reincarnation of the Messiah, but there was still the slight chance – actually, 1.618 by ten to the power minus thirty-eight – that something could go wrong.

SS3 was on his feet, vibrating from top to toe in his finest purple robe, leading the company in 'Jerusalem'. His job was almost done. All the planning behind the scenes, the committee-room wrangles, the coordination of countless precise details had come to this. His finest hour. And Fuzru sang along in the front row, confident that the master programs were bug-proof and mole-proof now that he had personally installed the new self-inverse security codes.

The chamber now settled to a steady rhythm as the third verse died away and a ripple of joy spread through the crowd like a Mexican wave. Even Tfozb put down her knitting. Attention focused on the space at the centre, and the lights dimmed until only a broad, brilliantly polished disc could be seen on the floor. It stretched and relaxed as if awakening, and seemed to hover in readiness as the safety screen below it was drawn back. The great crystal sphere rose up slowly from below, absorbing all light into itself, to the accompaniment of Handel's Oratorio on a great organ. Czosn had decided on this, not very imaginative but always a crowd-pleaser.

Everything became still as the countdown routine began. His fingertips brushed the keys with practised ease like feathers as the data flashed mutely on the monitor at Czosn's elbow: the XY chromosome equation, the experiential benchmarks, the latitude, longitude and moon phase ordinates… until at last the program locked into the parents.

EG.

CDP.

Far, far away it was springtime in the south of France and Scorpio was about to rise. In a dark wine bar off the Rue d'Antibes, the very large and heavily sweating American film producer Con Danny Prattsmuller was looking into Eleanor Glee's delicious cleavage, telling her he had a vision, and suggesting that she might like to audition later that night for his new surrealist art movie on the weakness of flesh.

Φ

There is an essential flaw in the job description of the night watchman. When the place one is supposed to be guarding, however high security, is finally still, so there is no activity and therefore nothing actually to watch, it is beyond the ability of the human brain to muster the slightest interest in the task. It's the same phenomenon that causes excessive drinking at cricket matches – one simply cannot concentrate when nothing is happening.

The guards at the FEW Directorate were not only bored witless, but being the only members of staff left out of the grand occasion they were also pretty fed up. It would just serve everyone right if, for example, someone came along and staged an amusing diversion by dressing up as Santa Claus so that when they were distracted other people came up behind them and tied them all up inside a big red sack after forcing some sort of cocktail down their throats. If that happened, for example, they'd be quite happy to go along with it.

Pru led the way stealthily on tiptoe along the empty corridors of the first floor and stopped at the Ladies cloakroom.

"Shall I go first?" she offered.

"Um, all right. We'll wait here for you."

"No, I mean this is it. There's a passage at the far end straight down to the lower basement."

"Hang on," protested Nigel. "That's not logical. We're on the first floor."

"Which is why," Pru retorted with a touch of superiority, "you would never have found it. It takes a woman's mind." They trooped in.

"Well, it takes a woman to be nosing about in the Ladies...I say, this graffiti's good, much better than what you get in the Gents. 'There was a blithe spirit called Lars, who was fond of observing the stars. But as Virgo moved faster his stool lost a castor and Pollux went right up -' "

"I do think we should get a move on," interrupted Harry, pushing Nigel on ahead. At the far end of the wash room and at the back of an empty linen cupboard, a thin crack could just be made out in the wall with a slight musty draught coming through it. Harry pushed gently on the wall until it yielded onto a dark, narrow passageway, festooned with cobwebs. In the distance, something squeaked. Their torches barely penetrated the gloom, so old was the memory of the place.

"Er, those little red lights up ahead...?" observed Nigel

"Don't be silly, there aren't any werewolves in Heaven."

"I don't see why not. Porphyria is a perfectly normal condition. See, light affects the skin and -"

"Anyway, the little red lights are little red lights. It's an intruder alarm – I found the trip switch in one of the cubicles back there. Don't worry, I flushed it. But it does look like they've tightened up the security."

The friends began to feel little knots tightening inside as the air of expectancy in the place grew. It had all been a bit of a wheeze so far, this running about the afterlife, but now it was getting altogether too serious. Reality was catching up.

They found the files easily, stacked up against a long wall in countless old cardboard boxes labelled 'Crunchy Nuts – This Way Up'. They were not indexed of course, but Ranjit had the uncommonly clever idea of asking his own original file to present itself, and it duly popped up like a piece of toast, singed at the edges. They each retrieved their own and pored over them for a while like old photo albums.

"Complete rubbish, this," said an indignant Pru, "not to mention sexist stereotyping. 'Cannot master emotional expression…fails to grasp male cues… wears restrictive underwear… ' And my GP's notes are here too. Seems I had the Coxsackie B Picornavirus once but he forgot to tell me. No wonder you never get to see your own notes."

Since it's impossible actually to destroy anything in Heaven, all their index cards except RJ's were ripped up, shuffled, and scattered among the cereal boxes. (They did try to find John Clarke's, thinking this might help somehow, but there was no trace of it.)

"I'm absolutely sure I paid those two parking tickets," grumbled Pru as they made their way back along the passage and along to her office. Nigel set to work at the computer, restoring Ranjit to himself.

"More new security codes," he chuckled. "Fuzru really is a berk. He's used the old self-inverse ones we did in college. No imagination."

Harry was subdued. It was the old feeling you get in the field when everything goes quiet before the Big Push, when the elements themselves hold their breath and you can't help a sneaking thought for your enemy and wondering what he has in store for you. The ethereal guerrillas' leader now gazed mutely from a window over deserted gardens, and felt out of his depth. The FEW was indeed a couple of levels up from where he should normally be, and the fact that Pru seemed perfectly at home here was humbling. This was not a characteristic that came easily to Harry.

"Right," he said, mustering as much authority as he could, "just what is going on here?" Nigel flicked through some channels. It was korfball on Channel Four. Then suddenly, using Czosn's password which Pru had found hidden under a poinsettia, they were into the RA-C. The screen filled with a thousand colours, jumping and flashing as if the machine couldn't cope with them, so bright that it hurt the eyes. Gradually the picture settled and Nigel toned down the contrast. Even so, the crystal sphere glowed like a hundred suns. They could dimly make out Czosn, head bowed over the controls, and Fuzru was just visible in the front row, appearing to look straight out at Nigel as if to say 'I'm here and you're not'. And there was also something vaguely familiar about the figure now entering the arena from a hidden door at the back and emerging into the light at centre-stage. He was of medium height, medium build, medium brown hair. But for the deep, dark eyes and the grace of his movement, he could well be John Clarke's twin brother.

The music swelled and its purity filled the little office where the watchers sat transfixed. Even RJ, himself again, was silent, mouth fallen open. The man moved slowly towards the crystal and, with only the briefest acknowledgement towards the assembly, stepped into it, sitting with knees drawn up to his chest, head bowed. A white bird fluttered from nowhere, the light catching the tips of its feathers and flashing penetrating laser beams to all corners of the chamber. Then there was a soft whirring noise as if some great machine were starting up, the note growing higher, faster, hypnotic. And a deep sonorous voice began to speak the ancient rite.

"Mine is the ecstasy of the spirit,
The cup of the wine of life.
Mine is the cauldron of desire,
And the mystery of the waters.
From me all things proceed.
Unto me all must return.
I am with you from the beginning.
I am attained at the end of all."

Harry and the others were drawn in by the voice, any thoughts of interfering with history – Sammy's urgent mission – completely forgotten. There was jelly in their stomachs and snakes where their spines had been. Now the sphere was pulsing as if breathing, growing smaller with each inhalation, and concentrating the figure within almost to a point. The voice continued.

"Darkest night and shining day,
East and south and west and north,
Listen to the words we say,
Take the cup that brings them forth.
Pentacle and sword and wand,
Cord and censer, scourge and knife
That never cuts the lovers' bond.
Waken, spirit, unto life."

The crystal was nothing but a swirling vortex of energy, enraptured faces now visible all around.

"King of Heaven, Queen of Hell,
Holy hunter of the night,
With all the power of land and sea
And all the might of moon and sun,
In sleeping minds the truth to tell –
My kingdom comes,
My will is done."

There was a soft murmur as the assembly responded.

"Eko, eko, Azarak,
Eko, eko, Zamilak,
Eko, eko, Karnayna,
Eko, eko, Aradia."

It was over. They sat back limply as the chorus faded and the crowd slowly dispersed. Only Czosn remained, as if melted into his keyboard.

"Hey, that is nice, man," Ranjit said at last, superfluously. "Why our dude Sam he so exercised 'bout it all, huh?"

"Ah, so Sammy's our mole, is he?" The sudden icy voice chilled them and they spun round as one to the door, where Czosn was loosening his tie and smiling at them. "It's a repeat," he explained, gesturing to the monitor. "As you can see, I am here in the pink. And you are there, red-handed." Pru stood hurriedly, flustered.

"I, er... that is, I didn't think it would... well, we haven't done anything, sir... we haven't taken anything..."

"Except," he replied calmly, "knowledge that was not yours to have. You disappoint me, my dear. I was even beginning to like you, and your flowerpots. But all the time it was our Sammy putting you up to it, eh?"

"You know him?"

"Oh, everyone here knows Sammy. Also known as Nftth. A harmless, doddering old codger. What's he up to now?" He removed his jacket and settled himself in a chair by the door, drink in hand, his eyes somehow fixed on each of them simultaneously. "Still playing with his pictures, is he? We Slavs have never trusted artists, they just can't help themselves being subversive even if it's just a Madonna and Shepherds. Counter-revolutionary."

"Now that's not fair," Nigel pointed out. "Take Caravaggio now – the harsh realism of the light in his David with the - "

"Well, whatever his game," Czosn interrupted, standing up and pressing a red button that hadn't been there before, "you're all too late." Two extremely large guards burst through the door and took up menacing if slightly unsteady positions either side of their boss. "It's all done. The child is on his way. Soon enough the boy will be a man, and at the Great Day of Declaration the whole hapless world will know."

"What?" asked Ranjit.

"What?" asked Czosn.

"The `apless world done know what, bruv?" Czosn looked at him as if he were a primitive life form hardly worth treading on let alone answering.

"Have you people not the least idea what you just watched on the video?"

"`Course, bruv. We is not stupid. Summat important, innit."

"Summat important, he says," Czosn mocked. "Is Manchester wet? Do rabbits like sex? Is chocolate pudding and custard nice? That, you hairy little scruff, was Maitreya – the Messiah, to you. The Second Coming's just been."

"Oh!"

"Wow!"

"Shit!"

Harry stayed quiet, thinking fast as he always did when danger threatened. It wasn't the guards that bothered him – he knew something they didn't. What nagged at his campaign instinct was the certainty that an organisation as rotten and inefficient as this couldn't possibly mount an operation as big as this and get it right.

"So… this, ah, D-Day…?" he ventured.

"All part of The Plan, meticulously prepared, nothing anyone can do about it now. Maitreya simply presents Himself on TV -"

"On TV?" Pru was incredulous at the banality of it.

"Certainly, eight o'clock on a Wednesday, prime audience. And then He'll do His trick."

"So it's like a talent show, then?"

"Not exactly, my dear. The details will be finalised later, depends on His mood. He might turn all the world's clocks back an hour, or wipe everyone's iPods, then get someone to shoot Him at point-blank range with a Kalashnikov and do a couple of somersaults. Then He will declare

Himself. So everyone will have to believe in Him, won't they? Absolute proof. World saved." He smirked quietly in his chair.

There was a total stunned silence in the room. It wasn't that the four friends had no thoughts on the matter. Indeed, they all unanimously now understood at last why Sammy had brought them together. And the power of this realisation was not something that could easily be expressed. It was the colonel who eventually took the lead, calmly standing to face Czosn, drawing himself up to his old clear-headed, stubbornly confident, dismissive of all alternatives self.

"But my dear chap," he began quietly, "what in Heaven's name is the point of life when there's no choice? How can one agree when there's no alternative? Belief? It means nothing when someone tells you what you have to believe." Prudence now stood too, side by side with him.

"The whole world?" she asked. "People are not statistics. People are human, with ordinary lives and everyday worries, struggling every day to make sense of it all." Now RJ joined them.

"Yeah, man, it am tough on the street, innit. An' the bruvvers, they do have to come togevver, an' fight for they rights."

"Being human is about ideals," added Nigel, "and making something of yourself…"

"And keeping going when nobody seems to care…"

"Being the best you can…"

"Peace an' love, innit?"

"Yes, old chap," Harry took it up again, "just where in your Great Plan is the mystery of love? Where is simple faith? What about the ache in a chap's soul that gives his life dignity? If a man never thinks for himself then he has no dignity, no backbone…"

"No fibre."

"And what happened to the promise to the poor and the sorrowful?"

"The hungry and the insulted?"

"If seeds never fall on stony ground…"

"And there are no lost sheep…"

"No bugs in the program…"

"And nobody can ever get it wrong…"

"Yes, look old bean, I say where's the point of life when there's no choice?" The four of them were standing shoulder to shoulder, a united front of philosophy, a single principle, challenging one of the most powerful souls in Heaven. Czosn sat looking back at them, completely unperturbed.

"Stuff the point," he said. "Everyone wants peace and justice, don't they? Well, nearly everyone. So now they're going to get it."

"But, sir," Prudence had something very much like tears in her eyes. "Life won't be… human."

"And a good thing too," her boss said.

Φ

In an entirely different world, the moon was high and bright and Evie was feeling a little sick. The Oasis had indeed been superb, the boeuf en daube cooked to perfection, the Chateau Grillet exquisitely chilled and the draught Guinness as dependable as ever. Yet still she had an uneasy inner sensation as the Gay Boy rocked gently at her mooring in Cannes harbour.

She was not given to superstition. But when she'd drawn that pair of eights alongside her ace and queens it was as if ghoulish fingers had closed around her neck. Hickok's dead man's hand. The other players had backed away as the involuntary gasp escaped her lips. Even Texas Dilly had refused to play on and had spent the rest of the evening in the bar, one hand inside his jacket. Enjoying a little glamour and celebrity here, a long way from NW3 and even further from Buckley Rise, Evie had at last tasted the sweetness of life. But now life was delivering its lesson and demanding payment. When someone-in-the-middle-distance is trying-to-tell-you something, there's nowhere far enough away to hide. The spectre of death (and on past evidence, private parts) was near again.

The Comte de Pennis had guided her with a gentle arm from the Municipal Casino and out along the pier to the boat. Even he could tell by her subdued daze that the tide was turning now. He blessed his instinct. It did have to be tonight, and sooner rather than later, while she was still vulnerable and he still had the strength.

Dawn was approaching. He poured them another drink and put on a CD of Italian opera. It lifted him a little. It would not be long now until he could return to those northern hills in comfortable, if not honourable, retirement. In the pocket of his dinner jacket, fingers closed on the ring combed from the beach at Juan les Pins, the seven zirconium stones given a final polish in gin that afternoon. In another pocket sat the special licence and the deed of authority for the bank. All was prepared for the final performance.

He knocked back the vodka and, closing his eyes, took Evie in his arms and kissed her. She clung limply to him and without a murmur of protest allowed him to unfasten the zip of her Cardin dress. It slipped silently to the floor. He stood back to reassure her with a practised smile, but her eyes were also closed, her arms hung down at her side and her small breasts sagged like wrinkled and undercooked fried eggs. He sighed and turned off the light. He would have to earn this money. With indecorous speed he undressed, opened the starboard window and carried Evie like a small sack of vegetables to the bed. She whimpered.

"What eez eet, ma leetle pastry? Are you not `appy?"

"Ooh, yeah... s'pose... an' you?"

"Evie, ma crevette, you make me zee `appiest man een all Fronce. We `ave zee moonlight, l'amour... " he hesitated, realising that he'd already done that bit earlier, "... we `ave each urthur. Zee last wiks `ave bin formidable. And now, your soft bowdy next to mine, eet makes me feel..." he searched his vocabulary in three languages but there were no words to express it, "...je ne sais quoi."

"Ooh, Count. You Frenchies an' yer saykwoy!"

"An' do you not feel a leetle surmthing moving eenside?"

"Oh oui, oui."

When she'd come back from the toilet he tried again, and went into his muscle control routine.

"You are a lurvely ladee, Evie, you are zee queen of ma `eart. I am zee `appiest -"

"No, listen, Count. You bin real nice to me, you make a girl feel real posh an' that. An' I don't want to disappoint you... but, see, you weren't at the baccarat table tonight..."

Outside, a slim dark figure slipped silently onto the starboard deck and edged towards the window. Moonlight glinted on the small Smith and Wesson as Sadiq Khan checked his watch. The Count had had long enough.

"...see, Professor Thorpe's system really does work an' I've bin using it for a week now. `Course, you `ave to count the cards an' keep yer mind on the job..." Gently, the comte shifted over and opened her legs. "...but some'ow that comes easy to me. Dunno, just a gift I s'pose. After a while you knows when the pontoon's up so you put more up front..."

The boat began to rock as de Pennis settled into his rhythm with gritted teeth. Sadiq Khan steadied himself by the oak railing, his stomach beginning to rise and fall in sympathy. And voices in the next boat tied alongside began to confuse him. There was a girl's light giggle of pleasure and another deeper, nasal accent.

"Again, Miss Glee, you've nearly got it... yes, yes, again please..."

The two boats rolled in harmony, faster and higher, perilously close. Khan was disorientated. He was not the only one. On a much higher spiritual plane, but descending rapidly, two infinitesimal crystalline spheres of brilliant light were arriving simultaneously from different directions. The souls looked at each other in surprise, then at the two boats, then back to each other with uncertainty.

"… an' even if the casino realises what's going on they can't stop you. `Course, the manager'll make the croupier shuffle up when you start winning, break the run, see? So then you only bet when yer losing, to bluff `em. Usually works…" She stopped in mid-prattle to stroke the comte's perspiring head a bit. Poor lamb, he was doing his best. "… or it did until tonight. The bastards double-bluffed me, didn't they?"

De Pennis' thrust faltered and he raised his head in dismay.

"You lost?"

"Mmm, two or three `undred."

"Ah, well that eez nurthing, ma leetle -"

"Thousand."

Suddenly feeling rather old and very weak, the comte's muscles gave up one by one and with a quiet sob he collapsed on top of Evie, all but suffocating her. The rush of her breath was joined by a long, low moan from the next boat. Losing his bearings and his patience, and spinning from one to the other, Sadiq Khan decided enough was enough. He lurched to the window, steadied his aim, fired twice into the mounds of flesh then spun round to fire again through the other window.

And as if in the very throes of death themselves, the two boats gave one final climactic heave in unison, toppling Khan overboard into the cold, murky water before snapping closed over him like giant nutcrackers.

Chapter Nine ~ Outlaws

"Enough talking," said Czosn. "The SGB can decide what to do with you lot. Guards!" The two men looked at each other but didn't move, avoiding his eye. Then one of them shuffled his feet.

"Well, sir," he mumbled sheepishly. "We're not sure as… I mean, in the circumstances, like…"

"Guard, arrest these people, I said."

"Well, no, sir. With respect, sir. Like the officer said, sir, and fine words they were even if I didn't understand them all… but there's no point, is there? All things considered, I think -"

"It's not your flaming job to think, man. I do the thinking here. Now - "

"Then with respect, sir, maybe it's you who should be arrested. sir." And to the cheers and congratulations of the others, Czosn was held. But that wasn't going to work, was it? He was not director of the FEW for nothing. Recalculating his position, he immediately created a new red button on the floor and stepped on it.

"Behind you!" he shouted, and another half dozen guards entered at the double, turning the tables.

"Ah, no. Behind *you*, I think," suggested Harry calmly.

"Ha! I'm not going to fall for that old aaarrrgh -" With a splintering of high-impact imitation polyurethane and a rousing chorus of the William Tell Overture, the SAS crashed through the walls in their HGVs, smoke bombs flying. They were a fearsome sight in black uniforms and shiny plastic masks. In no time at all, Czosn and all his guards lay in an untidy heap by the waste paper basket, completely convinced they'd been shot. It was a superb performance. Sergeant Glum, breathless but exultant, drew himself up and saluted smartly.

"Hoperation Rescue complete, sah! Sorry if we was a bit late, sah. Got your orders but it's a long way an' hard going. Had to yomp over Hastral Two. 'Fraid we lost Private Parker, sah. Like you said, belief not strong enough." Harry returned the salute and inspected the men, strolling calmly among the debris of the office with hands clasped behind his back.

"Fine show, Plonker, deuced fine show. Just in time actually. Well done, men. At ease. Ah, just one thing, sergeant. Why are you all wearing Mickey Mouse masks? I thought I said androids."

"Sorry, sah, best we could do at short notice. I, er, didn't know what a handroid was, sah."

"Never mind, sergeant, shows initiative. It certainly scared the enemy, what?"

"Not just them," Prudence pointed out, indicating Ranjit spread-eagled on the floor in abject shock.

"It's all over, son," barked Harry, reviving him with a judicious kick. Then more gently, "Sorry, son. No-one likes violence. I respect your principles but in the real world it's often necessary -"

"Nah, it ay that," said RJ, dusting himself down. "I jus' can't stand that mouse-dude, scares de pants off me, man."

The SAS exchanged uniforms with the guards and escorted the others out and far away from the FEW.

"I guess that's the end of my career," mused Pru philosophically as they turned north on the Edgware Road. "Brief, wasn't it? And I don't suppose I'll qualify for redundancy benefit."

"Never mind, my dear," Harry consoled her. "You had a job to do and you did it superbly. Mission accomplished. We know exactly what the enemy's plans are now. I'm proud of you." She smiled up at him and took his arm, and Plonker Glum shot him a furtive wink.

"We couldn't have done it without you, Harold. You were magnificent," she said. He blushed and coughed in embarrassment. "Just one thing, though…"

"Of course, what is it, my dear?"

"It's just that if you call me 'my dear' one more time, I'm going to shove your DSO right up -"

"You realise," said Nigel hurriedly, "that every SGB patrol in Heaven will be after us now?"

"But surely," said Pru, "they won't find us. We can always switch identities again, and anyway we tore up all the old records."

"I don't think I'm very keen on changing any more files, if you don't mind," muttered Nigel. He shuddered at the memory of RJ, persona non certa, with tufty whiskers and jolly ho-ho. "And anyway, we didn't."

"Didn't what?"

"Tear them all up. I left Ranjit's in Czosn's office. Sorry. So he's the one they'll be after, really."

"Oh, fanks, bruv. An' after all I done for you, innit."

"What have you ever done for us, RJ?"

"Well, no need to get technical, man." Ranjit paused in his tracks, feeling hurt. This afterlife had started off a real gas. He was into his machines and had something good going with Benny-boy. But nobody seemed to appreciate him, and all this fighting and fuse and Messies was doing his head in. The others didn't even notice he'd gone.

Φ

The Third Spiritual Secretary was trying to digest all that had happened, and was feeling decidedly dyspeptic. He paced his office furiously from corner to corner, even creating new corners to pace into, sat down, stood up, held his head in his hands and moaned, laughed, stared morosely into the vacuum beyond the window and finally, having run out of emotions, turned on his old friend.

"It's all your fault," he bellowed at Fuzru, sitting calmly by the desk and playing with a Rubik's octahedron. "You said the program was foolproof."

"Ay, yes," Fuzru pointed out reasonably, "but those people weren't fools, were they? If you ask me, this job's got Gibbs all over it."

"Who?"

"A slimy suck-up creep I went to college with. Nigel Gibbs. Oh, he can program computers all right. In fact, he can build them. But he was too much of a rebel, didn't fit in with the rest of us. No class."

"Well, if he can break all your security codes and tamper with the records, he's in a different class all right. Where can we find this Figgs?"

"PRU(NE)."

"Don't get semantic with me, Fuzru. I have enough of that already." He gestured to the other chair where Tfozb smirked and knitted, softly murmuring 'Another one for the basket'.

"The young gentleman is trying to tell you that Gibbs works in one of the Psychic Research Units."

"I'll get the SGB onto it." But even as he reached for the red Thought Transfer Module, SS3 knew it was probably too late. There was an aura of doom about him now. It wasn't fair. After all the aeons of planning and preparation, the argument and subterfuge, and getting it all on the road with the RA-C... who could have predicted the unimaginable synchronicity of two souls incarnating at precisely the same moment not four feet apart? People should allow themselves at least three times that privacy. The odds must run into... well, Czosn was going to get a taste of his own Deviance Method now.

"I shouldn't take it too hard," said Tfozb, surprisingly conciliatory. S/he was feeling magnanimous, with the total belief of anyone who has ever been a woman that they were right all along. "You can't be held responsible for the sexual appetite of an American film producer. And the Italians have always been a law unto themselves." S/he put down the knitting – a Cambridge University scarf – and gazed fondly into the past.

"I remember one trip to Venice, there was one gondolier who just wouldn't take -"

"You're supposed to be beyond all that sort of thing now," grumbled SS3. "Collective mind, remember? A Higher Being."

"Well," s/he snorted, "if you didn't have your head stuck up the ether and got a better grasp of human reproduction, maybe none of this would have happened."

"No need for smut," he replied lamely. Then, to no-one in particular, "What am I going to do?" Tfozb took it as a personal invitation, casting an eye around the office and making a mental note of the changes s/he would make.

"Well, first you sack Fuzru and put this Gibbs in his place."

"Fuzru?"

"Yes, boss?"

"You're sacked. Next?"

"Next we go and face the Planning Committee."

"Eh? They'll tear me apart."

"You can do it. Like your ex-friend said, you're the boss. And Duflc," s/he was somehow warmer now, standing up to approach him and laying a hand on his arm, "I'll be with you, all the way." He looked up in surprise. Despite their formlessness, things seemed to be shaping up.

Φ

When they reached the safe house, Harry and the others were met by two total strangers who introduced themselves as Winnie Khan and Luigi Mori but who couldn't explain how they'd got there.

"Something to do with sex," said Winnie. "That's what the young girl said, anyway, but it's never had this effect before."

"Er, which young girl is this, exactly?" asked Prudence suspiciously, watching them through narrowed eyes. She was not just being cautious. The odd thing was that the pair not only seemed quite unconcerned to find themselves dead, but for complete strangers they were also getting on extremely well. Indeed, they seemed made for each other. The count, relaxing in the depths of the green velvet sofa, put an arm around Winnie' shoulder as she continued.

"Oh, the dancer. Lovely young thing she was, so lithe and expressive. Silvery hair, beautiful nails. You should have seen her rumba."

"Si si, exquisite," agreed de Pennis, blowing an imaginary kiss.

"So where is she now?" asked Nigel, interested in all art forms.

"Oh, gone. Didn't I say? No, went off in rather a hurry actually, with that smelly old codg -"

"Sammy's gone too? Did he say where?"

"Just mumbled something about 'Below'. Said they were getting out before they got thrown out. Some sort of hanky-panky going on, if you ask me. Oh yes, he did leave a note for you, Evie, on the canvas over there, though why he couldn't just write it on -"

"What was that?"

"I said he left a -"

"No, you called me Evie," said Pru, taken aback.

"Yes, well isn't that your name? I'm sure the old soak said Evie should be coming. The name seems to ring a bell anyway. Do you know who it is, Comte?" He shook his head.

"I `ave nevur `eard eet."

While Pru and Nigel put the house in order, trying to digest these developments, Harry and his men (in civvies) escorted Winnie and Luigi out onto the M25, where they disappeared arm in arm like two lovebirds on the yellow brick road.

"...and zee Oasis at La Napoule eez zee best restaurant een all Fronce," the comte was saying.

"Do they have Senancole?"

"Mais oui. Only zee best for you, ma leetle temptress, ma Salome."

"Oh Comte, you Frenchmen and your little sausages!"

Φ

The Planning Committee was indeed in uproar, the peaceful dignity of the pure Unconscious thrown to the winds of panic.

"I said it was wrong from the start. You can't trust actresses."

"No, you said she had a nice bottom."

"Yes, but all the same -"

"That reminds me, anyone seen my copy of -"

"You and your prime numbers. If we'd gone for a palindrome, none of this would have happened."

"I blame Daniel, opening his big mouth."

"Well I blame computers. What's wrong with energy, I want to know?"

"And Ireland have got them at thirty-five for seven now."

"Meditation used to be a pleasure, but -"

"We think therefore we're not very sure and hence -"

"Why wasn't the mission aborted anyway?"

"Can't you guess? 'A woman's inalienable right', s/he said. Typical women's rights, just `cos they have the babies they think -"

"Yeah, where is s/he? I'm going to give her a piece of Mind."

"Whose plan was it anyway?"

"Not mine."

"Nor me."

"Nope."

"But you are," the unmistakable strident tone cut abruptly through the hubbub as Tfozb entered, "the Planning Committee, are you not? You did ratify SS3's suggestions, did you not? You do have collective responsibility, do you not?"

"Ah, well…"

"If you put it like that…"

"`Spose…"

With an imperious flourish s/he took her place among them and an uneasy calm descended.

"Of course," s/he went on quietly, "if you'd accepted my idea of a female Messiah -"

"Oh, don't start that again," protested Mxtth.

"Right," announced SS3, entering with as much authority as he could muster, "this is not the time for recriminations. Despite the hiccup-"

"More like a flobbering sneeze -"

"– life goes on. Maitreya has incarnated." There was a ripple of applause. "We're just not quite sure where, for the moment. We'll have to wait and see." There was a ripple of groans.

"A forty-nine year old part-time cleaner in a hairnet is not exactly comparable to a statuesque actress found naked with a corpse and who now has her tits on every front page of the western world, is she?" SS3 considered the matter.

"There are some differences," he conceded, "but we of all people mustn't be judgemental. Evie Gardner may be humble, but she is a single woman with some money coming to her -"

"It's been. I always said you shouldn't trust the Thorpe system."

"Vingt-et-un's got a lot to answer for."

"Not to mention soixante-neuf."

"No need for smut."

"Anyway," interjected SS3, having some difficulty keeping his grip, "the point is that we'll just have to be extra vigilant. See what turns up, as it were. I've decided we'll need someone to direct this operation, keep a check on policy coordination, oversee the extra Witnessing and -"

"I wish to apply, sir."

There was a collective swivel of head and raising of eyebrow towards Tfozb. SS3 hesitated. S/he hadn't mentioned this earlier, and while he was personally naturally above suspicious thoughts he couldn't help the inkling that s/he was Up To Something.

"Are you sure?" he asked. "This is not an easy job, and it's pretty uncomfortable down on the A1. Decisions, arguments, criticism…"

"I'm used to that."

There were no other nominations. The Planning Committee remained deathly silent in rock-solid unanimity, seizing its chance to get rid of Tfozb (so they thought). There was no need for a vote.

"Another thing," said SS3 uncertainly. Things were going altogether too well. "We now have a vacancy among the Elementals."

"Yes, shame!"

"Nftth of all people."

"Traitor!"

"Yes, well s/he'll be dealt with in the customary way once the SGB get onto it. In fact, after their purge I imagine there'll be quite a few vacancies here and there. So we need someone to supervise the appointment of -"

"Sir?"

"No, Tfozb, you've already got a job."

Φ

It was Prudence who eventually found Sammy's canvas in a corner beneath a pile of dust sheets, badly tuned guitars and preliminary sketches for a new abstract pop expressionist study of Apollo and the Corybantes. The cursor flashed dimly in the top corner beneath the words Vermilion Exuberant Ubiquitous Underwear.

"That's his final message?" sighed Harry, wandering over when she called out. "Not awfully helpful is it? Looks like this SEx has gone to his head. Round the twist without a paddle. He's sloped off and left us right in the -"

"Surely he wouldn't do that?" insisted Pru. "He did help us a lot, even if he was -"

"A senile pervert? You never know with these artist-johnnies. One-track minds, all flesh and symbolism." Pru's own mind was racing with unfamiliar possibilities about the wearing of gaudy French knickers. She was rather enjoying Heaven, especially since her records had been destroyed, and she'd begun to sense all kinds of sublimated urges she'd never known existed before. But she had to concede to herself that this idea, sadly, was not likely to be what Sammy had intended to convey.

"I'm not sure I even know what vermilion is," observed Harry.

"A brilliant red pigment made by grinding cinnabar," Nigel called out. "Mercuric sulphide. It's Latin."

"Who's a clever boy, then?"

"Little worm."

"Now, look here young chap -"

"That's what it means." Nigel came to study the message. "You know what? I reckon it's the same code Fuzru was using at the CPU. The initials spell KILL."

"Good grief!"

They put their heads together over a long drink and tried to fathom it out. Life was becoming decidedly dangerous not to mention violent, considering that this was supposed to be a place of eternal rest and atonement. Then Pru remembered something.

"Hang on, Sammy did leave another message, didn't he, with the Winnie woman – he said 'Evie should be coming'. So is he saying we've got to kill...? Harold, why are your eyes gleaming?"

There was a scratching at the window pane and they swivelled round as one to see Alison floating surreally outside, mouthing to be let in.

"Gosh, you lot aren't easy to find," she gasped, settling herself down as if after a very long journey. "You might have told me where you were going."

"Sorry, Ali," said Pru. "But it is supposed to be a safe house. And things have been ever so slightly hectic. See, we went off to the FEW and..."

"Yes, I know about all that. This weird old codger came through the NRC the wrong way. He was in a terrible hurry. But he put me in the picture and told me where you were."

"Sammy!" they chorused.

"That's him. And there was this dancer with him, lovely girl. Very lithe. You should see her -"

"Where did they go?"

"Well, that's the funny thing. Apparently there'd been some sort of boating accident and this chap was at death's door having an OBE. I was just going to give him the big Efficient Empathy welcome when this Sammy pops out from nowhere, fills me in, snips the chap's thread and shoots off back down the tunnel. So there I was left with this Arab gone before his time and not very happy about it, I can tell you."

164

"Brilliant!" smiled Nigel. "What an escape. But what happened to Giselle?"

"The dancer? Oh, he told her there'd be another one along in a minute and they'd meet up on the Riviera. And that's not all…"

Sadiq Khan had been understandably annoyed about his premature departure from Earth. After all, a terrorist has work to do, anarchy to ferment, ideals to tarnish. It's a secure job with plenty of perks for the psychopathically inclined. Yes, one accepts there are certain risks in this line of work, though being crushed between two heaving love-nests in a Mediterranean harbour is a bit unusual. Still, he had fully expected to recover and be back behind his gun within a few months. Instead, he had found himself at the Western Sector NRC of an afterlife he didn't believe in, and at the loose end of an umbilical cord.

Alison had been on duty alone, as Boris had been hauled off for questioning by an SGB given free rein to make a nuisance of itself. Sadiq being an Arab and Alison apparently being an attractive white female, Khan had lost no time in telling her his version of his life story. When he got to Evie and the Municipal Casino, Alison had put two and two together.

"… so what Sammy was getting at," she went on, "was that this Evie woman has to be stopped before she gives birth."

"But that's murder!" exclaimed Pru. "Harold, your eyes are gleaming again."

"It doesn't seem very moral," Nigel agreed.

"I don't see what that's got to do with it," the colonel said. "The enemy's the enemy. You do what you have to do. Look, suppose you found yourself in Hitler's bathroom with a loaded gun in 1939 when he was about to go to the toilet. Eh?" Nigel frowned, trying to get his head round this.

"Why would I be in Hitler's bathroom?"

"All right, in his kitchen, then."

"Are you saying Hitler went to the toilet in his kitchen?"

"You'd shoot him, wouldn't you? Surely anyone would."

"I wouldn't," said Pru. "I'd make us both a cup of tea and sit him down for a chat. But it's hardly the same thing is it, assassinating the mother of the Messiah? You have to admit the implications are different."

"Seems much the same to me, my… er, Prudence. Anyway, no-one actually does get killed do they? Just moved about a bit to somewhere else. So if we care about the future of human life, however dysfunctional -"

"Speaking of which," interrupted Alison, "where's Ranjit?"

Φ

There were others, far removed in terms of space, time and motive, who were nevertheless equally intent on eliminating Evie Gardner. Ever since Judas Skim's appearance on the BBC breakfast programme, the world's markets had been in crisis, several leading bookmakers had gone out of business and there were reports that the North Korean Chairman had mentioned the word peace twice during a game of snooker with a Chinese diplomat. Confidence in the City was at an all-time low and the moving average forecasts resembled the temperature chart of a patient with terminal chickenpox. The consumer boom was fizzling out like a damp November squib and the Public Sector Borrowing Requirement had vanished overnight. The British government was at its wits' end and there were absolutely no foreign military adventures available to divert the public's attention (unless you count Glastonbury's unilateral declaration of independence).

Moreover, Jim Khan's private life could hardly be called straightforward either lately. No sooner had he received the crushing news about his brother than Winnie had arrived home by air ambulance. Against all the odds it seemed at first that she was making a remarkable recovery, but there was a strange fixed expression on her face and a distant vacancy in her eyes. This might not have been unusual after five or six gins on a Friday night, but she wouldn't touch the stuff now.

"Her whole personality changed," Jim confided morosely to Ron in the Rising Sun. "Not interested in horses at all. The other evening I got some neighbours in for a spot of bridge; that always used to cheer her up."

"No good?"

"She made two penalty doubles in the first half hour, missed an obvious ruff in a three-diamond contract, and we were fifty pounds down by nine o'clock. It was like she'd never played before. And on Saturday she refused to cook the pork sausages. We always have pork sausages on a Saturday."

"My word, you are having a rough time. Whatever happened in France?"

"Amnesia. She can't remember a thing. When I tried to talk about it she just grabbed my shoulders, said 'I want my poo jar' and demanded that I find her dick. I mean, what's a chap to do?"

"How's she doing at the funny farm? Settling down?"

"Seems so. Lots of staring into space, she likes that. Thanks, Ron, you've been a good friend, sending Sylvia over."

"What are friends for?" They left Ron's car at the pub and drove back in silence to Hertfordshire for the weekend. Sylvia was warming a casserole, then there'd be time for a quick three-hander before bed. There was serious planning to be done tomorrow.

But Saturday proved frustrating. A decent financial strategy had been thrashed out by the time the pork sausages appeared, but it depended on a good deal of interest rate deflation and insider trading. Normally this wouldn't be a problem, but the peace disease was starting to infect the dealers and no-one would play ball. By evening they still hadn't even started on the outstanding question of Mrs Gardner's demise, so the two men turned to the one experience that never disappoints.

Jim had sold the horses. The big race meetings were only taking entries from rank outsiders since Skim's predictions had ruined the system, and betting had just become a sheer gamble. He'd made a good arrangement with the Soho restaurant. With the right herbs and the odd special Japanese ingredient, horsemeat could be turned into practically anything. In return he'd got the jacuzzi plus Yoko and Kyusha, and the job lot had been installed in the old tack room, overseen by head groom and nominal eunuch Jim Roberts.

There is something uniquely paradoxical about jets of soft bubbles rushing to and fro about one's nether regions, exploring the nooks and crannies. For while it is the outer surface receiving the treatment, it is the cerebral cortex reaping the benefit. Add to this the quiet attendance of one or two dewy-eyed young girls with long black hair and loose kimonos, and the suprarenal glands get to pump a good deal of cortisone. While Roberts attended to some stiffness in Sylvia's lower back in the new massage room, Ron and Jim began to feel fresh.

"Trouble is," began Jim, "no-one seems to know where this Evie creature is right now. Somewhere between Provence and Picardie."

"Assuming she's on her way back to England."

"Well, according to the Great Pink Guru she is. I've got my men onto it, there's plenty of refugee manpower in France. A matter of honour for them."

"Yes, of course. How is Sadiq? You flew down there didn't you?" Khan shook his head sadly. It had been traumatic to find his brother so utterly transformed. It wasn't the injuries that were upsetting; it was the man's inner contentment, his very disturbing wellbeing. He'd also taken to smoking a disgusting pipe and doing charcoal sketches of the nurses in the prison hospital. He couldn't terrorise a flea now. There must be some truly evil force in the world to have caused this, and Jim had sworn vengeance. After all, blood is thicker than water. Not to mention messier.

Ron stood up in the water like a surfacing hippopotamus, sending tidal waves rippling over the patio surround. He gestured to Kyusha for the lanolin and the girl immediately rose from the floor, slipped the kimono from her shoulders and stepped silently into the water to kneel at his feet, jar of oil in one hand, loofah in the other. As the girl slowly worked her way up his legs, something grew in Ron's mind.

"I say," he began, "you don't suppose this is all a bluff, do you? This Evie business. A blind to send us off in the wrong direction, to protect the sprog? I mean, the old bag is hardly likely mother-of-God material, is she?" Yoko was attending to Jim's muscles.

"Fuck me!" he exclaimed, uncharacteristically. "Do you think so? We've all fallen for it while all the time it's... well, who?" Ron shrugged, sending a convulsion through each roll of fat in turn.

"Someone in Skim's group, maybe? He's at the centre of it all."

"So it could be Sylvia? Or Winnie? Is that why she's acting so strange? No, you can't be serious – they wouldn't... surely..."

"Unlikely," agreed Ron. "But can we afford to take that chance? Who knows what they've been up to. Something's turned Winnie's mind, and Sylvia – well, she is easily carried away." As if in confirmation, low moans could be heard from the massage room. Even Khan was taken aback by his friend's implication. Admittedly, as wives the two women had long outgrown their usefulness but they were still wives. On the other hand, there was an awful lot at stake. Hardly a time for emotion.

"Perhaps I'll go and visit Winnie, then," said Khan pensively. "She always did hoard tablets, terribly dangerous when you're prone to depression. What about Sylvia?"

"Didn't you tell me your sauna door tends to jam when the heat's up?" Even Khan shuddered at the horror of the suggestion. He was seeing his friend in a new light, even allowing for him being a banker. "And then," went on Ron absently, pausing for a scratch and stepping from the water, "it could be that other one. What's her name?"

"Pene. Yes, she's young and pretty, apparently. At least, Winnie used to come home furious with her every week. Seems a pity to... I mean, there isn't enough beauty in the world, is there?"

"Well, bring her here, then. We can keep an eye on her, until we know for sure... Any ideas on how to keep her here, though?" Khan, stroking Yoko's hair, was beginning to feel himself again and his lips parted in the old familiar, terrible smile.

"Why do you suppose these girls stay?" He gestured towards Kyusha's pale, naked body, slim and unashamed and freely given as she softly towelled down Ron Golightly's extraordinarily disgusting mounds of flesh.

"It's in their character, isn't it?"

"Even the Japanese aren't that selfless, old boy. It's heroin."

Φ

The first bullet had scorched Evie's right eyebrow but the second had buried itself well and truly in the comte's already flaccid abdomen. He had surrendered at the height of the campaign and paid the penalty. Later, he would come to in hospital and confound the authorities by claiming in a Geordie accent to be a private detective with evidence of alcohol abuse in Heaven. At least he ended his days in his beloved northern hills of Italy after all, although an institution for the criminally insane near the shores of Lake Garda was possibly not what he'd had in mind.

Evie herself was completely unhurt, except for having the stuffing knocked out of her by the heavy collapse of her lover and, with it, her last lingering dreams of romance and adventure. She had lain trapped on the Gay Boy's bed for several hours while the entire local gendarmerie trooped around the next boat. Eleanor Glee's screams had attracted some interest, although not half as much as the sight of her, pink and squirming beneath the very ample and very dead Con Danny Prattsmuller. At one point there must have been forty officers there, not to mention the photographers of every national newspaper in the western world. Eventually Sadiq Khan had been noticed and fished out, and everyone had wandered off back to their hotels, stations and darkrooms. Silence fell on the gently bobbing craft in the harbour, and nobody even thought to look over the Gay Boy.

Around late morning, Evie managed to dislodge the comte and crawl to the vodka bottle. The spectre had visited her yet again, and with an awesome terror. No longer could she deny that there was something very odd about her life. A Purpose. She had had everything within her grasp – money, celebrity, adventure and love – and in one apocalyptic night it had all been snatched away, every last bit. That doesn't happen unless you have a Purpose. With resignation, she pulled on the Cardin dress, the last vestige of that life, and cooked up some eggs and beans in the galley.

By midday she felt sufficiently fortified to turn her attention to the comte. Miraculously, he was still breathing. With the clear mind that comes only in a crisis, she did what had to be done, sterilising the wound with the remains of the vodka and then going through his pockets. Somehow, she was not surprised to find the licence and banker's letter, which she burned, but the shiny little ring gave her pause. On the point of throwing it into the sea for the fish, she hesitated and then slipped it onto her finger. It was not sentiment – she would be needing money, since the man's wallet yielded only a couple of hundred euros, three credit cards, a faded sepia photograph of a fat, dark-eyed woman with six children, and a dry cleaning ticket. Finally she packed a small suitcase with anything that could be unscrewed, and slipped away unnoticed by the throng of tourists on the quay being entertained by the duty gendarme with the heroic account of how he had overcome the crazed assassin in an underwater struggle. The French are romantics.

But where to go now, and how to get there? Evie surrendered herself to the guiding hand of fate that had got her into this mess in the first place. It was perhaps the first truly spiritual act of her life. She found her feet turning towards the Municipal Casino and within twenty minutes was drinking black coffee in the Assistant Manager's suite.

Jean-Paul Lapelle had a soft spot for Evie (as anyone might for one who had made them considerably richer). It should be said that he didn't have many soft spots. He had heard every hard-luck story in the book and indeed the job interview had consisted of being strapped in a chair wired up to an electroencephalograph while watching videos of tearful children waving their fathers off to prison. The French are romantics. Evie explained her plight with such quiet simplicity, such humble fortitude, and with a suitcase full of such marketable onyx ashtrays and gold tap fittings, that he could not find it in his heart to refuse her. In no time at all he had acquired everything she needed – a bag of sandwiches and a flask, five hundred euros, and a bundle of assorted old clothes.

"Zay are ma warf's," he explained generously. "She weel not meess them. She eez also a middle-aged b... a ladee of your 'ight and shape. Also, take thees." He handed her a small package in brown paper, securely taped up and addressed to someone in Marseille. "Eet eez ma friend. We do a leetle business and ee go vairy often to Hingland. Ee weel do ze passing port for you. Et maintenant - " He locked the office door and turned back to her, rubbing his hands. " – you weel please be taking off ze clothses. Ma warf 'as nevur 'ad ze Cardin dress before." The romanticism of the French has already been remarked upon.

The next few days were among the strangest of Evie's whole life, and she'd had a few, not least because she only uttered three words during the entire period. One of these was 'Marseille' at the railway station, and the other two were 'Sod off' when Jean-Paul's friend had suggested she might be taking off ze clothses again. It crossed her mind that for one well past the first flush of middle-age, and who had never aroused genuine carnal passion in a man (even Stan kept his socks on), her body had recently become intensely desirable. She was still unaware of the subtle yet profound changes taking place within it.

Apart from this, nothing crossed her mind. She was living in a vacuum of total incomprehension, going through the motions, moving hands and feet about with no inkling of purpose, staring vacantly at the verdant French countryside shuddering past the grimy windows of the old Citroen truck as they made their way north by a rural and circuitous route. Evie was lost, literally and spiritually, abandoned to the power of the spectre, her brain suspended from duty. Like an empty Seven-Up can tossed into the sea, she bobbed along in the stream of cosmic consciousness.

Some of her state of mind could be put down to extreme hunger. Unaccountably, she found that she'd become vegetarian overnight. Lapelle's sandwiches had contained something shapeless and greasy but undeniably animal parts, so they had been tossed out of the train window. This being France, she had not come across anything else edible except a few dry croissants and a bag of overripe plums. Unmistakably, she was being purified, though the fact was lost on her.

The pure are not much fun to have around, so Jean-Paul's friend had had enough of this before long. Considering his social obligations fulfilled, he tossed her out when they reached Calais and juddered off in a cloud of grey smoke. It was late evening, and a light mist swirled in from the Channel bearing that distinctive continental aroma of rotting vegetables, unwashed armpits and Disque Bleu. Aimlessly, Evie turned down the Boulevard Jacquard towards the quay as the impassive Burghers stonily watched her progress. She crossed the bridge and staggered on towards the thirteenth century watchtower looming up ahead. It was becoming difficult to put one foot in front of the other, her head light and spinning. At last, Evie reached her catharsis.

In the middle of the road near the Place d'Armes, lights suddenly flashed from the sky all around and the strident blare of angelic trumpets filled the air. She fell to the ground and heard a voice.

"Ay up, missus, look where you're… well, flamin' Nora, it's Evie Gardner. What the `eck are you doing `ere?" Bill Shaddock, fishmonger and erstwhile Judas acolyte, jumped down from the cab of his van and came to help her up.

"I'm blind! I'm blind!" she wailed.

"Ar, well you're sittin' in front of me `eadlamp, missus," explained Bill, helping her to her feet and kindly folding his black plastic raincoat round her shoulders. "C'mon now. Ee, you do' look well." He guided her through a small throng of spectators and into the cab. "What brings you 'ere, luv?"

"I couldn't begin to tell -" she began, but another powerful and distinctive aroma from the back of the van had caught her breath and turned her stomach.

"Ar, the fish," explained Bill. "I come over every week, good prices, see, an' a few specials. Like them John Dories in the corner there, with the black spots. 'Course it's mostly bass an' skate an' cod. 'Ere, I got a few ling though." He reached back and offered her one, his eyes bulging with enthusiasm. Evie looked bleakly from the one ugly face to the other and felt tears finally begin to trickle down her cheeks.

One of the spectators approached the open cab window.

"Excuse me, only I saw what happened. You're English aren't you? Can I do anything to… oh gosh, I recognise you," said Benedict.

"Ay up, mate, you a friend of our Evie's then?" Bill greeted him cheerfully. "Ar, the lass is ok. I were jus' telling 'er about the ling. Hoover of the sea, I call 'im, sucks up anything passing. Disgusting little bugger. Now, your mackerel's the same. Lovely oily fish, he is. You just slit 'is skin in a few places an' rub gooseberry jam in, then grill 'im over a -"

Evie could contain herself no longer. All the tumultuous emotion and despair of her recent life welled up in a raging torrent, and with a great sob of the very soul she turned towards Benedict and emptied herself, through the window, of yesterday's plums.

"Ee, missus," said Bill softly and with real concern. "I know what's up with you, I seen it afore. You're pregnant."

Chapter Ten ~ The Wilderness

There was a collective groan as the fugitives realised there was nothing else for it but to move again. No tranquil Elysian Fields here. In any case, they were going to need Arthur's specialised tracking equipment and proximity to Earth. Alison was fussed over and, being the only one among them with a legitimate job and not under suspicion, seen off back to the NRC with cheerful waves and salutes.

"Plonker!" Harry shouted. Sgt Glum arrived at the double from the newly extended kitchen where the SAS were billeted.

"Sah?"

"Prepare the men, Sergeant, we're on the march in two jiffies."

"Yessah! Where to, sah?" The colonel drew himself up in the middle of his band of outlaws and coolly issued the orders.

"Two men in camouflage with concealed weapons will escort Gibbs here to World's End -"

"Eh, why me?"

"– where he will rendezvous at one Gandalf's café with a woofter called Adrian and a fine soldier of a dog called Bonzai. The five of them will set up an underground resistance network to harass the SGB."

"Right, sah! Corporal Sloan and Private Davey, in 'ere at the double. Leeft rye, leeft rye, 'olt!" Nigel was about to protest at being singled out for this dangerous mission but the sight of Private Davey's long hairy arms froze his lips.

"As for the rest of us," Harry went on, his voice rousing, "onwards! To Fortress PRU(NE)!"

Arthur Stone was fed up.

Since Nigel had disappeared off on that foolhardy expedition to the FEW he'd been on his own with nothing to do except play with isobars and tune in to Mrs P from time to time. This sort of solitary existence with a bit of spying and plotting used to suit him perfectly. But since Harry and Prudence had entered his life it all didn't seem enough somehow. It was a strange, disturbing mood that settled over him now. Perhaps he had grown, a subtle light entering his soul, making him aware of far spiritual horizons. Perhaps he had been touched by the soft warmth of true human friendship. Or perhaps he was just fed up because Stachov and Hurski had been round again to beat him up and break things.

He sat on the floor where they'd left him, among the crushed microcircuits of the new intruder alarm system, and wondered why, after so long being pointedly ignored by everyone, he had suddenly become an object of such interest to the police. The others must have stirred things up.

He was considerably relieved when they all arrived from Stanmore (having briefly been held up by a roadblock at Neasden, which they'd only avoided when Sergeant Glum had called in a favour from the Sappers who slung a pontoon across the North Circular Road).

"What did the SGB want?" asked Harry, helping Arthur to a chair.

"Vot do ze SGB alvays vant? To smash a few sings off sentimental value and biff me about a bit, off course."

"Good show, that's all right, then. They're not onto us yet. Well done, Stone."

"Sank you. It voz nothing. By ze vay... please don't sink me rude, I am very hospitable in private... but vot in ze name off Gott is half ze British Army doing here? Zey make me nerfous."

Harry introduced Plonker and his men and did a quick inspection for Arthur's benefit, before filling him in on the latest developments. Stone heard him out with mounting excitement, finally banging a shoe on the workbench in the traditional way of expressing emotion.

"Zere! I told you somezing big voz going on! Didn't I tell you?"

"You did, Arthur, you did," agreed Pru, picking herself up. It had been her shoe that he'd banged on the table and she'd still been wearing it.

"Zo vot do ve do now?"

"Right, here's the plan," barked Harry, taking up command stance beside a flip chart, baton in hand. "Gather round, men. And, er, lady. Sergeant Glum, detail half your men for the extension of our new barracks here. We'll need a bigger Ops Room, a Mess -"

"Ve already haf that," interrupted Stone, indicating the state of the floor.

"- a training ground, billets, that sort of thing. The men will be under the command of Captain Clearwater here." He patted Pru's arm affectionately.

"Sah?"

"Yes, Sergeant?"

"Beg pardon, sah. She's a woman, sah."

"Good thinking, Sergeant. That's why she's in charge."

"Barracks and billets, sah!"

"Good. The rest of the men will be under your command, Sergeant, building defences, alarm systems and weapons. I want this place impregnable. Sooner or later they'll come for us, men, and we'll be ready for whatever they throw at us. Right, Sergeant?"

"In pregnant, sah! But beg pardon, sah, only I'm not sure -"

"You have to be sure, Sergeant. This is the biggest Op there is. Remember your training, men, it's all about belief. You can do anything with belief. Belief and plenty of bullets."

"Yessah! Barracks, billets, belief and bullets, sah!"

"Any more questions?"

"Vell, just von or two small sings occur to me," ventured Arthur.

"Spit it out, man."

"Vell, you seem to haff forgotten zat zis is *my* Psychic Research Unit."

"It's requisitioned," replied Harry calmly. "War calls for self-sacrifice and you're first. Anyway, you'll be perfectly safe. All you have to do is keep a track on Evie Gardner until we can decide how -"

"Yes, vell zat is ze other sing. I haff no assistant now, because you haff sent Nigel off to ze café -"

"It was necessary to set up a -"

"– and he is ze only vun who knows how to program ze computers here. You tvit!"

"Ah," said Harry, sitting down, "I hadn't thought of that."

Φ

In the queue for the ferry, Evie began to calm down a bit. It was immensely reassuring to see a familiar face, even if it was thick-lipped, oily and with protruding eyes. It also offered her cheese and pickle sandwiches and a flask of English tea.

Bill couldn't help feeling sorry for her, and protective. True, the circumstances of their only previous meeting could not be thought auspicious for a long-term commitment, and he'd left Judas Skim's house that night pretty sceptical. But what if the old phoney had been right all the time? Bill Shaddock began to feel the same trickle of fear that Winnie experienced with her hand on the car door. It was getting late in the day to be converted, and he'd never been one for insurance.[19] Still, in his favour, he had volunteered to be the Messiah's father, even though technically he'd now missed the best bit of the process.

As the rumbling of her stomach and the jangling of her nerves subsided, Evie told Bill and Benedict her story, or at least the bare bones

---

[19] It is often thought that this sort of last minute repentance is pretty unfair on those who have been true believers all along and who therefore deserve priority in the New World order. But on the other hand, without it the New World would be denied most of its truly interesting characters.

of it – she left out the flesh. Bill's eyes widened and bulged even more alarmingly until there seemed a distinct possibility of them popping out of their sockets.

"Gawd, all that money," he gasped. "Bin an' gone. An' now you up the… sorry, missus, in the family way. Never mind, I'll get you home safe. The name's Shaaarrgh…" Evie's nails dug into his arm, drawing blood. With some heightened instinct of self-preservation she'd glanced in the wing mirror just as the two dark figures, hands inside jackets, slowly approached down the line of vehicles, peering into each one. Even in the darkness and at a distance she recognised the middle-eastern features and knew what they were looking for.

Later, as they hit the M2 and headed for London with Bill hanging grimly to the steering wheel, right foot pressed to the floor and furry dice swinging crazily from side to side, Evie wondered whether it had been such a good idea to hide underneath the mackerel. True enough, the gunmen had not spotted her at Calais. But then the Passport Control Officer at Dover had recoiled from her with such disgust, running from his post with both hands clamped to his mouth, that the whole ferryload of passengers had got out of their cars to watch. With Benedict himself struggling to stay behind them in his hire car, the black BMW was just a dozen cars behind him. Approaching Sittingbourne it was within fifty yards and gaining.

To his credit, as the first shot zinged off the rear bumper and the second smashed his wing mirror into a million sparkling fragments, Bill's loyalty only wavered slightly. It was true that his tenure of the high office of father-of-the-son-of-God seemed on the point of being cut short. A third shot missed the front tyre by a whisker. But on the other hand it had been a peaceful, uneventful and to be honest downright boring life so far. Up with the dawn, standing in a draughty shop all day slitting gills and chopping tails, with egg and chips in front of the TV later. He'd never managed to find that one special, caring woman to share his twilight years. All right, he'd never managed to find any woman willing to spend more than quarter of an hour alone with him. But now, with his engine screaming at its limit as he flung the van from side to side, his knuckles white, his teeth gritted, his thighs damp, Bill had some responsibility and purpose in life. And he had an idea.

"See, missus," he remarked, "that there BMW is a beautiful piece of machinery. Superb chassis, a lovely smooth ride. Nimble `andling an' plenty of power -"

"And only thirty yards be'ind us," Evie pointed out, shrinking into her seat as another bullet thudded into the back door. "Worrarwegonnado?"

"Ah well, first off you climb in the back, missus, an' 'old on tight." She looked briefly at the ling but did as she was told. Bill was checking the mirrors and road signs carefully. "Your Beamer can leave most others standing, no bother. No wheel spin, see? Mind, if it 'as a fault it's on account of it being so quiet. The speed can be deceptive, see?"

"It ain't deceiving me, Bill," Evie yelled, hanging on to a rack of skate for dear life. "It's right up our bum." Benedict's car had been forced to give way and he was hanging back, helpless to intervene.

"Ar, well do' fret, missus. You just stand ready by that back door, ok?"

"What? I'm not going to -"

"Like I say, the bends are evened out so easy," Bill signalled and turned onto the narrow slip road just as the other car pulled alongside, "that you tends to take the corners a bit faster than you should. You gets uncomfortable understeer, you might say, go a bit wide on a bend." The two vehicles were tearing down towards the island as if locked together. Bill forced the gearstick into third to gain a yard, the engine begging for mercy, and Evie was convinced the van would shake itself and them to pieces. "The power steering lacks a bit of feel, too, if you know what I mean. Now, put that together with a variable ratio rack what's meant to reduce your steering on full lock..." Bill flung the van to the left as they hit the island at the bottom of the slip road at sixty-five and they went round on two wheels.

"The door, missus. Now!"

Jammed hard against the inside of the van with apparently every internal organ in her throat, Evie obeyed. Box upon box of fresh French fish hurtled out to splatter and squelch on the tarmac, turning the corner into a deadly skidpan just as the BMW hit it. They had no chance. The car turned over three times before hitting the motorway bridge support with a sickening blow. There was an instant of terrible silence, then a great roar as the lightning flash of fire engulfed it and its occupants.

"...an' if you're not careful, you find yourself diving into a corner too soon, see? Apart from that," Bill brought the offside wheels of the van back to earth with a gentle bump and pulled up on the grass verge, "it's a lovely motor. Now, you don't get that problem with the old Ford. You all reet, missus?"

Benedict pulled up just behind them as Bill helped Evie out, and they all stood with arms round each other's shoulders watching the flames hiss and crackle. Evie buried her face in Bill's clammy neck and sobbed her heart out.

"There, there, missus, you're all reet now. We'll look after you. You an' the kid."

In the cab, they finished off the flask of tea and set off back to the motorway just before the flotilla of police and fire engines arrived.

"I'm sorry about your John Dories, Bill," said Evie, a hand on his arm and managing a weak smile.

"Never mind, missus. Plenty more in the sea, eh?"

Φ

Nigel had led the men to Gandalf's without mishap and settled himelf at a pavement table sipping something long, pink and harmless while Adrian and Bonzai, delighted to see him, set about discreetly getting rid of the other customers with a combination of leers and pants. Corporal Sloan went off to do some window shopping at the Army Surplus shops on North End Road, but Private Davey was not so easily distracted from duty and sat loyally at Nigel's side drinking a banana milk shake. His only civvy coat being a knee-length dark brown astrakhan, it wasn't long before a couple of passers-by had tossed some coins at their feet. Nigel sent him off to buy a new coat.

At last there was only one customer left and he was so morosely huddled in his own thoughts in a corner that they had let him be. It is the primary purpose of a café, after all, to offer sanctuary to those down on their luck or needing a breather from the family. As it happened, this particular act of charity was not only misplaced, it was to have profound consequences for the entire world. (It is as well to consider this possibility before embarking on charitable acts.)

The two conspirators had barely had time to exchange news, let alone conspire, when the morose customer got briskly to his feet and came to sit at their table.

"Mind if I join you?"

"Well, dear, I don't -"

"Oh cripes!"

"Hello, Nigel."

"Algol. Or is it Fuzru these days?"

"It's all the same. Well, isn't this nice, and after such a long time, if you know what I mean. And I was just thinking of you, too."

"Were you really? I'm terribly sorry but I was just on my way -"

"Life is full of such funny coincidences, isn't it? Like all my security codes being broken, which somehow made me think of you."

"That's too bad. But there's a very urgent -"

"Sit down!" As Nigel tried to get up he found himself firmly pushed back by the two SGB men who had suddenly appeared at his shoulders. Adrian gulped with incomprehension.

"Gracious! Where did those brutes spring from?"

"One in my position has a certain authority," remarked Fuzru offhand with a casual wave of his arm that emptied Nigel's drink over Bonzai's head. She stretched and bared her teeth, but realising that she was outnumbered slunk off to the back yard. Meanwhile Nigel was thinking fast, having learned a thing or two from Harry. His eyes narrowed.

"Yes, now what exactly is your position, Algae? One doesn't normally get Elemental riff-raff in these parts. You haven't, er, lost your job have you? Something gone wrong, has it? Something big?" Fuzru shuffled slightly in his seat as four SGB eyes also turned questioningly towards him.

"Might have. Just temporarily. Nothing to worry about now we have you."

This turned out to be a bit of a miscalculation. Now, the Third Spiritual Secretary may have been an old friend of Fuzru's, and a pompous fool, but you don't get to be SS3 by being actually stupid or by refusing to grab gift horses by the throat when they're presented on a plate. Things had not been going well since the last Planning Committee meeting, which is to say that things had been going altogether suspiciously smoothly.

There had been a queue of eager and suitable applicants for the vacant Elemental positions. Tfozb had initiated a complete overhaul of the education system, involving in-service Witness appraisal and replacing the Better Afterlife Authority with a new QUalifications And Karma Board, which would have a stronger voice in the Presentation Of Nurture Directorate. With uncommon vigour the SGB had been through the astrals like a dose of senna and completely filled Strangeways with shady characters, such as German philosophers, Italian prime ministers and anyone with the initials EG. Even Czosn had announced that he'd found the flaw in the Deviance Method while considering the problem of phyllotaxis in the sneezewort, and had started on the fourth volume of his trilogy (to be entitled 'Statistics Your Grandmother Could Do In Her Sleep').

So like the captain of a great ship in the eye of a storm, it seemed to SS3 that he was the only who knew they were in the middle of the greatest crisis there has ever been. To incarnate a Messiah into the wrong mother was bad enough. To incarnate a lesbian anarchist into the right mother was worse. And to have lost them both was about as bad as things can get. He could forget about promotion. And if he didn't get a firm grip and find a solution, he'd be following Fuzru down the back streets of Fulham.

When Nigel had been wheeled into his office flanked by two heavies and an insanely smirking Fuzru, it was as if the very clouds had parted and a deep Voice From On High had spoken. And the Voice said: "This is your last chance to get out of the manure." He turned on a sickly smile and gestured Nigel to a comfy chair.

"Ah, Fibbs from Troon, isn't it?"

"That's close enough, sir." Nigel was not about to get pedantic with someone coming on to him like one of the Holy Creatures of Revelation.

"You've caused a bit of bother in the old etheric electronics department, Figgs. Breaking codes, altering records, hacking the system to pieces?" He chortled at his own joke, like an Austin Allegro with a flat battery being turned over on a January morning. "You know something about these computers, don't you?"

"I can find my way around a keyboard, sir."

"And under one as well, I believe. A bit of a whiz at college, according to one of the files you haven't altered." He made a quick mental note to check his own PF later. "Strange, then, that you never got on in the business, eh? I mean, you could have had, well, Fuzru's job by now surely?"

Nigel recognised the trap immediately. Ever since his arrest, the speed and clarity of his own thought had surprised even himself, and a strategy had begun to form in his mind. He found that he had indeed learned much from the colonel. For one thing, strict mental self-discipline was keeping his ideas hidden from those around him, while for another he knew with total conviction that nothing could hurt him. So he'd winced and groaned a bit for the sake of appearances when the SGB handled him roughly, and even with superhuman effort forced out an apology to Fuzru. He could at any moment have slipped off to the new Kings Cross terminal, had he really wanted to, and spirited himself away with a new identity almost anywhere he chose. But he also knew, apparently better than Harry, that the others needed him if they were to have any chance of success. And if they didn't succeed, he could forget about ever tasting Bishop's Brew again and achieving the true, ultimate bliss of personal oblivion.

SS3 wanted to swallow him up in the system. But Nigel had one or two cards to play.

"Surely one of your talents can't be satisfied with menial psychic research, Biggles?" SS3 persisted. "You must know it's a dead end? Old Arthur Stone can mess about with cerebral politics and whip up the odd shower of frogs over Clacton, but it's not going to change the world, is it? And you must know as well as I do that intramundial communication is an impossible dream. Now, just imagine what you could do with the state of the art nuts and bolts here, eh?" He sat back expectantly. But it was Fuzru who reacted first, seeing the enemy metamorphosing into the prodigal son.

"Now hang on, Duflc. Really! The man's a criminal. He's been playing willy-nilly with aeons of spiritual evolution and ballsed-up the Second Coming."

"No, I haven't."

"No, he hasn't, Fuzru. Honestly, do calm down and... what do you mean, you haven't? Wasn't it you?"

"All I've done," said Nigel evenly, "is expose the weaknesses in the system. You should be thanking me. The security was pants and the hardware is generations out of date. The readouts don't even make sense. Only a Chinese waiter could understand EG HA PRU AL."

"You do have a point," confessed SS3. "We couldn't find any Chinese waiters in Heaven."

"And in any case," Nigel led with his Jack to draw the opponent out, "the Second Coming all looked fine to me, from what I saw of it. Lovely atmosphere, beautifully organised... er, was that your work, sir?"

"As it happens...," SS3 smiled modestly, off-guard. "You see, Czosn got hold of the wrong set of parents, something to do with deviance, I believe."

"Well...," he played the five, as a sacrifice, "I suppose I might be able to help, on one or two small conditions..."

"Now steady on, young fellow," SS3 asserted his rank, "I make the conditions round here, you know." In a fairly literal sense, this was true, which was a large part of the reason for the mess he was in. So Nigel casually tossed in the ace.

"...since I know who EG is and where you're likely to find her." The last bit was a bluff, of course, but a cast-iron one.

"I don't believe you," snorted Fuzru. "How could you?"

"Shall we say, a chance meeting put me onto her."

"A Chinese waiter?" SS3 asked, sensing he was losing control of the interview. "Look, all right, Boggle, suppose for the moment we accept what you say. Suppose, mind. What do you want – Fuzru's job?"

"Now, just a min -"

"Good heavens, no."

"Eh?"

"No? Then what?"

"I think Fuzru's perfectly placed where he is. He's earned it."

"I say, that's awfully decent of -"

"But perhaps I could be a sort of advisor... develop the next hardware generation... some input on security... streamline Analysis... run research programs for the CPSU..."

"A minute ago he was arrested," huffed Fuzru, "and now he's running the whole caboodle."

"And another thing," Nigel continued, "do call your gorillas off. I'm sure they've got better things to do, like finding John Clarke."

"You know about him too?" SS3's shoulders sagged. There was a sound like cracking knuckles but he waved the SGB men out.

"Sorry, I thought everyone knew about Clarke. Look, I'm just a back-room boy. The caboodle is all yours, sir."

"But Duflc," hissed Fuzru, "what he's asking for is instant promotion from Limbo to Elemental. Souls go through dozens of incarnations to get that, and most never make it."

"What the hell?" SS3 shrugged. "It's only karma. There are ways of paying it off. And modifying the records seems to be the least of Gibble's problems. All right," he turned to Nigel, "we'll give it a try. On probation, mind. I want results. I want the Second Coming sorted, priority." He got up.

"Just one more thing." He sat down again.

"Oh, come on, Fibbles. I've just given you the biggest job since Creation. What now?"

"This chap Czosn..."

"The shifty Slav? What about him?" He was the only one able to connect Nigel with Harry, Pru and the others.

"Well, correct me if I'm wrong, but I gather that this rather critical mistake you mentioned is down to him. Certainly not your fault, sir, how could it be? Nor Fuzru's." They weren't going to argue about it. "So might it not be a good idea to, er, move him somewhere? A long way?" The Deviance Method worked after all.

"Demotion?"

"Well, that might lead to resentment. Not good for one's development. How about a grant to go and write some more books?"

"You know, Tiddles, I think we're going to get on just fine."

It was one of the most significantly rare moments in human history. No less than three people had sat down as enemies, then risen again all believing that they had got what they wanted. Certainly, they all got what they deserved.

Φ

Evie had no idea where she was.

Nigel had no idea where Evie was.

Arthur had no idea where either Evie or Nigel were.

In fact, there was a list of people as long as your arm who didn't know much. Even Evie's newly-appointed high-power firm of city Witnesses failed to get a trace, much to Tfozb's disgust. Usually, one picked up on a soul's distinctive psychosociomorphology and homed in via the personal auric channels. But there was nothing distinctive at all about Evie, and her aura was still saturated with mackerel.

However, there were others employing more conventional tracking methods. Realising this, Bill set about making their task as hard as possible. They left the motorway at junction three and weaved across country, back-tracking south then circling up through Surrey and Berkshire, travelling at night and passing the daylight hours bedded down on an old blanket in the back of the van, tucked away under trees. It was neither comfortable nor romantic, but Evie felt safe with her menial, down-to-earth, ugly fishmonger. With that extraordinary perversity of her gender, she even began to feel some affection for him. When he had dropped her at Virginia Water to stroll peacefully in the June sunshine while he withdrew his life savings from the Building Society, bought provisions, a tent and sleeping bags, and returned for her in a second-hand Toyota, she was hooked.

"Well, missus," he shrugged, "they'd find the old van soon enough. Anyroad, the water pump were going." Evie didn't know much about men, but enough to realise that his vehicle is a piece of his very soul. This had been a supreme gesture. Bill Shaddock may have been an unlikely candidate for beatification, but he was catching up on the field fast. The rest of that day was blissful, spent snoring beside the Thames at the Wallingford Riverside Camp Site (two pennants) followed by an hour and a half in the showers.

Benedict could not be said to be at peace. After all he'd been through, all his efforts, his determined and faithful pursuit of instinct, against all the odds he had actually found Evie only to discover that she hadn't the faintest idea who Alison was. Yes, she remembered the somersaulting, crushed and broken body on the Embankment, when he told them his story, but that was the last of it. George P and Judas Skim were now Benedict's only links to her, she who was after all, let's face it, dead.

But far away and quite unknown to Benedict, a chap called Harry had put his finger on it. A man is not human without the mysteries of love and simple faith. It is the ache in a man's soul that gives his life dignity. And Benedict was very human. So, pausing only to exchange mobile `phone numbers with Bill and, holding his breath, to hug his new friends, he turned the hire car back towards north London.

Less than thirty miles away, Jim Khan paced his snooker room in abject frustration, not least because he had no idea how close Evie was. There were several other reasons for his state of mind, from money to his wife, and from Pene to his brother. The cares of the world were crowding in on him. Not only were the stock markets continuing their slow disintegration, forcing the WICH Corporation to review its product range, there was also the small matter of a wrecked BMW and its occupants to keep quiet.

But if his business world was teetering on the edge, his private life was spiralling out of control. Sylvia had been duly roasted and, for good measure, cremated as planned, but Winnie was still very much alive. True, she was behind several locks and keys with a diagnosis of psychopathic schizophrenia, but this was in itself an affront to Jim's simple philosophy of life and death. Moreover, he hadn't bargained for Ron actually going into mourning, and it's just not the same fun taking a jacuzzi alone. Or playing snooker.

His thoughts turned to Pene Marker. It had been child's play to get her out of London on the pretext of visiting Winnie, and to deal with the shock of her friend's terrible state with a couple of injections. But whatever the girl had experienced while cooped up with Skim seemed to have ruined her for anything either hallucinogenic or sexual. Drugs had no effect on her, nor would she have anything to do with Khan. On the other hand, she was perfectly happy to stay around and flaunt herself for the crippled vegetable that was Sadiq (whom the French had felt obliged to deport and whom Jim had felt obliged to import). He wandered moodily across the lawn to stand behind the invalid, loosely supposed to be his brother, as he worked with intense concentration at his easel.

"Do try to keep still, my dear, just a little longer," he was muttering, through teeth clenched on an old briar. Jim gazed beyond them to Pene's soft, lovely, naked body sitting thoughtfully on the grass beside her clothes and a wicker basket of fruit, shaded by a young oak. Such a waste. The artist must have heard his sigh and looked up.

"Ah, James. Do you like it? After Manet's Dejeuner Sur l'Herbe. But I don't know, I just can't quite the hang of French Impressionism. Not my century. All right, Pene, thank you. Let's call it a day; the light's going now so we'll try again tomorrow, eh?"

"No problem, Sammy. It's always a pleasure to pose for you." This was true, it being the first time in ten years that a man had looked at her body without wanting it for himself. She slipped on the short cheesecloth dress and wandered about for a while on the grass without doing the buttons up, just to annoy Jim. But his mind was no longer on flesh as he turned to confront his brother.

"Never," he hissed, "in my life have you called me James. It isn't even my name. What sort of brother of mine are you? And why did she call you Sammy?"

"Oh, just a little pseudonym," the other replied diffidently. "Artist's licence."

"Are you so ashamed of our family that you now change our names, brother? Where's your honour?"

"I lost a good deal in France."

"And we lost two cousins for the cause under the M2," retorted Jim angrily.

"What cause is that?" asked Sammy evenly.

"What cause? The one you botched in Cannes, the elimination of the old bag Evie Gardner." Across the lawn, Pene heard the name and looked up. "They were fried alive, brother, in fish oil."

"Did you say fish?" Pene said, walking slowly back towards them. Momentarily transfixed, Jim Khan watched the gently undulating approach of the small black forest above creamy thighs and wished to be the fly that had just settled on her left knee.

"He did say that," replied Sammy, since his brother's mouth was temporarily out of service. "It seems that James here got a message from something called a carphone that this Evie person was in a van full of fish. I didn't even know that cars could -"

"That'll be Bill Shaddock's van, I suppose," said Pene innocently.

Jim was back in business. Within twenty-four hours he knew more about Bill Shaddock than Bill did, including how much interest he'd forfeited by withdrawing his money at the Egham Building Society. He briefly considered letting the police do the donkey work of finding them, but they were so unimaginative – they'd only lock them up. Instead, more cousins were despatched to the Surrey borders.

For his part, Sammy realised with resignation that his own task was not yet over after all. The Khans were liable to cause untold mayhem. His mind was made up a day later when he overheard Jim on the 'phone.

"... so what do you mean, the trail's cold? They've been at Wallingford and Standlake... so check every site within a day's drive... yes, I'm aware of that, cousin. So use your head – Shaddock has a sister near Ledbury hasn't he? Well, then...and every antenatal clinic in every town... women over forty, that's right... You know what to do... yes, the injection... get on with it."

A wave of sadness overcame Sammy. He had hoped fervently that it wouldn't come to this but now the Terror was in the world again, the old familiar, desperate assault of Darkness. Within a week, the newspapers were carrying stories of the sudden and mysterious deaths of pregnant women across the south Midlands and into Gloucestershire and beyond. Some hideous, unknown virus, it was said. Twelve died, and panic began to grip England.

But born-again Bill was more than a match for Evil. The Toyota had already been switched again and the pursuers were hopelessly off track.

Sammy knew there was nothing else for it but to enlist Pene's help. It was a pity, for beauty should never be abused. He broached the subject as they reworked Picasso's Demoiselle d'Avignon with a bunch of grapes in the garden, while Jim was out rescuing some investments.

"I don't really know what's going on," he began, "but this Evie seems to be in some sort of danger. A friend of yours, is she?"

"Sort of," Pene replied, in some discomfort. "Do you think I could take these pyramids off my tits for a while?"

"Certainly, my dear. And take your leg out of there, too, it can't be good for you." She limped over to see how the work was going.

"Yes, I feel a bit guilty about it all. I mean, Bill and Evie are awful old wrinklies but I wouldn't want them to get hurt. And maybe Judas Skim was right all along, about the Messiah."

"Believe that do you? Well, you do seem to have been close to him."

"Didn't think about it much. It wasn't one of those things that came up between us. He believed it anyway. But look, didn't Jim say that you were supposed to find her?"

"Ah, well, my dear, people are not always quite what they seem, you know. Listen, I do have a few, ah, contacts of my own. Perhaps if I had more information we could find this Evie first and warn her." He crossed his fingers behind his back. "James doesn't tell me anything now.

He thinks I'm a bit wet. But he'd tell you, if you, ah..." He patted her soft, pink bottom in a fatherly way.

"Oh, I see. Do I really have to?"

"It's what he wants. It could be the only way, and you'd be so good at it."

"Oh, I don't know. There are lots of other girls -"

"No, you have the perfect posture. North-west London junior champion, I heard."

"That was years ago."

"You never lose the technique, my dear."

"Well, all right. I'll give it a try. But I'd better go and practise while he's out." Within a couple of hours she was making breaks of over fifty.

Φ

It was inevitable that Ranjit would get lost, wandering about the astrals on his own. Until recently, he may not have had an entirely lucid grasp of The Plan and everyone's part in it, but back there in Czosn's office before the mice crashed in he'd seen enough to get the gist. It was Big. And while RJ may not have been blessed with the greatest brain, what he did have was a huge heart. Even though he'd been dissed by his friends, he realised that they must not be jeopardised by a little thing like a file left carelessly on a desk. If they wouldn't go back for it, then he would, innit.

Finding the past seemed like a straightforward matter of retracing one's steps. But one size eight footprint in time looks very much like another. Sergeant Glum had led them sure-footedly over rough ground and through shadowy landscapes. So why was RJ now standing in the middle of a traffic island between two neon signs which stated 'Turn Left Only' and 'Shopping Centre First Right'? The littered pavements were thronged with people and the roads snarled with taxis, delivery vans and buses. It looked like he'd walked right out of Heaven.

He didn't exactly panic but a great uncertainty now gripped him. Not only did he not know where he was, he was also unsure of who he was. There had been a lot of changes lately. There was a saintly vestige here, a nuance of idiot there, while the truth lay on a desk somewhere else. He joined the crowd and surrendered to the flow, carried almost bodily into a shopping mall, perspex-domed and tinkling waterfalls, plastic sunflowers and smelly alleyways, Escher escalators and cavernous shops filled with rows of polyester on wire hangers. A burly security guard eyed him up and down. He pressed the hot chocolate button on a drinks machine and the paper cup filled with soapy water.

He tipped out the water and edged his way to the lift, pushing number three.

And suddenly there he was. It was quiet, empty, a soft muted vista of nothingness in which everything was possible. It was as if all that had been before was stripped away. RJ looked down at the paper cup he was still holding. He realised that it was only the empty space within each of them that made them useful, the nothing that made them real.

He stepped out of the lift and rubbed the gaudy colour and chaos he'd left below out of his eyes. His mind let go and he began to move forward effortlessly along a thread of a path that stretched out through the formless, silent landscape. He was going nowhere, and this was the right way.

Structures rose and fell away on either side and pale green canopies of shifting, living shapes filtered a cool light dripping from a sunless sky. Nameless animals scampered past and were swallowed up in the yawning undergrowth. Just ahead there was the slight movement of another figure walking out of sight before it could be recognised. Here was freedom. Here there was no machination, no Messiah, no God.

The others were in another place, enwrapped in plots and clever words and bright thoughts charged with ideals and beliefs. But RJ had no knowledge save that, like a newborn child before it learns to smile, he was alone. Yet if one is in a place where everything is possible, why not take advantage? If granted a wish, why not ask for unlimited wishes? For a start, a small grey manila card index file appeared in his hand. Then, with a wry smile, Ranjit decided that he would finish the job.

He went back down in the lift, out through the mall and into the street. He caught a number 142 back to his little observation room. Finding it completely trashed by the SGB, he decided to visit Alison instead.

Φ

There was a brisk knock on the door of the Operations Room and Glum entered, snapping to attention at Harry's shoulder. The colonel was poring over Adrian's map of Heaven, pushing little black and white tanks around on the table top. It helped him to think.

"What is it, Sergeant?"

"Thought you'd like to know, sah, we've caught two of the henemy snooping around outside, sah."

"Good show. Anything to say for themselves?"

"Some cock-and-bull story about a hurgent message, sah. One's a bit of a pansy if you hasks me, sah, and the dog just keeps swearing like a-"

"Did you say dog, Sergeant?

"That's right, sah."

Harry stopped playing with his stick and settled himself with a smile in his new black leatherette chair beneath the photo of Queen Elisabeth.

"I have a shrewd idea who they might be, Sergeant. I hope you've roughed them up a bit. Wheel `em in." Adrian and Bonzai were frogmarched in under double escort and deposited on the carpet at Harry's feet.

"Harry, at last. We've -"

"Silence, prisoner. Speak when you're spoken to. Right, thank you men, good work. I know these two. You can leave us now."

"If you're sure, sah." The soldiers turned on their heels to leave, Bonzai and Glum exchanging a parting snarl. Harry helped Adrian up.

"Sorry about all that, old boy, have to keep up appearances, y'know. They're fine men, very loyal." Adrian rubbed his sore spots.

"Hmm, bully-boys I call them, deary. Not very nice."

"Rough," agreed Bonzai.

Corporal Sloan and Private Davey had arrived back from their shopping trips; in snow-wash denim blousons and Levi twill Docker jeans, too late to prevent Nigel's arrest and removal in a large black van. The colonel made a mental note to put them on fatigues for the duration should they ever show up again.

"… so we thought we'd better get over here to warn you," Adrian concluded. "This place isn't easy to find, you know. A pretty low dive."

"It's the front line, man. There are no home comforts this close to Earth. Well, what a kibosh this is. What are we going to do without Gibbs?"

"Ah, well he did say something cryptic just before they carted him off. Whispered it to me, said to tell Arthur there's a Special Reserve Biscuit hidden in the lavatory."

It seemed unlikely that Nigel's final message to his boss should be so gastric in nature, but all the same Harry got the others together for a systematic search. As it happens, they found the backup diskette among the crumbs at the bottom of a cookie jar. It contained a lifetime's accumulated wisdom on hacking, including detailed instructions for altering PFs and a brand new security code-breaking program. Arthur put down his fog calculations and sat at a keyboard to try and make sense of it, while the others just sat in frustration. Momentous events were taking shape, Evie Gardner was out of reach, and they could do nothing about it. Bored out of his mind, Adrian switched on Channel Four for the Welsh

Domino Championships, and there was Nigel filling the screen with a cheerful grin.

"At last," he called, "there you are. I knew you'd turn it on sooner or later. This is the only safe way I could make contact."

"A bit risky, isn't it?" said Pru, instinctively looking around. "Won't someone be able to overhear us?"

"You don't imagine anyone else would be watching this, do you? Anyway, we haven't got long. The adverts will be on soon. And by the way, on the off-chance you might have been worried, and since you haven't mentioned it, I'm fine, thanks. I'm here on the -"

"Get on viz it, Gibbs," snapped Arthur impatiently.

"Charmed, I'm sure. Though you might want to be a bit nicer, Art, when you hear the news. First off, I've tracked Sammy to this place in Hertfordshire where -"

"Sammy?" the others chorused. "I thought the old blighter was out of it," said Harry.

"Well, he's back in it now and up to his neck. The contact's a bit hazy – they're still working on the old psychometric dual-resistive atpercent interferon principle here."

"Fancy that."

"Well, well."

"So I can't get too many details yet, but he's up to something." He played a five-blank and scored eight points.

"And where's Mrs Gardner?" demanded Harry.

"That's just it. They've smothered her with blanket security, Witnesses falling over themselves. There's some new woman in charge, all smarmy voice and tight corsets. Nobody here can get anywhere near Evie. There's nothing else for it – you'll have to go down after her."

"What? Earth?" Prudence was aghast.[20] The prospect of Hertfordshire was doing nothing to excite the inhabitants of PRU(NE).

"Oh, and by the way," went on Nigel, "there was just one other small thing you probably should know. You've all heard of angels, I expect?"

"Um, yes," said Pru. "But surely they don't actually exist, do they?"

---

[20] The single, solemn but indubitable reason why parapsychologists generally have a bad time of it, and that despite nearly two centuries of earnest effort nobody has ever been able to prove spirit communication, is that having got to Heaven and tossed away for good one's broken-down body, no dead person in their right mind wants anything whatever to do with Earth again, let alone go back there. Those not in their right minds are what keep people like Dora P in business.

"That's what I thought. But it turns out there's quite a lot of them, big butch chaps, all high-and-mighty and holier-than-thou. Sixteen hundred wings of green topaz, saffron hair from head to foot, on each hair a million faces and in each face a million eyes, you know the sort of thing."

"Of course."

"Well, usually they keep themselves to themselves, don't bother with the likes of us, up in their place beyond Elementary. Seems they like a quiet life. But with the Messiah business going wrong, the word is they're a bit fed up with us. Well, with you to be precise. So they're coming down to sort you out." A double-three took the game.

"What?"

"Eh?"

"Pyostri rvota!"

"If I were you I'd form the HGVs into a circle and hold out as long as you can. Don't worry, I've got a plan…" The picture disappeared, to be replaced by a government information film about how to disconnect the plug before going to bed.

"He's got a plan!" moaned Arthur. "Famous last vords."

But there was no further opportunity to insult Nigel, for at that moment the laboratory was rocked by almighty explosions, and ectoplasm-curdling screams reverberated through the PRU(NE).

Φ

Sammy exchanged his brush for a glass of Liebfraumilch, sat back in the cool of an English summer afternoon, and stared hard at the new canvas bringing all his intuitive powers to bear on it. To the untutored eye it resembled nothing more than a Tracey Emin cornfield. In fact, it was a map of AA approved campsites, each dot and stroke a snippet of information from Pene about Evie Gardner, Bill Shaddock and their desperate, shadowy pursuers. Art being the highest form of intelligence, he knew there had to be a pattern in the spiralling, swirling, backtracking paths. [21]

There comes a point in any act of true creation, creeping up subtly unawares like a thief in the night with unstoppable force, when suddenly the master key is in the lock and the ultimate form emerges. The future

---

[21] This should be a lesson to us all. Next time we go to an exhibition of pompous, pointless, self-indulgent modern art, we might do well to consider the possibility that the sheer rubbish before our eyes is actually the work of highly advanced Elemental spirits channelling vital esoteric information about the future of Mankind to us. On the other hand, it might just be rubbish.

arrives and nothing in the universe can prevent it. As he drained the glass, Sammy still didn't fully understand how. But all at once and with absolute certainty, he knew exactly where Bill Shaddock was heading and that they only had hours to stop him. If he made it, no-one on Earth would ever find Evie.

Φ

At just about the same time, Benedict was once again leaving Judas Skim's house with mixed feelings. Far beyond his own expectations, the Apache Agency (workforce one, company registration delayed in the post) had proved phenomenally successful. It was an idea whose time had come, and in just the right place.

With his ample experience of the advertising industry, Benedict had been able to tutor Skim expertly in What The Public Wants To Hear and What The Public Definitely Should Never Find Out. All enquiries from journalists and TV producers had been carefully directed to a new official-looking website which merely stated 'Thank you for your enquiry, it is being dealt with', and which was programmed to redirect the enquiries in turn to the Recycle Bin. The only newspapers and TV shows that actually got Skim had been individually selected and personally approached by the Apache Agency, their acceptance guaranteed by the very modest fees requested. What was actually making Benedict and Judas very rich, very fast, was the subliminal product endorsement deals that Benedict had secured from his old contacts. Things like 'In the New World Order it will be important for everyone to keep their homes spotlessly clean. For example, I myself use Spotto Detergent' and 'Should the Messiah approach you in the street, you'll want to look your best, perhaps in a clean white Armeenstek suit like mine'.

For his part, Judas Skim was both delighted and relieved to have someone alongside him who actually knew what they were doing and, in particular, with the skills required to eliminate his less than spiritual past from the public eye. In case the man should be misunderstood, it should be pointed out that he really did believe in his Message. Yes, reinventing himself in that lonely cell had started out as a bit of a wheeze, a ride on the waves of Aquarius. But he couldn't deny that there had indeed been some strange moments, usually alone at night and after two or three glasses of Jack Daniels, when he had felt himself to be overshadowed by... what? A Presence. Something like a small furry animal popping up on its hind legs and looking appealingly at him. There really was a Message to be given.

And now the message was being heard and he, Judas Skim, was literally changing the world. Well, the stock market anyway. It was all going well. All right, the mystical group of seven had been reduced rather suddenly to two, but that had still had its compensations. The further disappearance of Pene was disappointing and puzzling. But the spiritual life is nothing without mystery, and there were plenty of nubile young replacements behind the scenes of TV studios. And, after all, one is a pretty mystical number in itself.

Despite all this, Benedict could hardly be described as satisfied though, for the simple truth was that Judas Skim also had no idea who Alison was or where she might be. His psychic communication channel, it appeared, was a one-way street and quite often blocked by roadworks at that. It seemed to Benedict, on this cool Wednesday afternoon, that for all his determined effort and belief he was as far away as ever from finding the truth.

He was wrong.

In desperation (or was it Divine Inspiration?) he drove back to the bedsit, had a wash and a brush-up, and set off to Edgware. He was going to offer himself up as a disciple to Dora P.

Φ

Sergeant Glum staggered in, hands over his eyes and moaning.

"Permission to report, sah?"

"Go ahead, Plonker," said Harry, calm and composed. He was in his element, this was his moment in time. "And do put your leg back on, Sergeant, you look untidy."

"Right, sah, sorry, sah. We're hunder attack, sah."

"You don't say."

"I do say, sah. There's 'undreds of 'em, sah, all 'uge an' shiny with wings an' that. 'Urts your eyes something terrible, sah. All roaring an' belching smoke like great beasts, sah. 'Orrible, they is, 'airy an' eyes an' teeth an' brilliant gold like the sun's shining out of their noses, sah."

"I see, Sergeant. But apart from that, is there anything unusual about them?"

"Well, er, no sah, not really."

"Right, then you know what to do, Sergeant." Harry barked his orders with cool efficiency. "Operation Repulse. It's all a matter of belief, Sergeant. Just belief, man. This is it, the real thing, it's what we've trained for. They're only angels, after all."

"Hoperation Repulse, sah."

"That's right. Draw up the first phalange with mortars and automatic rifle support, three men on Bishop's Brew atomiser cannons and the rest in the HGVs and shiny red plastic combat suits. And yes, the Mickey Mouse masks, I think. RJ was right, they are more frightening than androids. Ok? On the double, man."

"Yessah!" A revitalised Plonker sprang to attention and saluted.

"And Sergeant -"

"Sah?"

"We're all behind you, man."

In fact, Adrian and Arthur were also behind several heavy tables and a big pile of electronic junk. Harry and Pru stood hand in hand in the eerie sanctuary of the laboratory as the awful battle raged around them outside, listening to the cries and the thuds, the whistle of the tracer, the terrifying screams of the HGVs as they turned to dive, the muffled roar of the apocalyptic cavalry charging. Pru's grip tightened and there was a lump in her throat.

"Can we hold out, Harry?" she said softly.

"We have to, my d…my dearest," he answered quietly, turning his face to hers. Their eyes met and it was as if the fighting had suddenly stopped. In that moment was perfect peace, as they both recognised a power greater even than all the hosts of Heaven and its far dominions. Pru's lips parted slightly as they moved closer to one another.

"Do give over, you two," said Adrian, popping up from behind a table. "The fighting's stopped. Have we lost?"

A jubilant Glum reappeared at the door, battle-scarred but with limbs intact.

"They've fallen back, sah! They're regrouping but we 'eld 'em off, sah!"

"Fine work, Sergeant. I said it was just a matter of belief, didn't I? The men just have to -"

"Beg pardon, sah, but the men was hall scared shi… silly, hactually. You should 'ave seen 'em, sah – all 'uge 'an shiny with wings an'-"

"You've done that bit, Sergeant."

"Sorry, sah. No, it were the dog as done the trick, sah."

"Bonzai?"

"That's right, sah. Like a demented monster she were, all snarling an' gnashing 'er teeth in seven places at once, effing and blinding like a navvie, silver 'air crackling with electricity, fierce has a lion an' fast has a cheetah an'…" He ran out of animals. "They was hall terrified of 'er, sah!"

"I've always thought she was possessed," observed Adrian. At that moment Bonzai herself reappeared, wearing a self-satisfied leer, and stretched herself out at his feet.

"Well done, that dog," said Harry. "Was it rough?"

"No problem. Like pussies in the park."

But then Nigel was suddenly on Channel Four during an action replay of a particularly tense moment with a double-five.

"Listen, you lot," he said briskly and with unusual firmness. His elevation seemed to have given him a mid-Atlantic tone. "So far so good but they'll be back in two and half jiffies. I've cleared a path to the NRC and Alison's expecting you. Her boss will be otherwise occupied. Good girl, that; knows her duty. So get out now while you can. Not you

Arthur..." Stone was already half way to the door. "You need to get the tracker onto Dora P in Edgware. There's another séance coming up. When they're all nicely settled, give them a blast of Colonel Bogey through the trumpet at a hundred and fifty to scare them out of their skins. Harry? As soon as one of them appears in the tunnel you take over, right?"

"Well, it's a rum do if -"

"Just do it. No time to argue. When you get to Edgware, head north and Sammy'll tell you where to go."

"But -"

"Go!" The screen went blank and they never found out if he was able to use the four-two. There were renewed sounds of activity outside and Harry quickly summed up the situation. He hadn't really got the faintest idea what was going on, but that had never held him back before.

"Sergeant? Captain Clearwater is taking command here. You detail two men and follow me. We've got another job to do."

"Er, where to sah?" Glum was having trouble reasoning all this out. He knew where he was with trumpets and Colonel Bogey but he couldn't quite see the connection with Edgware.

"I'll explain on the way, Sergeant. Basically, we're going to do SEx."

"If you say so, sah."

"But Harry," Pru cut in, agitated, "you don't know how to do it."

"Then I'll make it up as I go along," he reassured her. "Everyone else does."

They made their hurried farewells, not knowing if they would ever see each other again. Harry was going into the jaws of life. Who could tell what triumph or disaster lay ahead? Pru was almost beside herself, clutching his hand and struggling to control her inner torment. This most unlikely band of warriors was going right through enemy lines, carrying the hopes and destiny of the whole human race with them. More to the point, as far as she was concerned the human race could go stuff itself – would her Harry ever return, and would she still be there waiting?

He understood and kissed her softly, for the first time. It was also the first time in his life (and death) that he'd known the awful reality of love. Even Sergeant Glum seemed to understand, and gave them a moment.

"When you're ready, sah."

And they walked out without a backward glance.

"This is it, then, Colonel, sah!" Sergeant Glum sounded more cheerful, as only the truly ignorant can in a crisis.

"That's right, Plonker. This time we really are going over the top."

Chapter Eleven ~ The Late Messiah

Harry swung the old blue car down the slip road of the Scratchwood Services and out into the heavy northbound motorway traffic with his eyes firmly closed. A Belgian juggernaut shuddered past within inches in a flurry of spray, flashing lights and foreign oaths. It wasn't easy to readjust to Earthly conditions, one's judgement of timing and distance completely warped. This being so, driving a Renault Laguna on the M1 in a wet rush-hour possibly did not amount to the best conditions for reincarnation. Nor does having one's finely tuned military mind encased in the erstwhile body of a bakery assistant and part-time caretaker do much to improve matters.

He coaxed the engine into top gear and risked a squint in the rear-view mirror. Ranjit, in Dora's green two-piece with wisps of grey hair poking out from beneath a hideous flowery headscarf, was already asleep. Sergeant Glum, self-consciously fiddling with the top button of Kath's crepe-de-chine blouse with one hand while the other tugged at the hem of the figure-hugging printed cotton skirt, was still sulking. One could see his point of view. When the three bewildered souls, shaken from their bodies by Arthur's unearthly cackles down the trumpet, had peered hesitantly from the mouth of the tunnel at the NRC, Harry had summarily commandeered George's silver cord on the grounds that he was the officer and got first pick. George was the only male, too, and after all a colonel cannot be expected to ponce around in tight skirts and fishnet stockings. Not in public, anyway.

In point of fact, considerations of gender made very little difference in the matter. Taking vacant possession of another's body in this way, without even the preliminary course of FEW counselling sessions, is so indescribably uncomfortable for a spirit accustomed to the airy freedom of the astral that one might almost prefer to be a three-legged mongoose swimming the Atlantic in an Arctic survival greatcoat. Nothing fits or works properly. Arms and legs have lost their spring, internal organs grind and squelch like gearwheels in a custard factory, and everything is out of focus. One wonders what the attraction of the human body ever was. So for Ranjit and Glum the addenda of spreading bottoms and a couple of pendulous breasts apiece were irritating but the least of their worries.

The whole operation had actually gone more smoothly than Harry could have hoped for, given his previous ignorance of SEx. Nigel's plan, coming out of the blue as it did just when the battle with the angels and the Welsh Domino Championships were coming to a climax, had left little room for thought or manoeuvre. At first sight it didn't seem to have much going for it. On the one hand it meant deserting the troops, while on the other hand the chap giving the orders wasn't even an officer. On the third hand it sounded just too outlandish to work. But Colonel Harold Arthur Markham, DSO (Dec.), being a natural leader, knew that the cause was mighty so he just got on with it. And once they were beyond the doors, and surveyed the blackened and buckled walls of the PRU(NE), his resolve had stiffened further. When the enemy throw this sort of fire-power at you, you knew you must be doing something right. Pausing only to deliver a brief keynote address to the weary but jubilant SAS on the virtues of belief, determination and biting their ankles, he had pressed on with a cry of victory amid the rousing cheers of men and dog. The multi-splendoured angelic force, temporarily taken aback by the ferocity of the omnipresent Beast, had retreated and now parted like the Red Sea. The escape route was open for the briefest moment, but it was enough.

Yet it was Alison, after all, who proved to be the critical link in the chain, for Boris had tightened things up considerably at the NRC since the last Memo, 'Getting Fingers Out', had arrived. He had personally designed a new impact-resistant barrier and introduced a highly innovative multi-stage link-filter queue system that promised to revolutionise the whole death experience. The clerks were now on productivity-benefit contracts and Ziggie had been sent on indefinite leave at the furthest JOB Centre. Alison, with a new lease of life, had trained herself up to supervise the electronics. Indeed, this was how she got Nigel's tip-off, having tuned in to Channel Four during the afternoon lull.

Boris straightened his collection of paperweights and toured his Axminster, relaxed and satisfied, totally unaware that there were two essential flaws in the structure of his empathetically efficient empire. The first was that all the personnel save one were male. It is commonly believed that this isn't supposed to count for much in Heaven, but it is simply not true, especially at the extreme material edges. So when Alison staged her diversion by removing her uniform and going into a practice routine on the asymmetric bars of the new link-filter gates, the work of the NRC had ground to a halt. Boris at first tried to protest, but was then himself so captivated by the parabolic arch of the back and the tremulous ripple of the quadriceps in her triple reverse Kutuzov pincer dismount, that he joined the others like rats following the Pied Piper as the floor somersaults carried her round to the blind side of the building.[22]

---

[22] The survival of physical urges beyond the loss of the body is one of the most fascinating yet neglected areas of psychical research.

The second oversight was in the design of the barrier, totally secure against any assault from the outside. It simply hadn't occurred to Boris that anyone already in Heaven might want to go out the other way. It was the work of moments for Sergeant Glum and his men to dismantle the mechanism, and for the task force to secrete itself in the shadows at the edge of the tunnel.

It had been something of a surprise when, an instant before the critical moment, Ranjit had strolled into view. Looking around for Alison, and puzzled that the place seemed entirely deserted, he had wandered through the open barrier and spotted the colonel.

"Yo, main man! How's it haaaarrgh -" Harry had grabbed him by the arm, wrapped a cord round his wrist and shouted "Follow me!" RJ had had little choice in the matter.

Coming to in an Edgware back room had been an altogether more difficult experience. Hideous wallpaper, matching Dora's headscarf, screamed at their blinking eyes, cartilage and tendon twitched without control beneath heavy flesh, and Arthur Stone's cackle still reverberated around the plastic chandelier and ornamental cats. At least this had soon been followed by a deafening whoop of Bolshevik expletives down the trumpet as the friends back at PRU(NE) realised that Phase One of the mission had been successfully completed. There was also a rather emotional message from Prudence for Harry which could have been altogether too embarrassing had the line not gone suddenly, ominously dead.

The three men lurched about the room for a while to get the feel of things, while the rightful owners of their bodies shivered forlornly at the head of a growing queue at the NRC, wishing for all the world that they'd never dabbled in the occult. There were two others in the room. Fran sat frozen with apoplexy in her chair, eyes staring vacantly, mouth open, and would remain so for several hours yet. By contrast, the new disciple Benedict, having suffered such an overload of trauma in the last few months that absolutely nothing could now shock him, had a big grin on his face and was quietly applauding the new arrivals. Rarely in human history can anyone have had quite such a result in their very first séance. He made them all some tea with plenty of sugar, and slowly coaxed the gist of the story from them as they calmed down.

I dare say you can imagine for yourself his feelings when Harry assured him that Alison was safe and well, a heroine, at the other end of a tunnel, and had firmed up her gluteus maximi nicely.

Φ

"…and I still say it should have been a multiple of seven. It always has been before. None of this would have -"

"It's that woman's fault. Didn't I say so?"

"This robe needs washing. There's an itch all down my -"

"…and I hear they even found geraniums in the causality chamber!"

"What's wrong with an exponential power, anyway? I mean, the least you expect is to get the numerology right."

"Well, we missed the last one by nine hundred years, so surely -"

"…everyone knows you can't trust artists. All the trouble in history -"

"Artists and women…"

"… it was SS3 and his perfect child-bearing hips…"

"All over the front page of Le Figaro, and did you see on page five they had -"

"Settle down!" Resuming the Chair, Tfozb silenced them at a stroke with an even more strident voice than s/he'd had before. "What's done is done. Accidents are the price we pay for free will. It's market forces. Look, we don't want to go back to the old centralised determinism, do we – the autonomous CPSU, layers of bureaucratic councils, spirit uniforms, no incentives or aspirations, a leave-it-all-to-Fate mentality? We have a new world now."

"It seems to me," ventured Mxtth in the hush that followed, "that this new world isn't much different from the old world, except that misplacing a soul seems to be a minor detail to you."

"What exactly does that mean?"

"What I mean, Tfozb, is that we haven't actually had much of a say in any real decisions, have we? They've all been made by, ah, certain individuals behind the scenes, as they always were. What's the point of all your Working Parties when others have already decided their outcome? There's no communal planning because certain persons are carving out personal empires, and of course those certain persons never actually accept any personal responsibility, do they? While the good Elemental folk of the Planning Committee sit about like a collective quivering jelly, the ones who really cocked everything up are blaming market forces."

The quivering jelly sat back in awe, each one murmuring silently to themselves either 'I wish I'd said that' or 'S/he's for it now'. Not since the debate on Socrates had such vitriol been expressed among Elementals, nor in living memory had one of them ever made such a long speech. Even Tfozb was stung into speechlessness.

The Third Spiritual Secretary made his entrance, as ever, with perfect timing. He surveyed the stilled room with some surprise and instantly summed up the situation with his usual consummate skill.

"Ah, good," he beamed, "the peace that passes understanding. Now look, we're going to have to put our heads together on this one." This of course means I'm certainly not going to take the blame for this one. He did his best to sound jolly. "The news isn't entirely bad." This of course means brace yourselves for some almost entirely bad news. "As you know, the hound of hell was giving us a spot of bother, but I'm pleased to report that the PRU(NE) has now been overrun and all the fugitives are in custody…" There were muted cheers. "… except their leaders." Groans. "Security had already been tightened up at the NRC in anticipation of trouble…" More cheers. "… but all the guards were missing and somehow the criminals got back to Earth. Last seen heading north on the M1 in England." More groans. "However, our top security men, Stachov and Hurski, were despatched in pursuit…" Loud cheers. "…and were last seen heading east on the A4 in France." There was a collective scratching of heads in disbelief.

"So that means," Tfozb suggested, "that Evie Gardner is in real danger, doesn't it?"

"Well," SS3 spread his hands as if to show how clean they were, "that's your department, isn't it?"

"She's certainly safe from psychic attack, the Witnesses have that all wrapped up. But you know as well as I do that no-one's completely safe on Earth. There are always accidents and terrorism… we had been relying on Earth's ignorance, but now that these criminals have got through…"

"Ah well, there are always criminals. That's market for -"

"Surely we can stop them? What about some fog and a multiple pile-up on the motorway? That's usually pretty easy to arrange."

"Usually, yes. But weather control was being done from PRU(NE) and the equipment got a bit, er, smashed up when the angels…" His voice trailed off in defeat. "But on the bright side," he continued, desperately searching for one, "they're in a Renault Laguna so they may not get very far."

"You know what I think?" said Mxtth slowly. All eyes turned as one with expectancy. "It's all too much of a coincidence. These so-called criminals have thought of everything… no, it's been planned, every last detail, every mishap and plot and counterplot and red herring. I see," s/he paused for effect and looked straight at Tfozb, "a Hand of Fate in all this. It's like some individual has orchestrated the whole thing, written the script."

They shifted uncomfortably as if cold skeletal fingers were running around the room and getting underneath their robes. They looked at Tfozb, then at each other, then at themselves and finally under the table.

"Not me."

"No, never."

"Couldn't possibly."

"Nonsense!"

"Just a mo," said SS3, holding up a hand and frowning intently. It took an outsider to notice. "Isn't there someone missing here? Can anyone feel a gap... somewhere over towards... yes, the young chap who's always popping in and out... keeps very quiet... oh cripes! Oh Confucius! Oh my sainted Nelly! I thought there was something familiar about him..."

"Is there something wrong, Duflc?" demanded Tfozb. SS3 laughed gaily.

"Wrong? Well, in a manner of speaking. Sort of, perhaps. It's that prune from FIGS... I mean, the gibble from SPOON... no, oh dear, the mole from tiddliompom..."

"Get a grip, man! You mean Gibbs has been in on the whole thing and you didn't recognise him?" SS3 was quivering with the rest of them now.

"Well, you know how it is. It's collective persona here, sublimated identity, formlessness and all-for-one and one-for-Almighty Ada – I've just gone and promoted him!"

"Anywhere in particular?"

"Well, you see he did ask, and he seemed like a nice chap, very obliging and efficient, and -"

"Where?"

SS3 gulped, a long gulp.

"Head of the CPU."

"You mean -"

"Yep, his fingers are on all the buttons."

In the ensuing ripple the Japanese yen fell through the floor, Italy declared war on itself, and Scotland took their first innings lead over Australia to seven hundred and eighty-five with six wickets standing.

Φ

Harry struggled with the Laguna's controls and barely avoided being swallowed up by Hemel Hempstead, reflecting that stopping at Scratchwood for sausage, egg and chips had probably been a mistake. Their bodies weren't attuned for such a shock. He felt distinctly queasy but unable to stop the car, having somehow got them jammed in the outside lane between several tons of high-speed Weetabix and a National Express bus full of American tourists. It might not have been so bad if they had some idea of where they were going.

As Luton flashed past, they couldn't know that Sammy was less than seven miles away and concentrating for all he was worth. It was RJ, fast asleep and thus the least distracted, who received the orders. He moaned and shifted uncomfortably on the back seat before shaking himself awake with a whimper and throwing up down the back of Harry's neck.

"Bruv," he said at last, sitting up and scratching his belly as he peered through the grimy windows at the gathering clouds in the darkness, "I is not enjoying dis ride, innit."

"Settle down, that man," Harry muttered through gritted teeth, not enjoying it much either. "No-one said this would be a barrel of roses. Nasty business, war. A chap has to make sacrifices. Let's have some dignity."

"I'd like to see if you is dignified wearin' elastic stockings and bony corset, bruv." He lapsed into a sullen silence and inspected the contents of Dora's handbag, cheering up a bit with the discovery of two humbugs and a packet of Marlboro Lights. "Anyway, what I is meaning is that I jus' had this real bad dream, innit. I is being chased by dis giant haddock, man, all bloaty an' weasely, an' we is goin' round an' round an' round in circles in dis wilderness that goes on f'rever an' none of the signs, dey is not making sense, bruv. An' then there am our dude Sammy, innit, holdin' up a board as says 'Where It's At' an' there's loads o' happy smilin' people, but I can't get there `cos I is trapped on de road going round an' round an' - "

"That's it! That's Sammy's message!" shouted Harry, turning round excitedly and gouging half an inch out of the off-side wing on the central crash barrier. The car bounced back into a lucky gap in the middle lane. "Don't you see?" Harry went on, his spirits up now. "He's telling us exactly where Evie's heading. It's a brilliant description." He found an AA Handbook in the glove compartment and tossed it over his shoulder into Glum's lap. "Navigate, will you, Sergeant."

Sergeant Glum and RJ looked at each other mystified, wondering if the colonel had lost his marbles somewhere during SEx.

"Right, sah. Er, where to, sah?"

"Where to, Sergeant? Isn't it obvious? The ringroad, the wilderness, the signs that don't make sense, the happy people beyond reach... it's Telford!"

They swapped places at Newport Pagnell and, an hour and a half later, as the car pulled off the M54, RJ nudged Harry awake. He shook off the clinging fatigue and peered ahead into the darkness past Plonker's shoulders, hunched at the wheel.

"Status report?" he demanded.

"We is here."

"Thank you, RJ. Care to be a little more precise?"

"We is on de ringy road, goin' round an' round an' -"

"Good. Sergeant?"

"Sah?"

"No need to stand to attention when you're driving, Sergeant. Now, just keep on this road at a steady fifty, and tell me if you see a giant haddock."

"Yessah!"

For her part, Evie had gone uncommonly quiet. Bill Shaddock rubbed the sleep from his eyes and put a hand on hers.

"Nearly there, missus. There's this place I know, Sutton Heights. You'll be safe there, you an' the kiddy. Nobody ever finds it." She smiled back at him but didn't answer, a consuming sadness filling her heart. They'd come so far. They were nearly there. Yet she knew perfectly well that they wouldn't make it. The Spectre was upon her again – pregnant women know these things.

She wasn't sad for herself. Life had had its ups and downs, but you couldn't say this last year had been boring. She'd been a woman of mystery, a witness of death, a widow and a queen of the tables, rich and feted by society, wooed by a count (nearly), degraded and impoverished, shot at by terrorists and saved again. She had a baby within her and a caring man beside her – ugly and smelly, perhaps, but nonetheless caring. It was a pity he had to die too. She hoped it wouldn't hurt.

It was instantaneous. The Laguna caught them a thunderous blow at the side and the van toppled slowly, almost gracefully, down the steep embankment and turned over twice before coming to rest on its roof, wheels racing futilely. Sergeant Glum pulled up sharply and touched the trickle of blood on his face in surprise.

"Cor luvaduck, sorry, sah. I never saw 'im. Must've dozed off for a -"

But Harry wasn't listening. Pushing Ranjit's prone body off his lap, with a soldier's instinct he leapt from the car with an agility that defied the awful cramp in his limbs. Within seconds he was by the van and astride Evie, who had been thrown clear and was miraculously still breathing. Helplessly, she looked up through a thin red mist at the looming figure.

There was something strangely familiar about him, though she couldn't put her finger on it. On the other hand, weak as she was, she still recognised a sawtooth bread knife when a full moon glinted on its blade.

"I'm sorry, Mrs G," said the colonel flatly. "An unpleasant do. But there is a damn fine reason for it." He knelt beside her, thrusting the knife with long practised ease just below the sternum and up into the heart.

Meanwhile, in a squalid downtown Chicago apartment, Eleanor Glee's baby kicked inside her, as if to say, 'There's something you ought to know…'

Φ

When the Angelic Guard reached Research Laboratory One with the Third Spiritual Secretary, resplendent in his most official purple robe and gold chain, they were taken aback. The first surprise was that the room, normally cluttered knee-deep with instruments and bits of electronic thingummies-that-might-be-useful-one-day, was completely bare except for a bench at which Nigel sat. At one elbow was a bottle, half empty. Another surprise was that his voice was ever so slightly slurred.

"Ah! `S the great an' won'ful SSSSS3 an' frien's. Welcome to my hummle kingdom." He made a magnanimous sweep of the arm and fell off his chair.

"What happened here?" gasped SS3. Tidiness and cleanliness were not virtues normally associated with workshops, even on the Elemental level.

"Progress!" effused Nigel, getting to his knees and offering the bottle. The guards recoiled. "Progress'swot happened. All that stuff…" he waved at the bare walls, "`sall obshlit… obsolliteat… oblosh… `sall too old. All your boffins ushless. Still working' on th'old art'fishl inter-refrashununun lasher prinshpul."

"Yes," observed SS3, puzzled, "where are Doctor Jyr and Duflc and the others?"

"Shacked `em. All shurplush now. This's all you need. Ninety-eigthsh gen'rashun. Look." He waved a thin card above his head and pointed it at an empty corner of the room, where a hologram of Snoopy playing tennis appeared. "Shorry, wrong button."

The image was replaced by a graphic three-dimensional scene of a grassy embankment near Telford, shrouded in darkness. Besides Evie's body could be seen Harry (or was it George?) lying quite still except for a gentle, steady flow of blood from his wrists. His face was calm, with an expression rather like deep satisfaction.

"Shee?" Nigel turned back to them. "You's all too late. Evie'sh dead, `sall over. It wash all wrong. Life jus' wouldn't be th' shame. No myshtry, shee? You've got to have myshtry..." His head dropped and voice trailed off, and despite the total absence of tear ducts he started crying uncontrollably.

The guards raced forward to seize him and the ninety-eighth generation computer remote control fell from his hands, twirling gently down like an autumn leaf to land at SS3's feet. He bent to pick it up. But computers have a natural antipathy towards those born before their invention, and it was altogether inevitable that SS3 would grasp it too firmly and by the wrong edge.

The intramundial FX-escape activated.

The cosmos heaved, then fluttered, then settled again. There was Heaven on Earth at last, although there was also Earth in Heaven.

You may not have noticed, since it all happened beyond any measure of time, but you may now not be too sure whether you are alive or dead. Take a look around where you live and see if you recognise any of the characters and institutions described here. If you do, then you're probably in Heaven.

Sorry.

Epilogue

"… and after all is said and done, and all that's happened… well, it's just karma, eh?" said Adrian.

"Eh?" said Harry and Pru in unison. The friends were sitting at a pavement table outside Gandalf's, a light breeze rippling the chequered linen cloth. At their elbows were tall glasses of something cool and refreshing with green bubbles, topped off by magenta striped parasols.

"Karma. Fate. Some foreign chap was telling me in here one day, Indian I think he was. Once upon a time, there was this bloke Buddha, a great and import -"

"Yes, we have heard of him."

"So one day he was walking along the bank of a great river with one of his disciples – they're the people who -"

"We're familiar with the term."

"– and they saw this other bloke drowning in the river and shouting for help. 'Help, help,' he shouted. So after he'd come up for the fifth time, the disciple asked whether maybe they should save him, or let him drown `cos that's his karma. 'Ah, but not so,' said Buddha."

"Who's this Arbuthnot?" asked Harry. "You didn't mention him before."

"No, do keep up," said Adrian. "Buddha said 'No, it's his karma to be drowning in a river near two people discussing karma'. So there it is." He sat back with a satisfied smile, apparently having finished.

"Where is it?" asked Harry.

"What?"

"Well, did they save him or not?"

"Oh, I don't know. The Indian had forgotten that bit."

They looked at him with a mixture of frustration and incredulity. Harry smoothed his moustache and drummed his fingers on the table for a while.

"So what exactly was the point of the story?" he asked eventually, with admirable restraint.

"'S obvious, isn't it? Fate." Adrian seemed surprised to be asked. "If everything's all planned out anyway, there's no point in getting so worked up about it. You just do your own thing."

Having been a civil servant and thus with ample experience of impenetrable logic, Prudence had been following the discussion quite well, but couldn't help protesting at this point.

"Just a minute," she said, "that's not right. You can't do your own thing *and* have everything planned out. It's not rational."

"Who said Heaven has to be rational?"

"But that's how we are," she objected. "And if we don't know that everything's planned out by Fate, we have to assume it isn't, don't we?"

"Exactly my point," said Adrian. "So you just do your own thing."

Pru sat back perplexed. It wasn't the conclusion she'd intended to get to. Meanwhile, Harry was looking from one to the other in total mystification, although as a decisive leader of men who rarely had any idea where he was leading them he probably should have understood.

"Deuced if I know what you're on about, young man," he said, "and I don't suppose the drowning chap would have been very impressed either."

"Ah, well actually you're right there," nodded Adrian, "'cos I've just remembered he wasn't a Buddhist anyway."

"Rough, innit?" said Bonzai.

The Cast

Benedict

Advertising executive, mid-forties, living at first in Hertfordshire and then a bedsit in north-west London. Married to Mary who has an affair with his boss Michael. Aka Michael Benn, CEO of the Apache Agency.

Alison

Receptionist at the advertising agency. Late twenties, slim with long fair hair, pleasant, not beautiful. Run over by an ambulance. Aka Alla Krappskaya.

Harry

Colonel Harold Markham DSO. Early sixties, deserted by his wife Barbara (who later becomes Winnie). Commits suicide in the bath. Later, becomes George.

Pru

Prudence Clearwater. Spinster, civil servant. Dies of an aneurism on her fiftieth birthday.

Evie Gardner

Harry's housekeeper. Forties, married to Stan. Boring and dim, but chosen to be the mother of God. Moves to Burnt Oak, north London.

Anthony

Benedict's Level One Witness.

Ranjit

Late teens Asian, long black hair, beads and rings. Doing Witness work experience but takes over from Anthony. Aka RJ, later becomes Santa Claus, then Dora P.

Gabriel

The archangel.

Boris

Officer grade 3 at the Natal Reception Centre. Later NRC[4].

Jones

Officer grade 4 at the NRC.

John Clarke

An inoffensive soul with no records.

Stachov and Hurski Officers of the Spiritual Guidance Bureau police.

Tfozb An Elemental. Aka Marge.

Sxzbu An Elemental. Aka Nigel.

Nftth An Elemental. Aka Sammy.

Mxtth An Elemental. Aka Timmy.

Duflc The Third Spiritual Secretary, SS3, aka Claud. Chairman of the Elementals' Planning Committee.

Adrian Proprietor of Gandalf's café on Kings Road. Young, gay.

Bonzai A dog at the café, lurcher, long grey hair.

Fuzru A CPU programmer. Aka Algol.

Arthur Stone The director of PRU(NE), small and scruffy, ex-Soviet leader (aka VIL).

Nigel Gibbs Arthur's assistant, thin, long hair, computer genius. Aka Sxzbu.

Judas Skim Medium and self-professed prophet. Ruddy face, red hair and white Italian suits.

Bill Shaddock Judas Skim acolyte, fishmonger, ugly and kind.

Sylvia Golightly Skim's acolyte, housewife, married to Ron.

Winnie Khan Skim's acolyte, socialite, stud farmer, married to Jim; later, Barbara.

Pene Marker Skim's acolyte and lover, subeditor, young and sexy.

Mrs Dora P   Chairperson of the Orange Hill Road Spiritualist Church. (Later, becomes RJ.) Married to George. Her followers are Kath and Fran.

George P   Married to Dora, bakery assistant and caretaker (later, Harry).

Ron Golightly   Sylvia's husband, a banker. Director of WICH.

Jim Khan   Winnie's husband, a broker. Director of WICH.

Sadiq Khan   Jim's brother, a terrorist. (Later becomes Sammy.)

Czosn   Director of the FEW. Czech, mathematician.

Comte de Pennis   Suave Italian conman on the Riviera. Real name Luigi Mori.

Sammy   An aged artist, the sitting tenant at Sutton Lodge. Later, Sadiq.

Sgt Willie Glum   Aka Plonker, SAS unit, loyal. (Later, becomes Kath.)

Eleanor Glee   Porn actress.

Con Danny Prattsmuller   American film producer.

Others:

Mary   Benedict's wife.

Michael   Benedict's boss.

Stan   Evie's husband.

Ziggie   Jones' secretary.

A medium	Mousey, grey raincoat.
Snorker	Harry's army pal Smythe.
Gerry, Dora, Kenneth	Harry's Witnesses.
Gladys	Evie's sister.
Laughing Meerkat	Judas Skim's Sioux guide.
Jaimie	Senior Witness in charge at the Orange Hill Road Church. Scottish Presbyterian.
Heap Yellow Feather	Evie's Apache guide.
Mario	Skim's acolyte, a restaurateur.
Kath	Disciple of Dora P, later becomes Sgt Glum.
Fran	Disciple of Dora P.
Sid Crocker	Landlord of the Ratcatcher's Arms, Buckley Rise.
General Sir Charles Forsyth-Furbright	Late commander of the SAS.
Barbara Markham	Harry's wife.
A private eye	Working for Barbara, a Geordie.
Pte 'Nosey' Parker	SAS unit, weedy but likes shitake risotto.
Pte 'Chimp' Davey	SAS unit, long hairy arms.
Cpl Sloan	SAS unit.
Giselle	Sammy's friend, a dancer.
Yoko and Kyusha	Japanese jacuzzi attendants.
Jim Roberts	Jim Khan's head groom.

Jean-Paul Lapelle   Assistant Manager of the Cannes
                                     Municipal Casino.

Jean-Paul's friend   Drug-runner from Marseille.

www.ingramcontent.com/pod-product-compliance
Lightning Source LLC
Chambersburg PA
CBHW072055170626
46813CB00004B/1366